ALAN DEAN FOSTER

STUART

STUART

Novelization by
Alan Dean Foster

Based on the screenplay by
Nina Navarro and Sammy Oriti

advertising the services of Sylvia Jensen, the Queen of Realty. Not the Queen of Reality. To find someone like that you'll have to look in a different part of the Los Angeles basin. *Realty.* Home sales. A good business to be in in a place like Newport. I should know. Newport is my home. Always has been, hopefully always will be. But you never know. Life can turn strange for any of us, at any time, without warning. That's realty (sorry, reality).

Anyway—Newport. Great beaches, great restaurants, great people. There's even a terrific bakery where the merchandise is just for dogs. The Barkery also offers treats and coffee for people. Jensen, the realtor? There's another one. Sylvia's daughter Jen, she's in there a lot. She advertises herself as "the Pet Friendly Realtor". Smart gal.

All I can add is that if you're planning to start a family, this is definitely a great place to be. For one thing, your dog will love it! Why? Well, because Newport has the best dog park in the whole world, that's why.

Did I mention that the Pet Friendly Realtor also happens to be my best friend? Here she comes now. Right there, in that white car. The one with the slightly askew magnetic advertising plaque clinging to the side that reads—well, you already know how she advertises herself. Yes, it's the one pulling into the driveway over there. She's the greatest. My very, very best friend, Jen.

See those "Open House" signs she's carrying? Always thinking ahead, is Jen. Never know when your neighbor or the couple across the street might decide to list their place. Best to be prepared. Although I don't know why anyone would want to move away from here. But you probably already realize that's my opinion. Look—she's carrying two signs with one hand. Manual as well as mental dexterity. Me, I think I'm pretty sharp upstairs, but I can't carry stuff worth a darn.

I love watching her come home. Sometimes the suspense until the door opens just kills me. But that's all part of being in love, I

CHAPTER ONE

There are some who believe the "California Dream" to be an urban myth (well, at least a suburban myth). Sunny skies, pleasant climate, beautiful homes, beautiful humans. The truth varies quite a lot.

One place where the myth meets reality is the town—really the general vicinity—of Newport Beach. Chuck Jones, the animator who created the Road Runner and Coyote cartoons (among many others) grew up there when the houses on the beach were half a mile apart. Long time ago. Newport these days is an upscale community featuring a wide sandy beach that gets groomed daily and a handsome fleet of boats moored in its marina. John Wayne's boat, a converted WWII minesweeper called *The Wild Goose*, is still there.

This isn't about John Wayne's boat.

It *is* a lot about Newport. And its people. Some rich. Most just regular folks. It's also about...well, you'll find out. Not the joggers. Not the bike riders. Not the occasional busker or the fish market on the pier.

On one of Newport's main streets you'll see a huge billboard

In memory of Stuart Louis, the buddy boy.

suppose. I mentioned Jen's name but I guess I forgot to tell you mine. I'm Stuart Louis. Or as Jen calls me....

"Potato head! I'm home!"

"Potato head"? That's a favorite one of hers. I suppose, descriptively speaking, it's not all that far off. Oh well. As long as Jen's saying it, I'm good with it.

You could apply the moniker "potato head" to most Boston terriers, I suppose.

"Stuie Louie!"

That's more like it! Now, where did she put my leash? Right there on the hook by the front door just next to the kitchen closet, with the brooms and mops.

🐾 🐾 🐾

Putting the two For Sale signs down in the foyer, Jen was confronted by a dog that was small in size but large in personality. Black, white, and perhaps just a smidgen tuber-headed, he sat on his hindquarters holding a leash in his mouth. His nub was wagging, his butt was moving, and his eyes were as expressive as Chaplin's on a good day.

"Stuart, put your leash on, don't just sit there. Oh, right—no hands. Sometimes I forget." Crouching, she snapped the buckle on one end of the strap onto the terrier's collar, then straightened. "C'mon, let's go."

Once outside, the terrier made a beeline for the nearest tree, took a pee, and then headed for the white car. He strained at the leash even though he had neither the energy nor the mass to move even a small human. But one had to put in the effort. A demonstration of enthusiasm was demanded. To exhibit anything less might mean no drive for the day, no walkies, or worse, a potential trip to the vet. Always better to strain at the leash, even when it wasn't necessary.

☺ ☺ ☺

Me again. Don't worry about me. I know how to work it. Been doing it for some time now. See, Jen and I, we go way back.

Way back.

I was a Sweet Sixteen present. Tiny little thing, was I. Much smaller than the massive, domineering descendant of wolves I am now (believe that one and I have a used doggie dish to sell you). She named me immediately. I remember the following year, she took up the guitar. We used to wrestle on the floor. She'd giggle, I'd lick. Dogs don't have many inherent physical abilities—another consequence of not having hands—but we're masters at licking. Ask any dog owner. Or dog. Maybe licking someone's nose isn't exactly finding a cure for cancer, but it's non-invasive, doesn't cause stomach upset, and immediately improves the mood of just about any human fortunate enough to be the subject of such attention.

It took a couple of years for me to get the hang of balancing a treat on my nose. Jen would keep treats handy in a small bucket and bring it out when she wanted to play. I'd balance the treat until she gave the command and then flip it into my mouth (the treat, not the bucket). And they say cats have quick reflexes (bleh...cats!).

I'd do anything for Jen. Or a bucket of turkey bacon. What's on your bucket list?

We also have a better sense of humor than cats. Cats are just—well, they're spoiled. And sarcastic.

I mentioned Newport's best-in-the-world dog park. That's where we're headed now. I mean, I love Jen and all, but nobody wants to spend their entire lives in the presence of a single other person. Husbands need friends besides wives. Wives need friends besides husbands. Dogs are no different. We need time with our friends, too.

Cats. But I digress.

We've been driving in Jen's car for a while now and we're close. Near enough that I can see the park through the car window. Sometimes Jen lowers it so I can feel the wind in my face. When that wind is a sea breeze, like in Newport, a dog's meteorological delight is doubled. But she's careful not to lower the window too much. I admit I'm the excitable type. That's good for playtime. Not so good for, say, leaping out the window on the 405 Freeway at seventy miles per.

Hey, there's Ringo and his human, Hector! Gotta admit, Ringo is one fit and handsome canine. Noble, even by German shepherd standards. I suppose that's to be expected of a police dog. Ringo has medals for outstanding service with the police department (I'm not so sure about Hector, but yeah, probably). They're a fine team, those two. Of course, any human could probably partner with Ringo and win medals and promotions. He's the big dog on campus. But he'd never tell Hector that. Ringo is far too polite. Except when he's chewing on the leg of some mugger or car thief. His growl is intimidating. Sometimes he even scares me, without ever intending to. He just doesn't know the strength of his own bark.

See over there? Next to the three women sitting at the park table? No, never mind them. *By* them. The dogs who are playing nearby. Those are my bestest friends. As to the humans, well—the one who's as black as half of me? With the braided fur...I mean, hair? That's Wanda James. The one with the blonde hair who looks a little like an Afghan? Her name's Shapiro, Cindy Shapiro. And the last one, who's tan like a Boxer? Nina Gomez. That's Southern California for you. They're almost as fit as their dogs. Wonder what they're gabbing about?

🐾 🐾 🐾

"She's late."

Shapiro shifted her legs beneath the table. Though her comment referenced the missing member of the group of friends, her eyes were on a pair of lifeguards stationed atop a lookout on the beach. They were in their late twenties, same as her and her companions. For a moment she thought of unexpectedly developing a sore ankle and hobbling over to start a conversation, during which her supposedly injured leg would doubtless have to undergo a proper and close inspection. With a mental shrug she set the scenario aside. Maybe later. Maybe tomorrow. The weather would still be good even if she wouldn't be.

"She's always late," Gomez muttered. "I suppose I understand. I mean, real estate is one of those professions where you sit in an office all day following up on or hunting down leads, right? And then calling up those leads and trying to get them to let you drive them all over creation to look at houses they're not gonna buy." She shook her head sympathetically. "I could do it, if I had the patience. Which I don't."

"We know." James flipped her braids back just because, as she regarded her friend. "If she's *always* late, then she ain't late. She's right on time."

Shapiro sipped something from a small plastic glass. "So now you're a philosopher."

"Honey, I've always been a philosopher. I didn't have to take philosophy to tell me that's what I was. I've always known. It's all about your outlook on life. Being in control, understanding the world around you, keeping your calm on and your chakra straight and DAMMIT MARLEY DON'T YOU GO PEEING IN THAT KID'S SAND PAIL!" Lowering her voice, she coughed delicately into one closed fist and smiled. "It's all about maintaining a personal balance."

Enough about the humans! Bouncing around in the back seat of the white car, Stuart could hardly contain himself. The *other* three.

Marley there, the Puli? Hairy guy, isn't he? It's the breed. Maybe not the best coat for running around the beach, but he's fine in the rest of Newport and he doesn't get chilled from the over pumped aircon in Trader Joe's. Cupcake, the Pomeranian? She's no short hair herself. Unlike her owner, she comes by her hair color naturally. Funny, isn't it, how so many humans pick dogs who look at least a little like them? I don't understand that. Of course, Jen doesn't look anything like me. Fortunately for her. We're kind of like human-dog proof that opposites attract. As for Gizmo there, he's about as laid back as a male Chihuahua can be. Which means, not much. Sometimes I think he's going to shake himself to death. Whether from nerves or glee I never can tell.

So there they are: Gizmo, Cupcake, and Marley: my park buddies. Good friends, beautiful place, great weather. It's gonna be a swell day, I can tell. I just have to be careful not to piss off Ringo. Not that he would actually ever *do* anything to me or any of my friends. He's got too much class for that. Not to mention that if he picked on a Chihuahua, or a Pomeranian, not to mention a Boston like myself and word of it got back to his station, both the human cops and the other shepherds would tease him unmercifully. He'd never live it down. It's always good to know that one of the main things keeping a big guy from beating you up is that he'd look really stupid afterwards.

Also, Hector would put nothing but dry food in his dog dish for a month afterwards. For a dog, food can be a wonderful motivator. So can its absence. And Whoa! *Who* is *that*?!

Even viewed at a distance through the rear car window, she was gorgeous. Trotting through the park, she was straight and clean, a brindle beauty, and trotted along with her head held high, her ears pricked forward, and her tongue lolling teasingly.

Even though he hadn't seen a female Boston in some time he could tell right off that this lady was special.

I'd share a pig ear with her any day!

Pressing his nose against the window glass he could hardly contain himself, whining and making little barely controlled jumps. Had the window been down it would have been difficult for him to restrain himself. He would have, though. He and Jen had engaged in numerous conversations about the danger of jumping out the window of a moving car. Of course, she had done most of the talking. Well, all of the talking. Of one thing Stuart could confidently boast: he was a good listener. Didn't always follow through on what he was told, but boy could he sit still and *listen*.

That was one thing about humans. Even good ol' Jen. They love to talk. Love to lay down the law; sometimes gently, sometimes loudly and forcefully. Whereas dogs, or at least the smart ones like himself, were perfectly content to sit and pay attention, eyes wide open, panting patiently. What humans didn't know was that half the time, a dog's attention was actually elsewhere, pondering more serious matters like going for a walk, circling trees, chasing whatever nearby creature happened to be smaller and weaker than themselves, sleeping, and most importantly of all, what was for dinner.

Come to think of it, he told himself, except for the tree-circling bit, maybe dogs and humans weren't that different after all. One might even make the argument that a dog's outlook on life made more sense. At least there was no hypocrisy in their actions. And when they fouled up, dogs didn't make excuses. Whereas humans could go on and on and on about how they were not responsible for their actions.

By Turkey Bacon, he told himself, if I'm caught chasing off a seagull, I'll own up to it.

"Hang on, buddy. There's a spot." Reaching back, Jen rubbed

the top of Stuart's head. Something else humans and dogs had in common, he knew. He'd seen humans tousling each others' head fur all the time. But *just* their head fur. They were woefully deficient in hair elsewhere. Except for one thick-bodied middle-aged male he and Jen sometimes saw at the park who was almost hirsute enough to pass for a dog. What he was doing there without a dog Stuart could not have said. Possibly looking for the human equivalent of his own female terrier. Human-wise he appeared to be in good condition, though Stuart had doubts as to whether or not he could have, if challenged to do so, catch a squirrel.

Having found the one open parking spot, Jen pulled in, shut the vehicle down, and slid out of the driver's seat. It took one, possibly two, seconds for Stuart to bolt off the rear seat and past her, his gaze fixed on the female Boston.

"Stuart, *no!*"

He was free! No restraints this time. Nothing to hold him back. He was free to greet, to sniff, to lick, to run, to...*urk!*

He had forgotten the small matter of being leashed, the unyielding leather strap secured by a small bolt to his collar. That would not have mattered either, except that part of the leash whipped itself around the car door handle and snugged tight. His rear legs went out from under him, his eyes bulged, and if not for a well-developed innate sense of balance he would have landed squarely on his butt. As it was he found himself jerked up short and flipped around. All he could do was hope that the object of his latest affections had not been looking in his direction when the Keatonesque farce had occurred.

On the other paw, maybe she was the kind who appreciated a good pratfall. One could never be sure with females. They hid their true feelings behind smiles, wide eyes, and the occasional plaintive whine. Again, just like humans.

Not for the first time he bemoaned his lack of thumbs.

Humans thought it was their brains that had let them dominate their surroundings when really it was all about thumbs. Cats felt the same way, although they had succeeded in controlling their surroundings even in the absence of manipulative digits. Cats had developed other ways of manipulating their humans.

Unlike some dogs he knew, Stuart didn't actually *hate* cats. Mostly, he was indifferent to them. Or found their presence distasteful. They were stand-offish creatures, hard to make friends with and often featuring inexplicable personality traits. The few house cats he had met were friendly enough, in their way. The feral ones, though... Best to steer clear of them, no matter their size. And he had seen a few who would have given even Ringo a rough time.

It was amazing how much torque a dog could exert when properly motivated, and nothing beat motivation more than an attractive female. Jen had little choice but to follow along, holding her end of the leash, as Stuart pulled her inexorably in the direction of the female Boston he had spotted from the back of the car. From what he had learned of human behavior, he felt that putting leashes on human males during such encounters would have considerably ameliorated certain unpleasant aspects of such encounters.

There was no leash on the man walking the brindle, though he did have a guitar bag slung across his back. By human standards of attractiveness he would have qualified as appealing, though he was likely in his thirties and not his twenties. He was barely well-groomed and attired enough for people to see that he was not a vagabond, though in Los Angeles and in Newport in particular, neither was a clear indicator of someone's status. The perfectly dressed human with the two-hundred dollar haircut might be an impecunious hopeful while the apparent beach bum, the CEO of a billion-dollar gaming company. In Greater L.A. more than most regions, one had to be careful not to jump to conclusions based on appearance.

Another problem dogs didn't have.

"Stuart! Stop pulling so hard! Easy!"

Her admonitions fell on deaf, if exceedingly cute, ears as Stuart continued to half lead, half drag her toward the terrier and her human. Every time she would bark a command to slow, he would pull that much harder, and every third step forward she threatened to trip. It was not that she was weak. For a human female she was in excellent shape. It was just that Stuart's motivation to push forward exceeded her determination to slow him down.

"Hey, look out!" Ahead of her, the guitar-packing man and his Boston strolled blithely onward.

Run or stumble. It was a choice Jen's body made, even if her mind wasn't wholly onboard with the decision. As they neared the man and dog directly in front of her, her own eyes widened. Perhaps not quite as much as Stuart's. Her expression suddenly resembled that of a body surfer who realizes they are about to go "over the falls", that there is nothing they can do about it, and that within a second or two they were going to be physically helpless and mentally stressed.

"Left, left!" Since "Slow down!" wasn't working, it was the only command Jen could think of in hopes of staving off looming disaster. The command wouldn't stop a surfer from going over the falls, and at that moment it didn't work with Stuart, either. Dogs are great at responding to human directives. Except when they don't want to.

Directly ahead of her and all too near now, the man with the guitar bag abruptly halted and stooped to pick up an empty bottle. His intention was to place it in the recycling receptacle he had just passed. Turning, he saw the barrel and Jen at about the same instant. Lacking the reaction time of a good dog, he was unable to move as Jen, desperately trying to change course to any heading except the one she was on, slammed into him. They both went down, with Jen on top of him. The accident and the supine position that resulted left her feeling distinctly uncomfortable. Though dazed, he wasn't quite as disappointed. Meanwhile both terriers, now loosed, took off side by side into the park, trailing their leashes behind them.

As Jen struggled to catch her breath she simultaneously thought to call out to Stuart while making embarrassed apologies. It was the latter that emerged first.

"I'm sorry, I'm so sorry! I was trying to tell you to look out. Didn't you hear me yelling at you to…?"

Before she could finish, the man beneath her reached up to remove first one, then another ear bud. Faint music from both suffused the air.

"I'm sorry. What were you saying?" As he spoke, he twisted slightly to one side. While she didn't play linebacker for the Rams in her spare time, Jen was no featherweight. As he adjusted his position a loud *crack* sounded from behind him.

Startled, Jen hastily scrambled clear and stood. Brushing herself off, she then offered him a hand up. He accepted without hesitation. Her expression one of genuine concern, she leaned to one side, trying to peer behind him.

"Was that your back? Are you okay?"

"No," he muttered. "My neck."

The brief moment of possible enjoyment Jim had experienced with Jen lying on top of him proved fleeting, propelled on its way by the splintering sound that had greeted his attempt to turn and rise. After placing the ear buds in a pocket his expression sank as he fumbled to bring the bag he was carrying around to his front. Unzipping it, he removed the guitar it had held. That is, he removed the guitar neck, which had been divorced from the body of the instrument. Or rather, pieces of the body. Strings dangled loosely, hunting in vain for the bridge.

"My—guitar," he mumbled, adding a few choice adjectives under his breath.

Looking at him, she lowered her gaze. "You play guitar?"

There are times in every person's life when they say something out loud that they immediately wish had remained unspoken. Because said something instantly defines the speaker as a blithering idiot. It was Jen's misfortune to presently be experiencing such a moment.

"I used to." He turned the now open bag in her direction. The condition of the instrument formerly recognizable as a guitar revealed itself.

Her mouth parted in a little "O" of horror. "Oh my God! I'm so sorry. There was nothing I could do, he was pulling me so hard. I couldn't stop."

Glancing in the direction the two dogs had fled, his expression turned wry. "Yeah, I sympathize. Those Boston terriers, they're monsters. Pull like Clydesdales." He turned sharply back to her but she didn't flinch.

"Well, Stuart, his strength can surprise *me* sometimes." She nodded toward the guitar bag and its traumatized contents. "Now, about your instrument...."

"It's okay, it's okay." He feigned a show of indifference. "It's just a limited edition Taylor anniversary model. There's always next year." When she didn't immediately react he added, "For another anniversary. Model. Anniversary model."

"Oh. Oh, right." She essayed a little smile. It came out slightly crooked, which was not the effect she was trying for. Hoping to make things better she added, "Thank God it's not a Fender."

He listened, and did not quite grin, and shook his head sadly. Desperately desiring to make things right Jen struggled with her bag until her fingers closed around a stray business card. This she managed to hand to him without dropping it.

"Again, I'm really sorry. Here's my card. I'm Jen. Let me get you a new guitar. I insist."

He squinted at the card, hard to read in the bright shoreside sunshine. "The 'Pet Friendly Realtor'?"

She looked away, slightly embarrassed, sure he was going to

laugh. Why the reaction of a stranger should bother her she could not have said. Breaking his guitar; that was reason for embarrassment. Nothing else ought to have mattered. But it did, and it unsettled her that it should. She had just met the guy, probably would never see him again (did she want to see him again?), and should not have given a lump of dried kelp what he thought about her or her business card. What she actually said was....

"My mother's idea. The 'Pet Friendly Realtor' thing."

"I like it." This time when he smiled there was not a hint of sarcasm attached to his expression. He sounded as well as looked wholly genuine. "I'm Jim." Turning, he pointed to where his dog and Stuart were playing happily, gamboling in the grass and exchanging face licks. Leading the way, he indicated his own pet.

"And that's Sweetie Peters. What's your dog's name?"

"Stuart. Stuart Louis." Upon reaching the spot where the pair of terriers were playing, she squatted and smiled at the female. "I think Stuart really likes you, Sweetie Peters."

Her new acquaintance (the two-legged one), crouched down beside her.

"Hi, Stuart Louis." Turning, he met Jen's gaze. "I think she likes him, too. Licking is a more positive reaction than biting." He grinned.

Jen thought to respond to his comment directly, immediately thought better of it. Her decision was confirmed by the sight of another, very attractive woman waving at them from across the park. Since she didn't know the woman she assumed that Jim did, and vice versa. The faint bubble of possibility that had formed in her mind popped. She had work to do and it was time to move on. Time to put the awkward encounter behind her. She straightened.

"Well, gotta go! I wish I could say it was nice meeting you. Under different circumstances, of course. Let's get you a new guitar asap. Call me."

If she expected him to say "Forget about it", she was disappointed. If she expected him to say anything else, that was also a disappointment. It didn't matter. The collision and fall was just a forgettable incident in an otherwise ordinary day. One that had cost her a few minutes out of her schedule. If she were going to walk Stuart, which was the reason she had come to the park in the first place, it would be elsewhere. Away from this kindly if slightly scruffy guitar player and away from his admittedly well-groomed dog.

Stuart had other ideas, of course. This time she was the one doing the dragging, with both hands on his leash. He fought, he struggled, he whimpered, his gaze fixated on the female of his own breed. But this time he was no match for his owner's determination. Or her weight. Jim the guitar man headed off in the opposite direction with his own terrier trotting along beside him. As he was swallowed up by the crowd and the landscape she put him and their awkward encounter out of her mind.

Her friends offered welcoming smiles as she joined them at their table. Never one to mince words and as curious (which sounds better than "nosy") as she was straightforward, Wanda was the first to speak, nodding in the direction from which Jen had come.

"Who's the cute guy you leveled?"

"How should I know?" A quick glance behind her showed that man, guitar bag, and female terrier were now well out of sight. The dogs on the grass nearby belonged to her friends and she recognized them immediately. Reasonably sure that it was now safe to do so, she unbuckled Stuart from his leash. For an instant she thought he was going to take off back the way they had come, but he was only swerving as he headed toward his canine acquaintances. Before she could explain further, her friend Cindy helpfully spoke up.

"Just some new park guy," she informed Wanda. "Seen him a few times. Don't know him, either."

"His name's Jim," Jen told them. "He's also got a Boston, named Sweetie. Stuart went nuts chasing after her. Almost killed me."

Nina chuckled softly. "Yeah. We saw you tackle him. I wish I'd filmed it with my phone. You need to let me know in advance the next time you plan to flatten some strange dude."

"Not funny. I feel bad enough as it is," Jen shot back. "I smashed his guitar."

"Ouch." Cindy winced. "Money."

"I *told* him I'd buy him a new one. I don't have any choice, since I'm the one who 'tackled' him." Time to change the subject, she decided. "Anyway, I wanted to tell you guys Arthur wants me to meet him for dinner tonight."

The Greek chorus replied as one. "Oh, where?"

"That's the thing." Jen paused for effect. "He wants to meet at Pompeo's".

Wanda let out a soft whistle. "'Pompeo's'? That's serious. One drink there is thirty bucks." A huge grin spread across her face. "I smell a big fat ring coming."

Next to her, Cindy was nodding knowingly. "It's about time. You got seven years invested in this guy."

Nina was panting almost as vigorously as Stuart. "You gonna say 'yes'?"

Staring off into the distance, Jen pretended to be pondering anything other than the subject at hand. "I'm thinking about it."

"Of course she is," Cindy put in. "The guy's not bad looking. Also, he's loaded. And as far as anyone knows, he hasn't killed anybody. In L.A. that's a pretty good resumé."

Their laughter was interrupted as every mutt in the vicinity started barking wildly. Attention shifted away from Jen and each other to their respective dogs. The reason for the sudden explosion of yapping shot across their field of view. It was small, gray, super fast, and familiar. Identification was immediate.

"There goes Freddy," Wanda declared with obvious delight. "That is one crazy squirrel. Look at him tease those dogs. If there is such a thing as an insane rodent, he's it."

"Or else's he's just stupid," Nina put in.

"Or suicidal," Cindy added.

It didn't take long for several of the dogs to get fed up with just barking. They launched themselves in the squirrel's direction. Freddy's response was basically the squirrel version of "Eat tail!". A nearby tree provided immediate refuge and the added opportunity to tease the pursuing dogs that much longer. They clustered around the base of the bole, leaping and barking, while the squirrel peered down at them utterly unperturbed. The leader of the yapping, semi-hysterical pack was unmistakable. By now the commotion had attracted the attention of several other park visitors. It was becoming a bit much.

"Stuart!" Jen rose from her chair.

"Gizmo!" Nina was not far behind her friend. "Ven para acá!"

Cindy was a little slower than her companions to take action. "Cupcake! Don't you run off! I'm not chasing you today. Do you hear me!"

Wanda brought up the rear, her tone practical and no-nonsense. "Marley! You're too old for this! You're too old to be chasing anything except the food in your dish!"

Together, the three of them strode toward the encircled tree. A few passing pedestrians looked on before turning away. This was Newport Beach, and unless one of the barking dogs suddenly grew wings and flew up into the squirrel's face, it was scarcely worthy of notice. Even then, the uber-sophisticated strollers would doubtless have figured they were witness to some kind of cinematic special effect. In the L.A. basin it was often hard to distinguish one from the other.

As Stuart and his colleagues in the canine choir continued to bark furiously at the squirrel, it stuck out its tongue at them.

There was no mistaking the gesture: Jen saw it for herself. Just coincidence, of course. While Stuart was unlikely to hurt himself, enough was enough. Dogs could suffer heart attacks as readily as humans and he'd already had enough excitement for one morning. When she scooped him up in her arms his attention immediately shifted from squirrel to Jen and he began licking her face excitedly. As she turned away and tried to slow him down they were joined by a much more senior newcomer.

Nobody in the group knew exactly how old Mrs. Walley was. "Eighty, or somewhere in that vicinity", was Cindy's guess. Her hair was white and her Lhasa Apso, Angel, blind. The dog might be slow but her owner was not, although dear Mrs. Walley could sometimes be caught out not firing on all cylinders. Pausing beneath the tree wherein the chirping four-legged irritant known to everyone in the park as Freddy had safely ensconced himself, she squinted up into the branches and shook her head.

"That squirrel had to be Jesse Owens in a past life. Well-mannered little critter, though. Used to eat nuts from my Harold's hand. That was ten years ago. Any dog that catches Freddy should get a gold medal."

Jen forbore from mentioning that squirrels almost never lived beyond five or six years in the wild. It would only serve to confuse Mrs. Walley, who regardless of the subject under discussion never failed to mention her departed husband.

"Never gonna happen, Mrs. Walley. He's still too fast." She nodded in the direction of the ocean. "We'll find him dead under a tree, from a stroke or something. We'll put him in an empty Planter's Peanut can, family size, set it on fire and push it out to sea at night when no one's looking. A Viking squirrel funeral." When Mrs. Walley eyed her blankly, Jen sighed and changed the subject to something more familiar and comprehensible. "How's Angel?"

The older woman looked down at her dog and grunted. "Still

blind as a bat." At this the Lhasa promptly walked into a trash can, shook his head, and gingerly eased its way around the unseen but smartly felt barrier. Jen didn't say anything. Harold Walley was gone but their dog remained.

It was one thing dogs were for.

CHAPTER TWO

Townsend Realty was a busy place. Which was not surprising. If you're going to sell cars, sell expensive ones. If you're going to sell jewelry, sell expensive stones. If you're going to sell clothing, sell on Rodeo Drive. If you're going to sell Orange County real estate, sell in Newport Beach. Competition was fierce, with commissions often approaching those in such rarified corners of Southern Cal as Beverly Hills and Brentwood. Despite being an independent, Townsend managed to hold its own. The number of awards in the lobby attested to the success of the company and its agents.

One secret to that success, and a very California one, was allowing its agents as much freedom and individual leeway as possible. As long as you delivered, as long as leads were developed and sales were closed, you could come to work in a pirate costume or wearing clown shoes. No one had—yet.

Some agents would show up with their pets. In Southern California, virtually every pet is a "service animal". One agent regularly brought in her scarlet macaw, Bacall. The name derived from one of the bird's favorite call-outs. In contrast, a younger gentleman, excellent agent though he was, was constrained from placing his pet python Goomba on his desk while he worked the internet. Tolerant though they were, his co-workers drew the line at having reptiles in the office that weighed more than fifty pounds.

So common was the sight of animals in the various cubbies that no one so much as blinked when Jen and Stuart entered side by side.

"Hi, Ms. Jensen." The girl at the front desk flicked a glance downward. "Hi, Stuart."

The terrier acknowledge the greeting with a nod of his head. Of course, Boston terrier heads are always nodding, or at least bobbing, so it was hard to tell if Stuart was responding to the salutation or just chilling as he stood there.

They passed another agent. New, young, eager, efficient, he offered an identical greeting. "Hi, Ms. Jensen."

She halted. The terrier beside her feet peered upward, nubby tail wagging like a metronome set on allegro. The office had suddenly gone silent. Confused, the new agent became aware that everyone was looking in his direction. In front of him, Jen tugged her sunglasses down to peer over them.

Comprehension hit home like a CHP officer's lights flashing in one's rear view mirror while heading home on the PCH. The newcomer rolled his eyes and intoned solemnly.

"Hi, Stuart."

The terrier's tail increased a beat as he and Jen resumed their march through the office.

The largest office space, the one in the back of the building with the view of the small garden, was the purview of Sylvia Jensen. Not only one of Townsend's senior agents, she was also Jen's mother. As her daughter and Stuart entered, Jensen senior was pacing back and forth, eyes slightly glazed, her attention focused on the conversation she was having via her telephone headset. Being wholly occupied at that moment with a tenuous transaction, she failed to immediately notice her offspring's arrival. When she finally did she easily divided her attention between the ongoing conversation and what she knew her daughter had come for. Without missing a beat, she picked up an envelope from her desk and passed it to Jen as she continued to talk.

"You will have it by Monday. It's with the title company right now, so just wait 'til Monday, Mrs. Hyman." Rolling her eyes at her daughter, she sighed silently but visibly. "Yes, I know you want to move in right away, Mrs. Hyman. Yes, I'm sure you can start making arrangements with the movers. It's just minor paperwork. Nothing to hold you up. The former tenants were out completely several days ago." She whispered as she nodded toward the envelope she had handed Jen.

"Your commission. Eighteen grand. Not bad for a month's work." Her voice rose again as she redirected her words to the phone. "Yes, Mrs. Hyman. Yes, the title company will notify you directly so you can pick up the finished paperwork directly from their office, if you wish."

Jen and Stuart made it to the lobby before her mother, having finally succeeded in disentangling herself from the needy Mrs. Hyman, managed to catch up to them .

"Jen!" She turned as her mother slowed. The receptionist scarcely looked up from her desk. Controlled chaos was the order of the day at Homestead.

Sylvia showed her daughter a worksheet. "Here's a lead that came in this morning. I'll email you an electronic copy for backup, but there's nothing out of the ordinary about it. The guy asked specifically for the Pet Friendly Realtor." She puffed up just a little. "I'm tellin' ya, that was one great idea you had. Newport homeowners and pets go together like lox and bagels." She extended the single sheet of paper toward Jen. "Here's the address, it's on Alta Vista. Zillow has it at six thousand square feet, not including the four-car garage. Big bucks in the offing, go now."

Ignoring the worksheet, Jen waved her off. Stuart sat at her feet, panting briskly, anxious to leave. There were no trees inside the office, no other dogs, and certainly no squirrels.

"Sorry, mom. I have to get ready for a date. Can't do it right now. Set it up for tomorrow."

Sylvia made a little mou with her mouth. "And when are you going to send out the announcements indicating your independence from financial matters?"

Turning, Jen started to leave. Stuart was way ahead of her. Or as way ahead of her as his leash would permit.

"Some things are more important than money," she called back.

Her mother smiled slightly. "Some 'things'? Let me guess. Arthur?" Her expression showed her disapproval. "Men will always be there. Even Arthur." She waved the worksheet. "Unlike them, leads like this don't come along every day!"

Ignoring the admonition, variations on which she had been subjected to since she had turned eighteen, Jen looked back again and raised her voice just enough. "Ciao! Mañana! Set it up!"

Her mother yelled back. "If it's still set-uppable! If it hasn't gone to another agency by then!"

"I'll take my chances!" were Jen's parting words as she and Stuart exited the building. Turning back toward her office, her mother let out a snort.

"Might as well say the same thing about men." She increased her pace. She had leads of her own to follow. Real Estate, that is.

☙ ☙ ☙

When it comes to eating, cats are precise, finicky, and work to a plan. Or as Sylvia Jensen would say, according to a worksheet.

Dogs, on the other hand, operate according to the laws of

mess and madness. They approach a full dinner bowl on the assumption that their already pre-masticated prey is liable to rise up and slough away, or that an invisible ghost dog may suddenly appear to devour it all. Even if they had hands it's unlikely they would use them. Dog logic says; why put anything between food and mouth? It constitutes an unnecessary step and a waste of time. Food—mouth. Also, speed is of the essence, and if in one's haste to consume the contents of a recently emptied can some of the contents get splattered on the ground, why, the technical canine term for that is "dessert".

No outlier when it came to consumption, Stuart was happily scarfing up every scrap of guaranteed organic-no-filler-no grain-all meat whatever it was. It never bothered him that his canned food came in only two hues: dark, and less dark. Or that regardless of its origins the consistency was likewise one of two varieties: chunky with gravy, or pulverized with faux gravy.

When there was nothing left in the bottom of the metal bowl save his own reflection, he checked the immediate vicinity for any tongue-propelled scraps. This was followed by a trip to the nearby water dish. Slurping sounds suggesting the activity of a much larger creature filled the otherwise quiet realm of the kitchen. A quick glance revealed that he was still alone. No ghost dog haunted the dark space by the door and no scavengers emerged to check on the bowl. Satisfied that he was still master of his domain, he headed up the stairs in search of his beloved human.

The hall was deserted, as was the bedroom. Softly squelching aqueous sounds emerged from a smaller room nearby. Identifying them immediately, he headed in their direction. They were indicative of the presence of liquid, but not of drinking. He knew what they signified.

Jen lay slumped in the bathtub encased in white foam. She was in complete agreement with those who believed that a hot bubble bath was one of humankind's greatest inventions.

Furthermore, it was cheaper than a Maldives' vacation, far more accessible, and devoid of sharks and other discourteous sea creatures. She could not spare the time to enjoy such a bath every day, but this afternoon it was a necessity. Tonight promised to be special.

None of which would have made any sense to Stuart, who having already inhaled his dinner would not have cared anyway. Why humans chose to lie down on such things as raised sleeping platforms and couches and immerse themselves in water was a mystery he could not fathom.

Seeing him enter, she raised a soapy hand and pointed. "Stuart, there you are. Be a good boy and bring me my scrub bush."

Looking in the direction she had pointed, he turned back to her, baffled. That it was a command he had no doubt. That it was more complicated than "Sit", "stay", or "roll over" was also not in doubt. But as always, he was game. He just needed additional input.

She gestured again. The brush was hanging on a hook at the far end of the tub. "Go get it, go on."

While he could not parse the words "scrub brush", Stuart was adept at the process of elimination. It stood even to canine reason that "scrub brush" referred to an object. Since there was nothing else in the direction Jen had pointed save bubbles, water, tile, and exposed plumbing, he walked down to the end of tub, momentarily contemplated the long object suspended there, then grabbed it in his mouth and brought it forward.

Jen accepted it, confirming his decision. "Good boy," she said to him. Her words were all he expected, or needed.

A glance up and out the bathroom window revealed an overcast sky. Many were the nights and mornings near the beach when sunny Southern California was a misnomer. Expecting the invasion of the marine layer, Jen was not surprised. The weather, whatever it turned out to be, would not affect the course of the evening ahead.

"Getting foggy, Stuart."

Thus roused, he turned and rushed off, returning a moment later with one of a plethora of squeaky toys. The one he had fetched was green with heavy dye despite its manufacturer's claim of being composed of wholly organic materials. It had bulging eyes, a round belly, and splayed feet. Jen pursed her lips.

"I said it's getting foggy, not get froggy."

His fetch dismissed, he dropped the toy outside the tub. Perhaps Jen would chance a second request. She pointed to the bath towel looped over a nearby rack.

"Sorry buddy, no time to play. Possible important doings tonight and mama needs to look her best. Bring me my towel."

Just the words he had been waiting for. Before she could call him back he was out the door in a flash, returning a moment later with another toy. This one was softer and didn't squeak. While exasperated at the sight of the stuffed owl, Jen didn't let it show. She sensed the dog's eagerness and regretted having to deny it.

"Towel, not owl. You're too cute. I wish I had more time to play with you like we used to. I wish I had more time to...." She shrugged. "Adulthood has its downsides for humans, Stuart. Not so much for dogs."

Putting his front paws up on the side of the tub, what is of a tail flailing, he eyed her empathetically. This lasted for a minute or so before he began to whine. There were no words, but Jen knew immediately what he was saying, and it had nothing to do with toy frogs or owls. It was more important than that. Also more urgent.

"Oh yeah? Pee-pee? Hold on. Hold *it*."

The whining grew louder as she rose from the bubbles and wrapped herself in the towel, looking like a rippling tower of deli ambrosia. "Hold on, buddy!"

No time to dress. Given the urgency in his whining it was likely there wasn't even enough time to don a robe and make it downstairs to the front door. She looked around a little wildly. The toilet, he might miss. The bubble bath, she might want to rejoin. In the absence of any remaining time that left only….

Sliding open the bathroom window, she picked him up and held him out just in time. At such moments she almost wished she'd taken on a cat instead of a terrier. Almost. Imagine asking a cat to fetch you your scrub brush and towel. Not that a cat couldn't do it, or understand such a command. It was just that a cat was more likely to ask *you* to bring *it* a brush and towel.

The golden shower arrived in the vicinity of the front door at nearly the same time as Sylvia Jensen. Given her age and more than a tad startled, she dodged the brief downpour with alacrity. Either someone was watering with a polluted hose or….

A glance upward revealed her daughter gripping a Boston sprinkler. She recognized Jen immediately and Stuart despite the unflattering angle.

"That's illegal! Also disgusting!" Looking around, she was relieved to see no one was observing. As for Stuart, he was just relieved. "Take him inside!"

"So he can do what, mom?" For good measure, she gave Stuart a gentle shake and was pleased to see he appeared to be empty. "Pee on the carpet? In his bed? He's a dog mom! The world's his toilet."

"I was almost a part of that toilet. Remember that lead I told you about?"

From within the bathroom now, Jen called down. "Remember that I told you to set it up for tomorrow?"

"What do you think I'm here for? You need some paperwork because I arranged an appointment time for you to follow up on it. *Tomorrow*," she added sarcastically, "since my daughter's every wish is my command. Buzz me in."

The door responded sooner than she expected. Also louder

than she expected. More like a steady roar akin to that of a Falcon rocket lifting off. She took an involuntary step backward, regained her composure, and moved to grab the handle. She was mumbling as she let herself inside.

"You better fix that damn thing! I almost had a heart attack!" Although she knew her daughter likely could not hear her, Sylvia felt the rebuke needed to be said. Stepping inside, she closed the door behind her as Jen shouted down from upstairs.

"I'm up here! C'mon up, mom!"

*Work all day, put together paperwork for your daughter who can't even be bothered to come downstairs to open the door for you in person because she's holding her urinating dog out the window, wonder why you bother...*Sylvia knew why. She was just feeling a tad irritable at the moment. Maybe it was the near miss of Stuart's sprinkle. Who hangs their dog out the window to pee? She smiled to herself. Her daughter, that's who. The act had been almost as gawk-worthy as the perpetrator.

There is something many men simply do not understand. Preparing for a fancy night out is not a matter of "getting dressed". It is a ritual. The laying out of dresses, shoes, accessories. A ritual to which most men are not privy. It is a mysterious ceremony that is passed on from mother to daughter. Blouses, pants, shoes, socks, dresses, necklaces, rings, earrings— all shifted positions like electrons in orbit around a nucleus. One had to feel for any men drafted into observing and worse, into commenting. To a primate with both an X and Y chromosome, it was akin to trying to see into the ultraviolet. There was no way to make sense of it. The best a male could hope for was not to be asked the Dread Question of Death, to which there is no satisfactory answer.

"Does this make me look fat?"

In this instance the one male present was saved by his lack of perception as well as his indifference. Holding up two nearly identical black dresses in front of her, Jen postured, pivoted, and turned to Stuart.

"Which one do you think, Stuart?" Holding one out slightly in front of the other, she said, "Does this make me look fat?"

There are times when it is safer to be a dog than a man.

To Stuart's credit, he listened to the words and struggled to make sense of them, as he did with everything Jen said. What he heard was, basically, "Wooga wooga, tak tak, Stuart". This preserved him.

"Well?"

"Well hell." Sylvia had entered the bedroom and was watching her daughter. She nodded in the direction of the bemused terrier. "You proposing to Stuart? That would make more sense than Arthur Daly."

If the comment was intended to unsettle Jen, it failed. Turning to the dog she clasped her hands together, batted her eyes at him, and spoke in her best girlish Disney princess voice.

"I'd marry him in a minute. He's *so* handsome." Turning back to her mother, she simpered a second time. "Don't you think so, mom? Wouldn't he make a good husband? I don't have anything against short men."

"How about those with protruding eyeballs?" At this, and for no particular reason, Stuart let out a couple of excited barks, delighted to suddenly be the center of attention even if he had no idea why. Sylvia made a face at him.

"Hi, Stuart." Serious now, she turned away from dog and back to daughter. "Jen, don't stay out too late tonight, okay? Your appointment with Derek Jones on the Alta Vista property is at nine. I told him you couldn't see him today because you were busy with Stuart. You need to be in business mode. Not in post— well, whatever 'post' mode you end up in."

Jen sighed and nodded. She had been down this road before. The U.S. had Route 66 for a mother road and she had Sylvia. "Right, mom. Business mode. What other modes are there?"

Her mother wasn't having any of it. She was going to build her daughter's success despite the snark, despite indifference, despite any and all objections. Jen could waffle when she reached Sylvia's age. Secure, comfortable, able to do what she wished and go where she wanted. She would and could achieve all of that.

With her mother's help, of course.

"There's also eating mode and sleeping mode. That's it. No other modes. Not until your banker smiles every time you walk into their office. Then you can play around with other modes. And then I won't have to worry about you.

Jen's exasperation monitor went from a five to an eight. "Mom, this 'pet friendly realtor' was all your idea, not mine. This isn't Manhattan and I'm not selling ten thousand square foot penthouses off Central Park. Go easy."

Her mother put up a hand, thereby contradicting her own recent assertion. Apparently, there was business mode, sleeping mode, eating mode, and shut-up-because-your-mother-has-something-to-say mode.

"Let me ask you a question. Does the pet friendly realtor like the money she's making?"

Jen had no retort for that. "She's not complaining."

Sensing an opening, Sylvia pressed her advantage. "Would she rather go back to working in college cafes and singing pet friendly songs with Stuart for two dollar tips?"

It didn't matter that Stuart understood not a word of what was being said. The mention of his name always elicited a bark regardless of the context. Jen eyed him fondly.

"*He* would."

"Great! He can study to be the human friendly realtor's assistant. Business mode it is!"

Jen shook her head. "You watch way too much Tony Robbins".

Having won the argument and made her point, Sylvia was prepared to offer a slight (albeit meaningless) concession. "Maybe I do, a bit. I'm also thinking maybe you should slow down with the Arthur thing. Especially if it's going to complicate your professional life."

Jen made a face. "The Arthur thing? You mean the 'Arthur thing' I've been involved with for much of my adult life? We've been going together for seven years. I think that qualifies as more than a 'thing.'" She smiled, a young woman's thoughts turning to flights not of fancy but of fancy-colored stones. "In fact, tonight we're having dinner at Pompeo's. Where I expect he will pop the question." She met her mother's gaze. "I believe it will involve yet another mode you didn't list."

Sylvia was not impressed. "Really? How many times did you think the question was being popped before? You want me to jog your memory? I can't remember all of them, but I have a few choice ones stored away." Her smile twisted. "It's one of the things mothers do."

"You're telling me. Spare me the recital."

Her mother let out a snort. It was a lady-like snort, but sufficiently stentorian that no one listening would have failed to grasp its import.

"Pop goes the weasel maybe, but not the question from Arthur. At least, not the question you seem to be expecting."

Straightening her back, Jen flicked the side of her left hand toward her forehead as her tone turned mocking. "I hear ya loud and clear, sergeant! No happiness, no down time, no recreational activities. In bed and lights out by nine! It's war, realty is, and I need to gird my loins for battle. I have my marching orders and I will obey!"

"Don't be a smart ass." Sylvia wagged a finger at her daughter. "As for your loins, girded or otherwise, we've already talked about that. Just work hard and make money. I don't want to be one of these doddering old nags who worries about where her offspring's next rent payment is going to come from. Take it from a non-doddering young nag: money fixes everything."

Jen realized that if she didn't finish dressing and fixing her face she was going to be late. And she did not want to be late. Not tonight, of all nights. Also, she'd had just about enough mothering for one evening, business-oriented and otherwise. So when she replied anew, her words reflected her attitude—if not her heart.

"Did it fix things when dad left?"

It would have stopped a lot of women in their verbal tracks. Not Sylvia Jensen. She didn't miss a beat.

"Absolutely," she shot back. "I worked hard for everything we have. Where do you think you would've been if I hadn't? So I missed a school recital or two, or an occasional PTA meeting. We both live in nice places, in the nicest part of Orange County, we have plenty to eat, drive nice cars…yeah, money fixes plenty. Those who say it doesn't, don't have any. Look around you."

Perceiving Jen to be under threat, if only verbal, Stuart had commenced barking non-stop. Sylvia ignored him. Unusually, so did Jen, as she focused all of her attention on her mother.

"So I shouldn't get married because *your* marriage failed? Because you and dad couldn't make a go of it? Is that what you're saying? Is that your maternal advice? Because if that's the best maternal advice you can give me, I'll stick with business mode, thank you!"

Sylvia took a deep breath, calmed herself. "Jen, I'm just looking out for you like any mother would. There's no Prince Charming out there. It takes time to find the right guy. To be *sure*."

Jen likewise settled down, but she was not mollified. "Seven years isn't enough time?"

"I'm just saying. Don't set yourself up for a heartbreak. That's my best advice. It's easy to love someone. It's hard to live with them."

Having managed yet again to get in the last word, she turned and let herself out. Leaving behind a teary-eyed Jen who promptly flomped down on the couch. Stuart was up and at her side in an instant to lick the side of her face. Lick away the tears, the upset, and anything else a dog's loving tongue could manage. Bending toward him, she gently kissed the top of his head. It made her feel better.

Him too.

CHAPTER THREE

I f Pompeo's food was not particularly understated, the front of the restaurant certainly was. The Fourth Law of Fine Restaurants states that the quality of the food is inversely proportional to the garishness of an establishment's exterior. With quality inside there is no need to make the outside look like an architectural refugee from Las Vegas.

Exiting the Uber, Jen fussed a moment with her dress before heading toward the entrance. It was typically busy: groups of stuffed diners waiting for transportation or their own vehicles, others gathering and conversing animatedly outside. Pompeo's was a place to meet and to enjoy: both the food and the company of others.

Though her bank balance might be less than most of those present, Jen looked as good as any of them. Make-up, hair, attire: all approached the Jensen standard of perfection. Initially the doorman was amiably professional.

"Good evening, ma'm. Welcome to Pompeo's." He shuffled his expression. "Hey, I recognize you. You're the Pet Friendly Realtor. The ad on the side of the bus. Nice!"

Jen responded with a professional smile. Reaching into her

purse she extracted a small cardboard rectangle. It was eye-catching yet tasteful. You never knew.

"That's me. Here's my card if you ever need anything."

"Thanks. I may." He turned mockingly serious. "I'm looking for a dog house for my pit bull, Rambo."

"Haha," she responded flatly. "Funny guy, very funny."

He gave a little shrug. "I'm workin' the door at a restaurant. Not so easy to afford a place in Newport on my salary. But jokes are cheap, anyway."

She turned sympathetic. "Give it a few years. Never know who you might meet while holding that door. Never know what opportunity it might lead to."

"Thanks, ma'm. Good of you to say so. Anything else I can do for you while you're here?" He opened the door for her and she started in.

"Yes. Don't call me 'ma'm'. My mother is 'ma'm'".

He called after her. "Then what should I call you?"

"'Jen works."

Within, the décor was understated Tuscan. Stylish, but leaving no doubt as to what kind of food was served. Unlike a steakhouse, the conversation as well as the ambiance was subdued. There was no shouting to be heard and little whispering. The normality of it appealed to Jen.

Arthur was right where she expected to find him, at the bar. That he was chatting with a couple of attractive women did not trouble her. During the first year of their relationship it would have done so. After seven years she no longer worried. Her mother would have called her tolerance something unprintable. Jen didn't care. On the contrary, she found it flattering to know that while every single woman in the place might hanker for a howdy-do with Arthur Daly, especially now that he was thirty and still single, he was only there at all because he was waiting for her.

Noting her arrival he shook hands with each of the girls and headed toward her. As he wove a path toward the entryway, one of the two women left behind murmured to her companion.

"You should have made your move before *she* showed up. He's a catch."

Her friend replied without speaking. Instead, she flashed the business card Daly had handed her. It was enough to spark a toast.

"Sorry I'm late." Feigning more indifference than she felt, she looked past him and toward the bar. "Who are they?"

"Who?" He looked over his shoulder, then back to her. "Those girls? Just some girls from the office. And you're right on time, so no need for apology." He grinned down at her. It was a marvelous, masculine grin. He had good teeth, did Arthur Daly. And much else besides. "Hungry?"

"I'm starving." She did not add that conflict with her mother always stimulated her appetite. Not appropriate subject matter for a dinner date—and perhaps more than that. Inside, she was fizzing with anticipation.

A hostess led them to their table. It was isolated, private, quiet. Perfect for intimate conversation. Arthur always knew how to arrange such things.

"I have some exciting news and something very special for you." That smile again. Had worked for seven years, she knew. She took a deep breath as she sat down. Before either of them could say anything else a waiter appeared beside their table. For once she wished Pompeo's celebrated service would dial it down a notch.

"Would you like to start with a glass of wine, sir? I suggest our award-winning Chianti-infused Lambrusco, just in from the Vatican."

Most men would have made the decision outright. Not Arthur. He was considerate and thoughtful as well as good-looking. Jen found herself thankful she *had* arrived on time and not left him alone at the bar any longer with the two attractive women from his business.

"What do you think, Jen?"

Her response was not as sophisticated as she would have wished. Her knowledge of wine extended to liking it. "The Vatican?" she murmured.

"Hmm, interesting," Arthur added, so that her comment would not be left hanging out to dry.

The waiter was too professional to do anything other than explain politely.

"The Pope, sir. His side business." He winked.

It was enough to explain but not to sell. Tonight at least, Daly preferred to stick with the familiar. "How about the Barbaresco? Still in the cellar?"

Playing his part, the waiter gazed off into the distance. "That was a well-received vino, sir, but sadly the northern Italian winter froze the harvest."

"So the vineyard purchased German grapes and…well, it just wasn't the same," Arthur surmised aloud.

The waiter actually wiped away a tear. As for Jen, she looked bewildered as the two men entered into a connoisseur's discussion of grapes, climate, and vintages that left her yearning for a quick trip down the chardonnay aisle at the supermarket. When they finally concluded the oenophiliac rondelet, the waiter's admiration was unbounded.

"Bravo, sir! Compliments on your knowledge of the humble grape. And yes, very, very sad about the Lambrusco." Leaning in, he whispered confidentially. "I *do* have a bottle of the Brunello."

Arthur made an off-hand gesture. "Not necessary. I'll just have the Malbec."

A quick nod, and the waiter turned to Jen. "And you, madame?"

At least he didn't say "ma'm", she thought. To hell with it. "I'll have what the Pope had."

"Good choice." He stepped back and bowed slightly, as if auditioning for the part of a mustachioed sommelier in a 1930's Busby Berkeley musical. "I will return with your drinks."

As soon as he was out of earshot, Arthur leaned forward. "Jen?"

Folding her hands on the table in front of her she looked deep into his eyes. Or as deep as the restaurant's subdued lighting would permit. "Yes, Arthur?"

At the tables nearby, couples were toasting, leaning toward one another, holding hands beneath the tablecloths, and in general savoring being in one another's presence. One slightly older gentleman handed a small box with a curved lid to the elegantly dressed woman seated across from him. Jen could just make out the contents as the woman opened it and exhaled delightedly. Earrings. Expensive pair, from the way they refracted the light from overhead. The dining room positively reeked of romance.

"I have been holding off telling you this for a while now," Arthur began, "but waiting for the right timing. The right day, the right moment."

She was breathing hard and hoped he didn't notice. "And?"

Reaching into his jacket's inside pocket he pulled out a small jewelry box and held it out to her. It was not all that dissimilar to the one that held the glittering earrings she had just seen shared by the couple nearby. The words accompanying the presentation spilled easily from his lips.

"And…I was made partner!"

Not only did the anticipation that had been building in her go out of her like air from a balloon, what remained was equally shriveled and limp. She struggled to process the twist the conversation had taken. Or maybe it hadn't actually taken a turn. Maybe it had shifted only in her imagination. The reality was disconcerting. So much so that she hardly knew how to respond.

A distant voice, far off and generic that might have been hers, mumbled a response.

"Partner? But you're already the...."

He interrupted before she could finish, as he often did. She was used to it by now—wasn't she?

"I know, I know, but now I've got more responsibility, control of new business, voting rights. I'm on my way to running the company, Jen! Only Martin and Goldberg are above me, and Goldberg's probably going to retire next year."

"Congratulations, Arthur. That's wonderful." Her tone was flat. If he noticed her disinterest he didn't remark on it. He could be very self-involved at times, could Arthur. In fact, he could be self-involved a lot of the time.

"So," he continued, moderating his excitement slightly, "I wanted to give you something precious."

"Precious?" She was having a hard time focusing. The evening was not going as she'd hoped.

He opened the jewelry box he was holding and turned it toward her. It contained a small gold locket. It was well-made but not especially fancy. It did look quite old. There were no gemstones set atop it, much less anywhere else on the box. She pointed.

"What—is—that?"

She didn't have to admire it and gush over it. He was doing it for her. A passing stranger might have thought it was a gift from her to him instead of the other way around.

"It's a locket." He paused for emphasis. "With my picture in it."

"A locket with your picture in it?" Dimly, she was aware that repeating what he said did not constitute an exchange of views, much less a conversation.

"Yeah." He set the box down on the table. "Since I'll be going away, I thought you would like to keep me close to your heart."

"Away?" There, she was doing it again, she told herself. "Where are you going?"

He puffed up like a penguin in a snowstorm. "There's a new venture that could be worth millions. Martin was going to supervise the deal but he passed it along to me. That shows you the kind of confidence he and Goldberg have in me. Also, how old they are. So, I have to go up to San Francisco. You know—due diligence. Meetings are scheduled for every day and I have to absorb a lot of information, financial and otherwise." He tapped the side of his head. "Plenty of room on the ol' hard drive. I'll master everything, the deal will go through, and then the rest of the company will have to rely on me for everything. It's a lot of work, but the end result will be that my position within the company will be untouchable."

Though she heard everything he said, all Jen could mumble was, "San Francisco?"

"Yes. I'm leaving later tonight." Not a word about inviting her to join him. Nothing. Not that she could have left Stuart and her own work on such short notice anyway but—it would have been nice to have been asked.

"Tonight?" Surely, she thought through the fog of unreality that now suffused her brain, she could think of something to say that didn't echo him.

"I know." His expression was sympathetic. Whether it was also genuine was another matter entirely.

She giggled. It was a totally unexpected response. As she did so she was studying the immaculate cutlery that had been neatly laid out on their table. Fortunately for the new partner of Daly Enterprises, the knives on display were designed for butter and were not sharp.

"I thought it'd be better to tell you over dinner," he rambled on, "and maybe you could come visit in a few weeks. I'll make some time despite my schedule. We'll go out, maybe take in a concert, try a new restaurant or two. Unless you just want to stay in and cook. I'll have an apartment."

Mechanically, as if something else was moving her hand, she

picked up the locket and dropped it in her purse. "A few weeks?" Pushing back her chair she rose and took a step away from the table. "Well, thank you for the gift. I will surely keep it close to my heart. In fact, I know just the place to keep it." Looking around, she located the entrance to the bathrooms.

"Excuse me, I need to find the ladies' room."

The facility was as spotless and elegant as the rest of Pompeo's. Pausing in front of one of the sinks, she studied the face in the mirror that was looking back at her. It was an attractive face, a kind and forgiving face. She then began, softly and angrily, to cry.

"What's wrong, honey?"

Turning, Jen found herself face to face with Mrs. Walley. It required a moment to fully identify the older woman since Jen had only previously encountered her at the dog park, clad in sweats and sneakers. She was dressed beautifully now. Understated but classy. It was a bit of a shock. The second one of the evening.

"Mrs. Walley? Fancy seeing you here." Using a towel Jen dabbed at her eyes.

Noting the younger woman's distress, the matron tried to be as upbeat as possible. "Oh, Harold and I used to come here all the time. One of our favorite restaurants. I come from time to time to reminisce. And to eat, of course. The food is wonderful. Did you know they make their own pasta on site?" She hesitated, wanting to help, not wanting to intrude. "You're upset, dear. It didn't go as you thought?"

"Not tonight." Jen sniffed, then frowned uncertainly. "How do you know anything about it?"

"I saw him hand you the little jewelry box. But I didn't see him put anything on your finger. For that matter, I didn't see you put anything on your finger." She smiled reassuringly. "It's never the one you think, Jen. Sometimes, the one you're looking for is right under your nose." She looked away, backwards in time. "There was this fella. Good-looking, athletic, steady income. The kind of man any woman would be glad to have. That was the trouble. There were too many women happy to have him. Harold, now… he maybe wasn't movie-star handsome and he maybe didn't drive a fancy car, but the only thing in the world he was really interested in was…me. That makes up for a lot of looks and money, my dear. *If* you can find someone like that."

"You may be right. Because it sure isn't Arthur." Fumbling in her purse, she pulled out the locket to show the other woman. "I really thought he was proposing tonight and all he gave me was this stupid locket. That, and a lot of talk about himself."

She held it up to show Mrs. Walley, but the older woman was gone. Vanished. Jen frowned. She hadn't seen her leave. Oh well. Seniors could surprise you like that. Move faster than you thought possible.

Might as well wear the damn thing as keep it in its box. It took a bit of wrestling to get it fastened around her neck. At least it hung properly against her chest.

Arthur was waiting at their table. He did not seem upset by how long she had been gone. Something, perhaps, to his credit. On the other hand, he didn't ask if she was okay, either.

"There you are." He gestured at the table. "The wine is here. Let's toast to success in Frisco, yeah?" Noticing that she was wearing the locket, he smiled approvingly. "It looks great on you. But then, everything does."

Her glass was half full (no, she told herself…half empty). Picking it up, she raised it towards him. "To success!", she declared. To herself she added, so softly he could not hear, "Business mode."

🐾   🐾   🐾

It was hardly a shock that since the evening had not gone as she had hoped, it did not end as she had planned. Nor did she bother to inquire as to whatever else Arthur might have had in mind. Fortunately for him, he was so wrapped up in and overcome by his promotion that he could talk of little else. Fortunately, because if he had suggested even the slightest little cuddle she would have, she would have.…..

The wine she was drinking now in the quiet of her bedroom was of a far more modest vintage than what they had sipped at Pompeo's. Disdaining a glass and fully intending to finish the whole thing anyway, she clutched it by its neck as she strode back and forth across her bedroom. Occasionally she paused to put the bottle to her lips and take a most unlady-like swig.

Sitting alertly on the edge of the bed, Stuart tracked her every move. As she stomped to and fro his head followed her as if he were watching a player at Wimbledon. Meanwhile Jen continued to vent continuously. Well, not continuously. Her ranting was periodically interrupted by the need to imbibe more wine. Her tone flipped back and forth between mocking and bitter.

"More responsibility. Voting control. I'm going to run the company." She executed her fifth impressive guzzle. "Oh, and by the way, I'm going to Frisco. Except that I'm so dumb I don't realize that ninety percent of the people there hate having it called 'Frisco'. But I'm going to run the company, so I can call it Frisco, instead of 'the City'. So anyway, I got you this stupid locket to keep my stupid face close to your stupid, stupid, *stupid*…!

Realizing that she was breathing too hard, too fast, and that even someone her age could have a heart attack and that it certainly would be a waste of a good heart attack to have one because of a certain Arthur Daly, she got control of herself.

"Seven years," she mumbled. "After seven years, all I get is a locket with his picture in it. Seven years of emotional support, of cheering him on as he rose up the corporate ladder, of being there for him when he needed someone. Seven years of often putting aside my own interests to help him out. Seven years of…of….”

Her voice trailed away as her gaze shifted to the mirror above her dresser. There were a lot of pictures there. Herself with Stuart, herself with Arthur. Many pictures of just Arthur. Many more of just Stuart. She staggered toward the dresser, the bottle hanging loose from one hand. Consumed subsequent to the finer wine she had somehow managed to down at Pompeo’s, she was now according to the laws of the state of California (not to mention her knowledge of her own capacity) thoroughly and officially drunk.

One by one she removed the photos of Arthur from the dresser top and took them out of their frames. She then committed them mentally if not physically to that particular hell that is reserved for such ignoble male representatives of the species, and one by one, ripped them up. She was careful to drop the resultant fragments in the trash can that was snugged up against the dresser. To have simply dropped them, even soused as she was, would have been to sully the carpet.

“It has to be the Pet Friendly Realtor thing. It has to be.” That’s it, she thought weakly. Blame something else. Blame yourself. Not dear, sweet, affectionate Arthur. Come to think of it, her mother could be dear, sweet, and affectionate. She shook her head, finding the comparison invidious.

“Seven years.” Clutching the locket that still hung around her neck, she addressed the reflective panel before her. “Mirror, mirror, see this locket? Tomorrow morning I will hock it!”

It was enough to make her laugh. The laughter quickly spilled into sobbing. Then laugh-sobbing, which threatened to make her choke, so she went quiet. Pouring some remaining wine into a glass, she sat down on the floor next to Stuart and took a more modest sip. If she were lucky, she would pass out before she finished the bottle. If not, there was another bottle in the fridge. She craved unconsciousness, and it was only a matter of time.

The face looking up at her was winsome and plainly distressed. There was no judgment in it: only concern. It was almost human.

"Looks like it's just the two of us, Stuart. As always."

It took her three tries to get the locket open. At the sight of Arthur's picture, the terrier growled. Putting his front paws up on her thigh he began to lick her face. It was an indication of how far gone she was that she could not tell the difference between the dog drool and the wine that was dripping off her chin.

"You know, Stu, I just realized I don't even know if I really love Arthur. I'm sure I did at one time, but it's been so long I can't really remember. I mean, he's nice and all, and good-looking, and has a good job—one that's apparently getting better. Something he never fails to remind me of. We're comfortable with each other, and it sure saves a lot of time that might be wasted dating guys I *don't* know anything about." She shook her head slowly.

"I'm just so *used* to him. There's a certain reassurance in familiarity, y'know?" Stuart's head cocked to one side. He was a great listener, Stuart was, even if he didn't entirely grasp what she was saying. Or even if he didn't grasp any of it. Right then, that was what she needed. Someone to listen.

"I'm holding on regardless whether there's any chemistry or not," she continued. She was now slurring her words to the point where the terrier understood them as well as most humans would have. Her voice rose.

"*Your* picture should be in this thing, not his!"

Arriving at a small epiphany, she abruptly rose, sat down again, found her footing, rose again more slowly, and wobbled over to the dresser. Hunting through the contents of the top drawer uncovered many of the same items likely to be found in a purse. The only difference was that there were more of them.

The scissors she finally seized upon were not large, but they did not have to be. Not for the task that had suddenly washed over her mind. It did take her several missed attempts before she finally managed to get her fingers around the edges of one of the pictures of Stuart that was taped to the mirror. Working very carefully and occasionally snipping nothing but air, she finally managed to trim the photo from a full-size image down to a portrait. Wetting the tip of her free index finger, she used it to slide the grinning image of Arthur out of the locket. She had to put her face a few inches from the open locket in order to slip the terrier's portrait inside, but when she was done and it was secured in place she was more than a little pleased with the result.

Refilled glass in hand, she staggered back to the bed and flopped down beside her ever empathetic pooch. Holding out the open locket, she showed it to him. He did his best to track it because she was having trouble holding her hand in one place.

"Look, Stuie. This is how it should be. Now *you* are the one even closer to my heart." She let out a most unladylike, booming belch, giggled, frowned at the glass of wine, started to set it aside, shrugged diffidently, and downed the remainder of the bright liquid in one long swallow.

"Mom was right. She's always right. That's the problem. That's what's so hard to deal with. I'd feel better if all that rightness weren't—wasn't—coming from her." As she leaned toward Stuart her face broke out in a wide, sloppy grin. The sort of expression you'd expect from a circus clown, if there were any such thing as a circus anymore. Damn technology.

Stuart's response was instinctively canine. He licked at the edge of her wine glass, sampling.

Sleepy. Why was she so sleepy? It couldn't have anything to do with the lateness of the hour, the stress induced by the overwhelming disappointment of the evening, or the fact that she had consumed enough wine to set the average French street mime to babbling stupidly. Perhaps all three. She fiddled with the locket, twisting and twirling it between her fingers.

"You want to know something, Stuart? I wish one day I would

meet a guy just like you. Someone who wants to be next to me as much as you do. Someone who cares more about *me* than about his job, his prospects, his car, sports—anything and everything. Don't mean he has to ignore any of that. Just puts me first. Unconditional love, you know. I resnooze—I refuse to believe that's just a line from a book, or the movies. Has to be a *guy* somewhere who believes in it, too." She went to take another slug of the wine, made a face at the empty glass, and resumed blathering.

"It can't be that hard. He has to be out there somewhere, a guy like that. They can't all be married. Guy like that." Her expression hardened. "The anti-Arthur. Four-leaf clovers exist. He's got to, also. I mean, I'm a good person. I make a decent living. Arthur's not the only good catch floating around. He's not the only attractive one. I'm attractive, too, right?"

Stuart had been staring at her throughout the entire tirade. At that moment he chose to move to one side. This allowed Jen to see herself in another mirror, the full-length one attached to the closet door. Staring back at her was a young woman who was indeed attractive. Unfortunately, that attractiveness was presently hidden behind a face drawn by sobbing and masked by a Niagara of runny makeup, compounded by hair that would have won first prize at many a Halloween contest. Her mouth opened wide in an "O" of horror.

"*Oh—my—god!*"

She dropped her glass. Having only a short distance to fall and carpet to land on, it did not break. This was fortunate as, trying to catch it before it landed, a reaching Jen overextended her already compromised self and followed it to the floor. Lifting her head, she was greeted by the less communicative end of Stuart. The other end was engaged in licking the last dregs of wine that had spilled from the glass. Wrinkling up his nose, he let out a (for his size) prodigious sneeze, which scared him, and he promptly fled under the bed. Normally, Jen would have followed up with an inquiry as to his well-being. Her present well-being being anything but well, she did not. She was out cold, the locket clutched in one hand. Catching the light from overhead, the curved and inscribed golden surface glowed.

Or maybe it was something else.

❧ ❧ ❧

Her alarm didn't sound right. What she was hearing was more akin to a song, a proper melody. It almost sounded like Verdi's Dies Irae. Except Jen didn't know the music from the Verdi Requiem. She'd heard it as part of the score for *Mad Max—Fury Road*. It certainly got the attention of strangers, especially if she let it play out. It did not emanate from her bedside clock, which when it went off did so with a very much more workmanlike *clank*.

Phone. Light in room. She realized she must have slept through the clock alarm. On—the floor.

Oh god.

She sat up fast: the first bad idea of the day. But she did not fall over. Or throw up. Moving much more cautiously, she rose to what she took to be a vertical position before commencing to search for the source of the Mad Maxed-out Verdi. Helpfully, the phone was right where it belonged; on her bedside end table. Right next to the overlooked clock, which read an unhelpful quarter to nine.

If she had been more awake, she would certainly have muted Facetime.

It was bright and busy in the Townsend Real Estate Agency. No office was brighter and busier than that of Sylvia Jensen, who sat behind her desk in full business mode as the phone in front of her rang and rang, calling insistently for someone to replace the musical sound with a voice.

"She better be on her way," she growled to no one in particular.

Someone on the other end of the call finally answered. It took Sylvia an instant to realize it was her own brood. Her eyes widened as she stared at the phone.

"Geezus! What the hell happened to you? Did you get hit by a bus?" Though the background behind Jen was distant and fuzzy, that was enough for Sylvia to identify her daughter's surroundings. "And when did your bedroom become a war zone?"

"Please—not so loud." Either Jen was presently unable to hold her own phone steady, or else the phone was stable and it was the rest of her that was unstable. Wincing, she mumbled something barely intelligible. "Not today, Satan. Not today."

"What did you say?" Unable to grab and shake her daughter through the phone, Sylvia had to settle for aural outrage. "You have a five million dollar potential listing in ten minutes. You need me to break down the math for you? Huh? Then clean yourself up and get out the door." She took a deep breath, added. "*Now!*"

She didn't bother to wait for a response and hung up. Either her daughter would make the appointment in time to salvage it or she would not. If the first, then the conversation (if such it could be called) would be quickly forgotten. If she failed to appear to meet with the prospective customer, Sylvia would throw the listing to somebody who *could* get there. Maternal love ended where seven figures were involved.

Jen did not so much slide out of bed as shuffle off the metal coils. That she landed on her feet instead of her ass was a sign that all might not be lost. The address of the listing, the big listing —it actually wasn't all that far from her own. Like anywhere in Southern California, the price for real estate went up exponentially the closer one got to the ocean. That someplace like Jen's modest domicile could exist only a few miles from a multi-million dollar home was the norm, not the exception. She might be a few minutes late to the appointment, but not enough to kill a possible deal. The potential seller could wile away a few minutes on the internet, or whatever their choice of time-killer happened to be.

Though she would have preferred to replace the face that stared groggily back at her from the mirror, that was not an option. A quick wash and rinse resulted in a better visage than she had any right to expect. Minimal makeup, no jewelry, arranged hair so that it didn't look like you spent the morning standing behind the engine cowling of a 737 waiting to take off, throw on some clothes—no, not sweatpants and shirt—shoes next, and *where was Stuart?* After last night she wouldn't have blamed him if he had decamped to the farthest reaches of the small backyard. Sometimes it seemed like everyone in SoCal needed therapy, including their dogs. Not cats, though. Cats do not go through stages. They are either entirely sane or homicidal. With felines there is no in-between.

"Stuart!" No sign of him. Last she remembered, he had squeezed under the bed. Most likely he was still there, sleeping off her drunk. Someone should, she told herself. She ought to look for him, she knew, but she was already in the kitchen and there was no time, no time.

It would have to be dry food: there wasn't a spare moment to so much as open a can. Usually when she dumped dry food into his bowl he would come running, but not this morning. Dare she pause long enough to make coffee? She could live without blood. She was less sure about caffeine.

The fridge supplied cold salvation in the form of a chilled can of double-strength iced coffee. She didn't even bother to look at the brand; just grabbed at it, slammed the fridge door shut, and bolted, shouting as she ran.

"Stuart! Where are you, buddy? Breakfast is in your bowl. Sorry, dry, no time to open a can. Double rations tonight, and treats." Racing to the front door at a run, proud of herself for making it without taking a header. Jen Jensen, Olympic house runner.

"I gotta get to work, Stu, but I promise I'll be right back to take you to the park. Business mode first, then dog mode. Treats —if you don't pee on my bed!"

Outside then, a necessary pause to make sure the door was shut and locked behind her, and then to her car. She would make the appointment in time—depending on whether or not she encountered any cops along the way. As she slid behind the wheel she tried not to think about being stopped. Because being stopped would mean missing the appointment for sure, and missing the appointment would mean having to deal with her mom's reaction, and….

There was no time for fear, she told herself firmly. You have nothing to fear but mother herself. Mom fear is the mind killer.

She put the car in gear and shot out onto the street. Fortunately, it was as empty as the wine bottle she had left behind on the floor in her bedroom. Or the hole in her heart that an unthinking Arthur Daly had put there.

CHAPTER FOUR

In her absence, the house that Jen had fled in Business Mode was dead quiet. Nothing moved within. Not a mouse, not a louse, and since she had left, not a souse. The TV was silent and so was the plumbing. There was a slight humming, but it came from the refrigerator and was not in any way sentient.

Within the master bedroom a limb slowly emerged from beneath the bed. It was dark beneath the box springs, but not as dark as the dog that had wriggled under there the previous evening. The limb terminated in a hand. A perfectly normal human hand. Hand and arm were followed by the rest of a perfectly normal human body. Male, its head featured long black hair and a matching beard. The body was also quite naked. Letting out a wide yawn, the unclothed figure ambled on hands and knees toward the stairs. These it descended in decidedly clumsy fashion; half crawling, half stumbling.

No matter. Reaching the kitchen, the figure spotted dry dog food in a nearby dog bowl. The usual food in the usual place. Crawling over and only momentarily inconvenienced by the presence of his beard, the male figure dipped his head and took in a mouthful of the colorful shapes—and promptly spit them out.

Odd. The dry food had never before tasted quite so much like cardboard. And how did he know what cardboard tasted like? Maybe Jen had left something else out for him to eat. He was very fond of leftovers. It didn't even matter leftover what. It was all edible. Except, apparently, the multi-hued gravel that presently filled the dog bowl.

Crawling past the kitchen's full-length mirror, he could not miss the reflection of a strange naked man. Whirling, he started barking. It was a peculiar bark, off-key and much deeper than his usual warning. Confused, he went quiet. A downward glance revealing that his paws were now hands confused him a good deal more.

Emitting a terrified yelp, he scrambled backwards away from the demonic mirror and began scrambling around the house. In the course of running his body began to rise of its own volition, shifting from a horizontal posture to a vertical one, until he was running on two feet. He was making a poor job of it, too, listing like a drunken sailor, bumping into furniture, and knocking over one object after another. Of one thing he was certain: when she got home, Jen was going to be pissed. He felt scared and frightened and lost and way, way off balance. He needed away from the horrific situation in which he now found himself.

Bailing up at the front door, he scratched at it furiously. "Jen! Jen! Je…!"

His mouth opened wide. The sounds coming out of him were neither bark nor whine but human. And comprehensible—he understood them. If he could make human sounds, maybe he could form human words.

He knew how the door worked. Reaching down, his human fingers contracted around the knob. Twist—that's how Jen does it—twist, and pull.

The door opened wide and he dashed outside, nearly tripping

as he did so when he started to drop to all fours before catching himself. Anyone seeing him emerge would have thought he was an ordinary man suffering a medical episode. He was suffering an episode alright, but one no medicine on Earth could alleviate.

His tree! At least his favorite tree was still there. *He* might be different, but the tree was not. Half running, half stumbling, he made a beeline for it. At first he tried lifting his left leg. Although the mechanics worked, it didn't feel right, somehow. Also, standing on one foot left him unstable. So he peed flat-footed. Peeing also felt normal, even though the flow seemed to begin a long, long way from the ground.

"Jen!" He let out a long, mournful howl. It was still sufficiently doggish to reassure him. He was still him. Or him still he. The raging confusion that filled him extended to syntax. He was he, for sure—but what was "he" now? "Where are you, Jen!"

Another long, drawn-out howl drew looks and the occasional gasp from a passing mail lady and a neighbor taking out the trash. Even in SoCal, where a tolerance for the outlandish was the norm, his actions exceeded anything the neighborhood had seen on television, the internet, or in film. A much younger onlooker might have reasoned that the man pissing on the tree was nothing more than a state-of-the-art special effect. Adults knew better.

"Hey!" the neighbor taking out the trash yelled accusingly, "put some clothes on, and pee inside the house! What are ya? An animal?"

The insult only intensified Stuart's whine. A bit defiantly, he indicated the collar around his neck. "I'm not allowed to pee inside the house. She doesn't let me!"

Now, there are certain quarters in Southern California where this entire scene would have been greeted with nods of understanding, but Newport Beach definitely was not one of them. Pausing briefly on her route, the mail lady offered her own take.

"Hey, Tarzan, I ain't complaining, because I never see anything abnormal on this route and everybody needs a change of pace once in a while, but as an official postal employee, if you don't go put on some clothes I'm gonna have to alert the police."

In response to this threat, and having concluded his dialogue with the tree, the naked male figure scurried back inside the house. The expression on his face was pitiful.

Handing the neighbor a fistful of adverts, the mail lady sounded disgusted. "I don't mind a nude guy now and then, especially one flashing a decent bod, but not when I'm at work." She nodded in the direction taken by the unclothed refugee. "I met the gal who lives there a couple of times. Needed signature on packages. Don't remember seeing *him*."

"I wouldn't know," the neighbor replied stiffly. "I try avoid other peoples' business."

The mail lady nodded. "I know she got a dog so maybe the guy is pet sitting?"

"Or maybe he escaped from somewhere." The neighbor shrugged. "As I said; not my business."

"And I've got a route to finish." The mail lady moved off, the neighbor headed back into his own domicile, and save for the faint smell of urine, the neighborhood was once more as before.

As if the listing for Derek Jones was not near enough to the beach to justify its price tag, its square footage was. Jen pulled up behind a pair of luxury vehicles that occupied part of the paved circular drive. A single glance at the mansion was enough to impress her. She could only manage a single glance because the sun hurt her eyes. Perhaps if the beams hadn't penetrated clear through to the back of her skull. Or so it felt.

Phone. Where was her phone? A moment of panic ensued before she found it and called her mother. Sylvia answered immediately.

"You look marginally less awful than fifteen minutes ago. Tell me you're there."

Ah, a mother's comforting tone. If your mother is Maleficent. Setting aside the tart retort that lingered on the tip of her tongue, Jen replied as if nothing untoward had occurred this morning.

"Just got here. There are two cars in front of me, each one of which cost more than my first house. This place is huge!"

"Yeah, and so is the commission if you sell it," her mother reminded her. "Now get in there! Make it happen. And maybe put on some dark glasses. That must've been some bender you were on."

She hung up before Jen could reply. Or explain. It didn't matter. She could only take on one fight at a time and right now that fight happened to be with sunshine. Another reason to put on dark glasses. Defiantly, she demurred. Bloodshot or not, clients always liked to see an agent's eyes. Many believed it enabled them to tell when a realtor was dissembling with them. This was, of course, an abject falsehood.

"Oooo, brutal," she muttered.

As she exited the car she was greeted by the owner, Derek Jones. Barely in his thirties, handsome, fit, he flashed a set of teeth fit to make a Deinonychus proud. Setting canine protocol aside, the Golden Retriever that accompanied him immediately jumped on Jen, putting both front paws on her stomach before settling back down onto all fours. His owner was instantly impressed.

"Wow, he likes you. Avery rarely does that. He's usually much more reserved with strangers."

"He must smell Stuart." Bending, she ruffled the retriever's ears and scratched the top of his head. It never entered her mind that the dog might react in an other than sociable manner. Living with Stuart had sensitized her to canine moods and she felt she could read them instinctively. Unlike the males of her own species, she reflected morosely. She didn't let her thoughts intrude on the moment, however. Business mode, she reminded herself.

"Who's a handsome fella?" she cooed to the retriever. "Who's a big boy? Avery? Yes, yes you are!"

Jones was more than a little captivated. "Wow, you really are pet-friendly. And clearly, pets respond in kind. I'm Derek. You must be Jen." He indicated the manse looming behind him. "I have coffee brewing. My own personal Goroka blend. Drink coffee?"

She straightened. The appointment had hardly gone anywhere but already it was going well. "Like, a gallon a day."

He laughed and gestured for her to follow. "I'll be interested to see what you think of my fusion." He looked to his dog, who was busy sniffing each of Jen's shoes and her kneecaps one after the other. "Come, Avery!"

At the double front door, one side of which was open, he slowed. "Come on in, but be aware of...."

The foyer was spotlessly clean and tastefully decorated. Before she could take it all in, a barrage of high-pitched screeching assailed her ears. In her present recovering condition the sound went through her like knives. The shape of the foyer amplified the cacophony. Putting her palms against her ears, she winced. The racket would have been deafening even sans her hangover.

"Holy Moley," she gasped, "what the hell is *that?*"

A moment later she saw as well as heard the source. The pair of excited Sulphur-crested cockatoos stood side by side on a giant perch. As near as she could tell they were completely unrestrained. Derek had to raise his voice to be heard over the otherworldly screeching.

"Not holy moley, but you're close. I should've warned you sooner." He nodded proudly toward the beautiful white birds. "That's Holly and Molly, my two love birds."

"You mean, *loud* birds. I thought love birds were smaller. A *lot* smaller."

"Oh, you thought I meant *Agapornis.*" He grinned. It was, she decided through her discomfort, a very pleasant smile. "Those are members of a different species entirely. I wasn't being technical."

"So relieved to hear it." Rubbing at her temples in an attempt to massage away the remnants of her hangover, she followed him into the living room. Like the foyer, it had the air of having been kitted out by a professional decorator. In addition to some fine landscape photographs and attractive bric-a-brac there were also trophies in a glass-fronted case and several large framed pictures of Derek, clad in a uniform she immediately recognized.

"Baseball player. Angels, cool." She turned away from the photos and back to him. "Still play?"

He led her into the kitchen. It was bright and airy, like everything else about the house. It was, Jen decided right then, the cleanest, neatest bachelor pad she had ever seen. She quickly caught herself. Of course, that didn't mean he lived alone. Just that he was alone then, at that very moment. He might have regular maid service. He quite likely had periodic visitors on a non-professional basis. Single guy, major league ball player, highly unlikely he lived a monastic lifestyle. But she was impressed that he could brew his own coffee.

"Cream, sugar, something else?" He was pouring black brew into a pair of mugs.

"Black's fine. Especially this morning." Taking the proffered cup, she sipped gratefully. "A little strong for my taste, but really nice flavor."

"I still want to see where it's grown and processed." As he leaned against a counter, Avery rubbed up against his legs. Reaching down with his free hand he petted the retriever, who was loving every second of the attention.

"To answer your question: yeah, with the Angels five years now. Starting shortstop. Still making it with my glove more so than my bat, though my average isn't too bad. No biggie. Everybody has a job. When I set up this appointment with your mother she said that you couldn't come yesterday because you were busy with your dog. Tell me about him. I love animals."

"I can see that. Stuart?" A warm grin spread across her face. "Nothing much to say. He's just the greatest Boston Terrier in the world, that's all. Did you know they're the first American breed?"

"I did not know that," he confessed, plainly charmed. "Learn something new every day."

"Yeah," she went on, "they're called the American Gentleman. Have a look." Pulling out her phone she showed him a favorite picture. Then another favorite picture, and another. Because whatever picture she was showing of Stuart at the moment was her favorite picture of him.

Derek did not have to feign interest. He was genuinely curious. "Because they look like they're wearing a tuxedo?"

She nodded as she continued to scroll through photos. For the moment, Business mode had given way to Admiring Stuart mode. Matters of real estate had momentarily been forgotten.

"Probably. Also, their demeanor. Bostons are very polite, gentle, forthright. And that's just a few of their qualities. No offense, Avery," she said to the retriever. Leaning up against Derek, he scarcely acknowledge his name. "Stuart has a moral code I don't see in most people. The love of my life and a shining example of his breed. He looked down at the retriever. "That's exactly how I feel about Avery."

☙ ☙ ☙

He was gradually finding his balance. It was not as if he hadn't balanced on his hind legs before. He was agile enough to do that while waving his front paws in hopes of acquiring a treat. He even had experience hopping on them. But running was a new skill he had yet to master. Not to mention having prehensile thumbs. They tended to hang loose until he actually had to grab something. Even that took some practice.

Last night. He remembered last night. She had held out clothes in front of her but had chosen to wear something else. Searching through her closet he came across the two black dresses she had held up in front of her before deciding to go with a different look. Emulating her actions, he decided against either. They were too cold, and smelled of laundry.

Laundry, *yes*. Sniffing around the room, it took him only a moment to locate the dirty clothes hamper. It smelled familiar. Homey, reassuring, musky. It smelled like Jen. He opened it, banged his fingers when he forgot to hold it open, and began fumbling within.

It had been awhile since the front door to Jen's house had slammed shut behind the naked stranger. Now it flew open and a singular figure emerged. It was still male, still bearded, but this time fully dressed. Although the choice of couture was debatable.

He had barely been able to squeeze his much larger and differently apportioned frame into Jen's pink jogging suit. The result resembled a misshapen, bipedal tomato. Having seen her often wear sunglasses, he had also donned a random pair of those. After a quick look to left and right, an exercise Jen had taught him, he crossed.

Having concluded the pedestrian portion of this part of her route and coming down the street in the opposite direction was the same mail lady who had encountered him earlier. Her eyes widened.

"Oh no! Not on *my* route!"

Holding onto the wheel with one hand she hunted through her glove box with the other. Pulling out a red flag, she waved it in the jogger's direction before bringing the truck to a noisy halt. Before he could make a move to get away, she threw the flag at him. His confusion was palpable. Should he run, or presume she was playing fetch? In which case he needed to pick up the flag and return it to her. Except he was momentarily stymied by how far the flag was from his mouth, and was not sure dropping to the ground to pick it up in his teeth was at that moment the correct thing to do.

Confronting him, the woman was wagging a finger in his face. "Is that you again, Tarzan? Making me throw a penalty flag. When you gonna learn the rules?" She glanced down. "Go get some shoes on your feet now. Believe me, there's places around here you don't want to be going barefoot."

"But I always go—barefoot around here," he protested. "And her shoes don't fit me."

"Neither do her clothes." The mail lady was shaking her head at the incongruousness of his appearance. "That outfit is pretty unisex, though I'm not sure the color suits you. And it's about three sizes too small. You look like an alcoholic housewife."

"I do? Thanks! I'm going to the park to find Jen." Seeing that she was not going to do anything to stop him, he headed off in that direction.

Bending, the mail lady recovered her flag. Had she yelled "Sit!", events might have proceeded differently. Stuart was nothing if not reactive. But it did not occur to her to say "sit" or "heel" or anything else to which he might have responded. Besides, she was running a little late and had more junk mail to deliver.

❧ ❧ ❧

The meeting had gone well, Jen knew. Considering the sprint required to make it on time and the consequence damage to both her physical and mental image, extremely well. Not only was she intrigued by the potential sale, the same might be said, at least a little, of the potential seller. As the Pet Friendly realtor she had caught an immediate break upon discovering that the prospective client was also a pet lover. His own dog, Avery, was a charmer. The less said about the twin air raid sirens on the perch in the foyer, the better. Even Jen had her limits. To each their own, she firmly believed, but personally she expected pets to provide love and companionship: not deafness.

As they walked back to the front door she continued her sales pitch.

"...and Derek, Townsend will be taking all legitimate offers, which will result in the sale of your house for top dollar. It's a fabulous place in a great location and we have many clients looking for homes like this. I have to compliment you on how well you've kept the place up. I would've thought...."

"What?" he interrupted her. "That as a professional baseball player I'd be having wild parties here every night, with people swinging from the chandeliers and throwing up on the carpets? We're not all like that. I'm actually a pretty quiet guy. I believe in focusing on my work." He grinned. "I reserve the wild parties for rental spaces. On the road."

She regarded him uncertainly for a moment, then smiled. "Okay, that puts me in my place. Speaking of finding places, that's what I do. And buyers. I'll find the right one for your house. Plus, I'll make a huge commission."

There was nothing he could do but admire her forthrightness. Besides, she carried around pictures of her dog. "I like it. Let's do it!"

She nodded once. "When I get in the office today I'll set up an appointment to finalize the paperwork."

"Sounds good." He gestured back toward the house. "See you later, then. Got to feed Avery. He sheds when his food is late."

"That's not a problem with Stuart," she replied. "Real short hair, so he never needs a cut and I never have to sweep up after him."

🐾　🐾　🐾

There are places in the world, and in the United States, where the sight of a bearded man wearing a too-tight pink jogging suit and florid sunshades would provoke a multitude of nonplussed reactions among the local populace.

Southern California is not one of these places.

Feeling more confident in his new bipedal stride with each step, Stuart made his way down the familiar commercial street. Despite the mental displacement caused by viewing everything from a new, higher angle, from time to time he recognized shops and cafes he had visited with Jen. One in particular drew his immediate attention.

TOTALLY CLIPS HAIR SALON

Putting his face up against the glass, he peered through the front window, searching for Jen. He couldn't see her. Maybe, he mused, she was in back, getting her fur groomed. Opening the door, he let himself in, sniffing as he went.

The girl at the front desk flaunted tats, piercings, and an attitude that suggested that if a tsunami had begun rolling in off the nearby bay she would scarcely have bothered to look for an inner tube. One side of her head was shaved, the other cropped so that the hair drooped tastefully down over her left eye. Exerting maximum effort, she succeeded in raising her gaze from the tablet in front of her to the peculiar figure that had ambled in through the front door. The fact that he was continuously and unabashedly sniffing of his surroundings as well as the empty air did not unsettle her. In fact, if left up to her she would have been perfectly content to let him snuffle to his heart's content. However, there was the small if regrettable matter of her job to consider, and other patrons of TC might not be so understanding.

"Can I help you?"

Though radically transformed, Stuart was as open as ever. "I'm just sniffing," he told her. As if that explanation was necessary. "Can you smell Jen? Jen Jensen? Was she in here today?"

"Yah. She was here, and she didn't smell anything, either.

Then she went out the door. Like you should right now." For emphasis she put a hand on the desk phone, as if she was prepared to call someone. The police, for example.

As a feint it proved unnecessary. Utterly missing both her sarcasm and the implied threat, he wagged a non-existent tail. "That's great! Thanks!"

As he departed, the receptionist took a moment to consider. She didn't know Jensen well, but from what she could recall of that particular customer the woman did not strike her as the type to keep the acquaintance of bearded men who dressed in skin-tight track suits. With a shrug she put the encounter out of her mind and returned to perusing the string of music videos she had assembled on her tablet.

As he walked, vertical Stuart drew only an occasional sideways glance. Offering casual greetings to passers-by sometimes sparked greetings in return. Also the infrequent dirty look. He offered the same hellos in equal measure to the small dogs he passed. Anyone observing his progress might have remarked that not a single one of them barked at the affable if oddly dressed stranger.

There, what was that? A touch of scent on the sea breeze. Familiar, overpowering in its strength, unmistakable. Not Jen.

Bacon!

Following his nose led him to an outdoor café. As it was one he often visited in Jen's company he had no compunction about stopping opposite the table occupied by a couple enjoying their breakfast. Why should it be a problem? Surely the staff would recognize him.

His momentarily overwhelmed senses masked the realization of what he had become.

Squatting down nearby, he gazed at the bacon on the man's plate. There were eggs and toast as well, but their aromas paled in comparison to the perfume of pan-crisped pig.

Although general safety concerns and common sense deem

interaction with the plethora of prevalent weirdos inadvisable in Southern Cal, sometimes circumstances require that such rules be broken. The diner, who heretofore had ignored Stuart's presence, finally felt compelled to say something.

"Do you mind?"

The strangely-clad visitor squatting nearby made puppy eyes at him. To the diner that proved even more disconcerting than the other man's begging posture.

"Be nice, Frank," said his breakfast companion. "He looks hungry. See? He's not even asking for money. Give him your toast or something. We can order more." She smiled at her husband. "Be socially aware. Besides, we're at the beach. Poor fellow probably sleeps under the pier."

The man let out a grunt. "Looks pretty well-groomed to me. It's not like his clothes are hanging off him. Oh, fine." He turned toward the eager Stuart. "Would you like some toast?"

The crouching figure shook his head. "No. The turkey bacon."

Turning back to his wife, the man cast a jaundiced eye. "Denise?" Her puppy eyes were almost as effective as Stuart's.

"Just toss it at me," he whined.

The woman grinned. "Toss it at him, Frank."

Her husband gaped at her. "Really, Denise? You gotta be kidding me." He indicated the remaining strip of bacon. "I wanna eat this."

There is a tone women employ when dealing with men that involves the slowing of time. Einstein somehow missed it when concocting his General Theory of Relativity. It belongs to the General Theory of Relatives, but that remains to be mathematically proven by an as yet unnamed scientist. The theorem carries with it implications all its own. Denise utilized it now.

"F—r—a—n—k….."

With a sigh he picked up the strip of bacon and swung it too and fro in front of the waiting beggar. Stuart's head went from side to side as he followed it, until its owner tossed it into the air. Tracking its flight, he adjusted his head to catch it in mid-air. Growling softly, he devoured it in seconds, then straightened and took off. Both diners watched him go, more than a little shocked at the unexpectedly savage behavior.

"I can't believe you did that, Frank."

Her husband gaped at her, at a loss for words. He was not the first man to be caught out by such a reaction. Nor would he be the last.

The Barkery was busy, as it usually was that time of day. Cindy served customers one after another, running credit cards and, rarely, taking cash and making change. One reason customers enjoyed their visits so much was due to the antics of Cupcake. Cindy had trained her to pick up small neatly wrapped bonus treats from a tray and deposit them in customer's Barkery bags. The Pomeranian never deviated from her duty until Cindy gave her the command to disengage.

Until now. Espying something outside, the dog started barking uncontrollably. Gazing in from without, Stuart met the Pomeranian's eyes. Nearly starting to bark in response, he thought better of it. Besides, there was no sign inside of Jen. He moved off, resuming his search.

On the counter inside, Cupcake sat up and made prayer hands with her front paws. Looking past her, Cindy frowned at the front window. Who had her dog seen to cause such a commotion? She shrugged. Whoever it was, they were gone now.

"Who was that, Cupcake? Did you scare him away? You are so fierce!" She eyed the wall clock. "Break time. Wanna go parky?"

In response, the Pomeranian started spinning excitedly. But not entirely for the reason her master believed.

CHAPTER FIVE

I t had been a good morning, Jen decided. In spite of the rushing, in spite of having to listen, however briefly, to her mother's harangue. The fact that Sylvia had been entirely within boundaries to read her daughter the terse riot act did not make it any easier to accept. What she believed to have been a completely successful meeting with the client soothed any hurt feelings or concerns. She was already imagining what she would do with the commission on the sale of the ballplayer's manse. A new, fancier car, perhaps (it would be a tax write-off anyway). Maybe that vacation she'd always dreamed of, to the Amalfi Coast or Polynesia. After her crushing dinner with Arthur she needed a vacation.

Still a little hung over, she winced slightly as she got out of the car. Both her lingering headache and all thoughts of vacation vanished when she noticed that the front door to her house was open. Reaching into her purse she pulled out the lavender cylinder of pepper spray she kept handy. Gripping it tightly, she tiptoed warily through the entrance.

"Stuart?" she called. Tentatively at first, then more forcefully.

"Stuart—come here, buddy." Her voice rose to an unnatural pitch and she added, in case anyone was listening, "*I have pepper spray*"!

She advanced further. "Where are you Stu?"

Reaching the kitchen, she noticed that the food she had put out in the morning for him was untouched. Walking more quickly now, she commenced a thorough search of the house. Everything appeared to be intact and untouched. Clothes, drawer with her jewelry, the electronics: everything was exactly where it belonged. There was no sign of an intruder. There was also no sign of Stuart.

Her voice rose once more, but it was different this time. Rather than challenging, a note of panic was creeping in. "Where are you? Stuart! Oh God—where is he? Stu, don't play with me! I swear, if you're hiding somewhere…. No more games, Stuart. *Where are you?*"

The initial note of panic had become a full symphony. As she exited the house and slammed the door behind her she saw that one of her neighbors was watering his outdoor plants and ran to him.

"Jerry, have you seen Stuart? I think he got out."

The man shook his head. "No. But there was a weird guy peeing on your lawn this morning. Naked. A friend of yours?"

"Naked? Let me think. Oh yeah—probably my accountant. She turned thoughtful. Thanks, Jerry. If you see Stuart, please take him in and call my cell phone. He knows you, he'll come to you."

Seeing her distress, he tightened his mouth and nodded. "If I see him, I'll offer him some bologna."

She brightened. "That'll do it. He loves bologna." Turning, she hurried back to her car.

In twenty minutes of driving up and down the streets where they usually went for walks she saw three cats, a dozing owl, numerous children, other pet owners happily walking other dogs, and a renegade chipmunk. But no Stuart. She was about to retrace her steps for the third time when a new thought struck her.

"Of course!" she muttered aloud. "Where *else* would he go?"

Flipping a U-turn, she headed west, driving slowly as she leaned out the window calling to him. Occasionally she drew the odd glance from other drivers.

"Stuie Lou! Potato head! Horse boy!"

None elicited a response save for one man going through a dumpster at a construction site, in whose proximity she rapidly accelerated.

At the dog park, Jim the guitar man and his Boston Sweetie Peters were picking up bottles and cans and depositing them in municipal recycling bins. Well, Jim was picking and tossing. Sweetie Peters mostly watched. As he performed this charitable public duty, Jim sang along to the music coming through his headphones. Sang softly, so as not to rattle the good citizens of Newport who often frowned on solitary men wandering about singing to themselves.

He stopped as he saw a figure running toward him, then braced himself when he recognized her. On the previous occasion when she had run toward him it had not ended well. But this time Jen slowed before reaching him. At the expression on her face his initial uncertainty turned to worry. She was frantic about something, and he doubted it was him.

"Hey Jim! Oh my God, I'm gonna…." She stopped in front of him and bent over, resting her hands on her knees as she struggled to catch her breath.

"Are you okay?" Confident now that she wasn't going to run him over, his initial wariness turned to concern. "You look like you're going to pass out."

She straightened, took a deep breath. "Stuart's gone. He got out this morning, I don't know how. I was sure I closed the door when I left. Sure! But—I had a lot on my mind. Big sale potential and my mother on my back about it and…and…I can't find him. I'm gonna have a heart attack."

The guitarist was appropriately shocked. "Oh no, that's horrible! You've asked around? Nobody's seen him?"

She shook her head. "No, and enough of the regulars around here would recognize him instantly if they had. Please call me if you see him. You know how friendly he is. He knows you and Sweetie. He'd probably come to you if you called him. I'm a nervous wreck."

"For sure. I have your card. If I see him, I'll try to get a hand on him. Either way, if I see or hear anything, I'll call you." His tone changed. "You work with Townsend Realty, right?"

"Yeah, why?" She was still working at breathing.

"They posted a sign this morning." He pointed to the far end of the greensward. "They're building a shopping center here at the park." Confused, she gave him a blank stare. "Where the park is now? Where we are? It's going to be a shopping center?"

"Really? That can't be right. I'll look into it." She peered around wildly. "Right now I gotta find Stuart." Without hesitating, she reached out to give him a quick hug. A presence at her feet caused her to look down and back off. "'Sweetie Peters', right? I'm sorry, I didn't mean to ignore you." Kneeling, she stroked the terrier and rubbed her head. The dog responded enthusiastically. Just as Stuart would ha….

The unexpected close-up of Jim's footwear gave her pause. She'd seen exactly the same pair in a shop in the Newport Mall. They were Gucci sneakers. Nine hundred bucks the pair if she was remembering correctly. That couldn't be right. Must be knock-offs. Really good-looking, first-quality knock-offs. And why was she studying a guy's shoes when she needed to be scanning the park and the nearby beach?

Not all that far away from the anxious Jen and the enigmatic sneaker owner, Stuart had located Cupcake, Gizmo, and Marley as well as their owners. Ignoring Cindy, Wanda, and Nina, he was making a mess of the pink jogging suit as he cavorted on the grass with the three dogs. They were all over him: licking, pawing, barking and whining for attention. Something had drawn the canine trio to him, and it wasn't his beard.

Sitting at a nearby table, Wanda looked on with amusement. "You watching this guy rolling around in the grass? I hope he knows a good dry cleaner."

"Gizmo seems to like him," Nina commented, "or he'd be growling his head off. He's usually wary around strangers, unless he's luring them in with treats?"

"Maybe he is." Cindy was studying the man-mutt interaction more closely than her friends. "He kinda looks like the guy who was peeking in the window at the Barkery today. Have you guys seen him before?"

"Not me." Wanda made a face. If he was wearing the same outfit the memory would've stuck with me."

"Same here." Nina felt herself softening toward the stranger and his antics. The beach area was a rest home for weirdos, but anyone who got along this well with her dog was worthy of tolerance in her book. "His beard is all over the place but the track suit isn't a Goodwill special, so maybe there's more to him than appears."

"Naw." Wanda gave an airy wave of her hand. "This is Newport Beach. You never know what you can find in a Goodwill."

"Oh so?" Cindy's look was arch. "You know that for a fact?"

The ensuing argument momentarily took their attention away from the visitor and their dogs. Had it not, they might have noticed that the stranger was mouthing words at the three pets. That in itself might not have piqued their interest further. The responses of their pets certainly would have.

"I knew it was you, Stuart!" Cupcake chortled. "There's enough of your smell, no mistaking it." None of them were shocked at Cupcake's avowal. To a dog, smell is a far more important source of identification than sight. She didn't even have to whiff his human butt.

"How is it even possible?" Flabbergasted, Marley walked slowly around the man lying on the grass. Cupcake was right: though it looked human, there was enough of the scent that was unmistakably Stuart.

"I don't know." The subject of all the sniffing was still in a daze. "I went to sleep with four legs and woke up with two." Holding out his hands, he gazed at them in renewed amazement. "Instead of my front legs I've got these human things." He reached tentatively for Cupcake. "I bet I can pet you."

"Whoa!" She retreated a couple of steps. "Let's not presume on our friendship, Stu. Besides, I'm not sure how I feel about this whole transformation thing."

"*You're* not sure." Stuart rolled over onto his back. The sky, at least, was unchanged.

Gizmo decided to probe further. "So, you can talk human? I saw you talking to our humans over there. They understood you?"

"Yeah. I'm getting used to it. It…," he rubbed his jaw, "it kinda hurts my throat."

"But you can still talk to us," Marley observed sagely.

"Obviously, flea house." Advancing, Gizmo put his face close to Stuart's, took a couple of sniffs, and murmured, "Can you hook us up with some tacos? She-who-fills-the-bowl only lets me have a taste when she buys them for herself. Habla Español?"

Stuart turned his head toward the chihuahua. "Huh?"

Marley explained patiently. "He's asking if you speak Spanish."

The human's brow furrowed even as his head turned quizzically to the side. "I don't think so. Wait, let me check." Sounds came from his mouth. They were garbled and unintelligible. "I don't think so," he concluded. "Jen doesn't. At least, I've never heard her speak it. I did listen while she tried to speak French to a potential client. It sounded like cat-speech."

Gizmo was plainly disappointed. "Hijole. Then you won't be able to get the good tacos for us. They don't sell them to gringos."

Abruptly, Stuart rose and headed toward the table occupied by the three women. The trio of dogs watched him go.

"Well now, what do you make of that?" Cupcake murmured wonderingly.

"'There are more things in Heaven and Earth than you ever dreamed of in your philosophy, Horatio,'" Marley intoned solemnly. His companions eyed him askance.

"Who's 'Horacio'?" Gizmo wondered aloud.

"Sounds like that hoity-toity Pekinese whose human only brings him here on Sundays, and that just for an hour," Cupcake opined.

"Where did you pick *that* up?" Gizmo eyed Marley questioningly.

"There was a Russian wolfhound in the park one day when you guys weren't around. Huuuge sucker, but kinda glum. You know the type. We sniffed, we barked, we chased a ball, we chatted. He started quoting some of his owner's reading material to me. Shakespeare, and Dostoevsky."

"Doesto—what?" Gizmo asked, frowning.

"I didn't get it all, but apparently it translates perfectly into Dog." As the stranger approached, the three women tensed in anticipation.

"Oh boy," Cindy muttered, "here he comes".

"He doesn't *act* dangerous," Nina opined.

"Yeah," her friend replied. "Just don't let him sniff you."

Before Nina could respond and Wanda could snark, the visitor was standing too close to ignore, brushing grass off the now seriously stained jogging suit.

"Have any of you seen Jen?" he asked politely.

That prompted a double take among the assembled women.

Weirdness they expected, but not something so straightforward. Wanda looked the stranger up and down.

"You know Jen?"

Nina was studying him more closely. Thanks to Wanda's query she was now able to confirm what she had suspected when he had first appeared.

"He must," she murmured. "He's wearing her clothes."

"Everyone owned that kind of jump suit," Cindy commented, adding, "Maybe not always in pink."

Lowering her eyes, Wanda gazed at her friend. "Who *are* you?"

They were interrupted by the sudden arrival of another, much smaller quadruped. Running up to Stuart, Freddy raced twice around his ankles before taking off, leaving a trail of sonic squirbling noises in his wake. Raising an arm, Stuart pointed at the retreating squirrel.

"*You*! Freddy! Your days are numbered!"

Bolting after the rodent, Stuart puffed and wheezed as he chased the squirrel around the park. For some reason, he couldn't catch his breath. Normally, he could have run like this for an hour. But then, he reminded himself as he ran, things were not normal. As he pursued the squirrel, which occasionally glanced back at him to launch an insulting squeak, Stuart realized how much he missed running on all fours. Hands were nice and all and certainly had their uses, but running on two legs was a fool's mission. Or a human's.

Watching a grown man chase a squirrel around the park did nothing to improve the women's opinion of the stranger. Their dogs, however, were beside themselves with excitement.

"Get 'em, Stuart!" Marley whooped.

Next to him, Gizmo could hardly refrain from turning rapid circles. "Andale, andale, amigo! Looking for squirrel fajitas, with peppers and onions!

"And avocado?" Cupcake inquired.

Gizmo halted his spinning long enough to reply. "Sin avocado. No bueno for Señorita Pooch."

"Who's 'Senorita Pooch'?" Cupcake was visibly puzzled.

"Horacio's girlfriend." As he peered down at her there was a hint of sadness in Marley's voice. "Sometimes I wonder about you, girl."

She took no umbrage at the mild reproach. "I'm a Pomeranian, not a brain surgeon."

Having recovered from their initial shock, the three women were now enjoying the spectacle.

"Wow, look at 'em go!" Wanda slapped a hand down on the table. "Damn, this dude belongs in the NFL chasing running backs. I've never seen a man run that fast before."

"Only when I ask my husband for money," Cindy observed. "Do they draft mental cases in the NFL?"

"Do they draft anyone else?" Nina said.

They were so busy trading bon mots they failed to remark on the collective sigh their dogs issued as the squirrel rocketed up a tree trunk and out of his pursuer's reach. Though not bent over from exhaustion, Stuart was breathing hard. But then, so was Freddy. As all squirrels knew, near death experiences, especially those involving pursuing dogs, was exhilarating. It was something fixed in the DNA of both species.

Cindy's attention had been drawn away from the last of the chase by the ringtone on her phone. It was Jen, who was looking for the three of them.

"We're here at the park," Cindy informed her friend.

"I see ya," came the reply. "I'm here, too. Walking over your way now."

Cindy frowned at the phone. "You sound upset. What's wrong?"

"You won't believe what happened." Jen sounded out of breath. What was it with everyone running to exhaustion today?

"You're engaged?" Cindy asked her.

"No, worse," came the reply. "Stuart is missing."

Putting up her phone, Cindy shielded her eyes, looking to the north toward the parking lot. It took her a moment to spot Jen. At the same time, the realtor zeroed in on her friends and broke into a jog. She arrived at the table out of breath.

"Jen!" Cindy looked askance at her friend. "What've you been doing? You look like you ran all the way from Long Beach. What happened?"

Leaning on the table, Jen fought to compose herself. Emotionally she was a mess, and she wasn't in such great shape physically, either, after searching for Stuart all morning.

"Short version? I came home after work—which went well, by the way—and the front door was open. I could've sworn I shut it. Anyway, I went inside and looked everywhere."

"Burglary?" was Wanda's first thought.

Jen shook her head and droplets of sweat went flying. "Nothing was taken. Everything was where it belonged and it didn't look like anything had been disturbed. Except—Stuart was gone. Also, a neighbor saw a naked man peeing on my lawn." Her cheeks bulged. "I think I'm gonna throw up."

"There's a strange guy here been asking for you, Jen. Maybe he knows something about Stuart's whereabouts. I get the feeling he knows you." She pointed. "You know him?"

Squinting into the park, the anxious realtor saw a bearded man approaching. His appearance was unfamiliar. As opposed to the grass-stained track suit he was wearing, which was very familiar indeed. She gaped at the stranger.

"Is he wearing my...?"

"Track suit!" Nina finished triumphantly. "Ha! I said that was yours."

The eyes of the oncoming figure widened as they caught sight of Jen standing beside the table and he broke into a run. Jen's eyes widened even more as the man leaped and wrapped her in a bear hug. Both expressions were matched by those of her friends as the pair tumbled to the ground and the man began licking their friend's face.

"Jen!" Stuart's joy was boundless. "I'm so glad I found you!"

Pushing and shoving, she struggled beneath him. "Hey! Get off of me, you freak! And why are you wearing my track suit?"

Rising from around the table to go to the aid of their besieged friend, the three women did not hear Stuart's sincere reply.

"It's the only thing that fit. Everything else was too small. And too clean." He smiled happily and plucked at the top of the jumpsuit. "This one smells like you!"

"Oh my God, you *are* a freak!" Realization hit and she gaped at him. "Are *you* the naked man who peed on my lawn?" As her friends gathered around, wondering how best to help, she began hitting him. "Oh my God, *you* took Stuart! Where is my dog? You better not have hurt him! I'll make you wish you were dead!"

With the women striking at him, albeit rather ineffectually, the hapless Stuart curled into a ball. This allowed Wanda to jump in and pull Jen away from him. Cindy took one of Jen's arms.

"Okay, okay, let's all calm down. Nobody knows anything about anything—yet."

Nina stepped between the berserking Jen and her target. "Jen! *Calmate!*"

Meanwhile, Cindy had let go of Jen and was waving toward a familiar figure in the distance. "There's Ramos!" Waving and jumping up and down failed to get the officer's attention.

Breaking free from her friends' grasp, Jen started walking as fast as she was able in the policeman's direction. Left alone for a moment, Stuart sprang to his feet and hurried after her. Looking back and seeing him in pursuit, a panicky Jen accelerated.

"Help! Officer!"

Behind her, Stuart was pleading desperately. "Jen, it's me, Stuart! I don't know what happened. I don't know *how* it happened. I—I don't even know for sure what I am. But I do know one thing: I'm *me*. You have to believe me." He tapped his chest with both open palms, Tarzan-like. "It's *me*. Stuart Louis!" He accelerated toward her again.

She kept backing away, again. Holding out both arms to maintain some distance between them lest he start licking her face anew. At the same time she did her best to sound threatening. She wasn't very good at it.

"Look, buddy, I dunno who you are, but you're gonna go to jail. You stole my dog *and* my clothes and nobody asked you to fertilize my lawn. I'm pretty sure all three of those things are illegal, even in LA. My dog… he better be okay!"

Finding the byplay between their friend and the insistent, obviously deranged stranger far more interesting than anything they had seen in weeks, Jen's friends looked on in silent fascination. Had they taken a moment to look down, they would have noticed that their respective dogs sat side by side, perfectly still and equally entranced.

"He's okay," the most peculiar man insisted. For a second time he danced the Tarzan patter on his chest. "Stuart is here." There was unmistakable sadness in his voice. He hit himself harder. "He's in *here*," he all but whimpered.

Something, she was not sure what, made her stop. That same something caused her to peer deeply into the stranger's eyes. What it was she could not have said. She knew only that at that one moment, at least, she was a little less afraid. But still no less angry.

"Where? Where is he?" This time she managed to sound, if not threatening, a little intimidating.

A note of exasperation was starting to creep into the stranger's voice. Exasperation and frustration. "*It's me Stuart, Jen!* Just put a piece of bacon on my nose so I can prove it."

She gaped at him. If nothing else, the guy was not your garden-variety nutcase. Considered as a bowl of Fruit Loops, he was definitely missing all the marshmallows.

"Prove…what?"

Exasperation finally overcame him. Honestly, humans could be so *dense* at times. Even Jen. "You have to put the turkey bacon on my nose," he explained patiently, as if talking to a puppy, "so I can do the trick!"

Unsurprisingly, she started backing away again. Had they been on the beach, she would have run into the ocean. A glance revealing that Officer Ramos and Ringo were now heading in their direction reassured her. She waved frantically at the cop. Finally seeing her, he picked up the pace, Ringo breaking into an eager trot and ready for action.

"Officer Ramos!" She alternated her attention between the approaching cop and the stranger imploring before her.

"Jen! Please!"

Dropping to his knees, the stranger began—whimpering like a dog. *Exactly* like a dog. It was at once unsettling and touching. Remembering something important, he began to sing. He had a pleasant, mild tenor, not at all drug-addled.

"'Stuart, you're the one who brightens up my day. Stuart, you're the wind that blows dark clouds away'."

She stopped waving at Ramos to stare at the man down on his knees. Not only was the way he was singing striking, so was the prayerful manner in which he held his hands out in front of him, the way his head was cocked to one side, the way…the way…

Unconsciously, she found herself singing silently along with him, he mimicking the words of the song.

"Only you can make my heart beat like a drum." She whispered the lyrics along with him, the two of them perfectly in sync. When the song ended, she could scarcely speak.

"Who—who are you? How do you know that song? How do you know that *I* know that song?" A light sea breeze had sprung up, ruffling her hair and his. She had a sudden unnatural urge to comb his dark locks back with her fingers.

He stared unblinkingly back at her, his voice soft. "It's *me*, Jen."

He rose. This time she didn't back away. Just gaped at him. Among her friends there was an outburst of whispering. It was accompanied by unbroken stares and much hand-pointing.

"Don't you remember?" Hesitantly, he took a step toward her. "You got drunk last night because Arthur didn't propose."

She could not have fled now had she wished to. In fact, she couldn't move much at all. She could only stand and gawk. "Who *are* you? No way you could know that. No way anyone could know that."

Noting that the policeman and his dog were now less than a dozen yards away, Stuart continued hurriedly. "You even switched pictures in that locket you're wearing, with mine."

She was shaking her head slowly, gradually being overwhelmed with disbelief. "What do you mean, 'with yours'? *Stuart's* picture is in here. Look, look for yourself."

It took her several tries to get a grip on the locket, several more fumbling with the latch to pop it open. Inside was a picture of man. Decent-looking, smiling, all but wagging an unseen tail. It was Stuart, all right.

The same Stuart who was standing before her now; bipedal, beard, and all.

Letting out a shriek, she collapsed forward, fainting in his arms. Reaching out, he caught her instinctively. Ramos and Ringo were very close now and he hadn't a clue what to do next. Ringo was beginning to growl softly. At least Ramos didn't have his service revolver out. Behind Stuart, Jen's friends rose as one from their table. Cindy and Nina made no attempt to intervene, but Wanda started forward, gripping her drink cup tightly.

Marley stepped directly in her path, causing her to nearly trip.

"Hey! Watch it, dog. Get out of the way!"

Every time she tried to go around him, Marley somehow managed to get in her path. She tried but was unable to avoid all that fast-moving fur.

Bending toward the unconscious Jen, Stuart gave her face a

long, tender lick in an attempt to rouse her. It was a technique that usually worked and it did not fail him now. Eyelids flickering, she came around to find herself blinking up through half-glazed eyes at—who?

"Stu—Stuart?" Her voice was weak, a not-uncommon condition among those who have recently suffered serious shock.

"Yes, it's me." He held her firmly, finally finding himself in a situation where hands exceeded paws in efficacy. "Potato head."

Half-conscious, her lips trembling slightly, she could do nothing but stare up at the man. At the knowing smile, the bright eyes, the very slightly exposed tongue. He was panting a little and….

"It *is* you. Oh my…."

She fainted afresh. Or more properly, she re-fainted. Difficult to say. Finally finding a way around Marley because the dancing dog stepped on one of his own long braids, Wanda resumed her advance—only to back off as Hector Ramos and Ringo arrived. Ramos didn't waste any time confronting the man in the oversized shades and pink track suit.

"What's going on here?" He jerked a thumb back the way he had come. "I saw Jen waving and came over."

"Not sure," Stuart opined. Jen continued to lie limply in his arms. "I think she's taking a nap."

"Is that a fact? Here, let me see." Stepping forward, a wary Ramos removed Jen from the other man's grasp and laid her gently on the ground. "Ms. Jensen? Jen?" Gently, he turned her head from side to side, then checked her pulse. Though everything seemed normal, it wasn't.

Using the back of his hand he tapped the unconscious woman first on one cheek, then the other while her friends looked on anxiously. Jen's eyelids fluttered. With the officer using his right arm to support her, she started to sit up. She recognized Ramos immediately. She also recognized his K9 unit, Ringo. The ferocious police German shepherd was several yards behind his human partner, standing on his hind legs and shaking hands with the man who called himself, who possibly impossibly *was*, Stuart Louis. As her eyes tried to focus, Ringo gave the Stuart-man a playful lick on the right cheek. Stuart-man promptly licked the German shepherd right back.

She fainted away for a third time.

Ringo was whining softly and making happy dog noises. Stuart listened attentively.

"Stuart, bro, I have never seen a deal like this. I take your explanation for what it's worth, but himmel! If it happened to me, would I look like Schwarzenegger?"

"Is he German?" Stuart inquired. "Or a shepherd?"

"Austrian, if I remember correctly. Sheep not involved."

Stuart nodded thoughtfully. "Same thing then, I think. You'd be buff, just like you are now."

Dropping back down to all fours, the police dog gazed up at Stuart. "But I'd still bark, I think. Buff-bark, that'd be me. Power eater, power lifter. Don't believe it's going to happen, though."

"Being human isn't all that you imagine." Holding out his hands, Stuart rotated them back and forth at the wrist. "Try running with *these* things."

Jen having regained a semblance of consciousness, Ramos was helping her to her feet. "Fainting could be a sign of dehydration or pregnancy." Aware that he might just have put his booted foot in it, he hurried to add, "Then again, maybe it's…."

She cut him off, excited. "Dehydration! That's it. I had a few drinks last night (*plus a whole additional bottle of wine, you fibber*) and whew hoo! Should've have mixed it with some fizzy water or juice or something and made spritzers. No wonder I…" She eyed him uncertainly. "I passed out just now, didn't I?"

"Several times. Can you stand okay?"

She nodded, chewed on her lower lip.

"Then excuse me a minute." Leaving her by herself, he walked over to where Ringo had the stranger cornered. *Good dog*, he thought. Doing his job. Although Ramos had seen Ringo herd disreputables before, and something wasn't quite right this time. The dog seemed awfully relaxed to be on guard. Halting, Ramos looked the stranger up and down. He did not recognize him as someone he had encountered in the park area previously.

"Fancy looking outfit you got there, cowboy." Ramos took note of the grass stains. "Been playing some park football?"

At this Ringo barked sharply. Not at the stranger. At his partner. It threw the officer off-stride and he forgot what he was going to say next.

Jen came forward to stand beside him. "Uh, that's—Stuart." She hesitated. Parts of her brain were still declining to function properly. Hardly surprising, under the circumstances. "An old friend from—college."

Ramos frowned. "Stuart? Like your dog?"

"Exactly." Finally, Stuart thought happily. Someone got it.

Despite Jen's apparent recovery Ramos wasn't quite ready to let it go. "From college, huh? Are you a professor, Stuart?"

"No." He eyed Jen, his countenance a vision of contentment now that he was back in her company, regardless of the inexplicable circumstances. He was happy once more. Although bacon would have improved the situation. "We used to sing together."

At this observation the most extraordinary expression came across Jen's face: a mixture of love, delight, and abject terror.

"Oh," Ramos continued. "Grad student, eh? You do look like the musician type."

"Thanks," Jen murmured.

"Not you." Addressing her, Ramos nodded at the man in the pink track suit. "Freddy Mercury over there." He turned back to her. "Come to think of it, where is Stuart? The four-legged Stuart. Your dog. I never see you without him."

At this Stuart answered the question by pointing at himself. A frantic Jen waved him off. Her gaze shifted away from him, away from Ramos, and toward the road. Several scooters went by, then a cluster of elderly men riding bicycles more expensive than the average citizen's car, then a truck flaunting an ad for Alta-Dena dairies.

Aware that Ramos was watching her closely, Jen stammered a response.

"He's, uh—with my aunt. At her farm. Having, uh, some cows…."

Ramos's expression tightened. "Some cows?"

"Uh, yeah. Some cow farm in Alta Dena. He plays with the cows there, you know. They play. He thinks he's a herding dog, tries to herd them. My Aunt Sally took him there for a change of scenery, for some fun."

The officer looked uncertain. "Can't see a Boston terrier trying to herd a bunch of cows. Or play with them. He'd be about the size of a cow's forehead."

"Yeah." Jen readily agreed. "That's why it's so much fun watching him try."

As they continued talking, with Jen continually trying to switch the subject away from Stuart and Ramos doing his best to ascertain if the woman he thought he knew casually had lost her mind, Ringo was busily sniffing Stuart's human leg. The suit's faint smell of Jen did not throw him, nor did the lingering Spring-fresh aroma of crushed grass. He had been trained to distinguish between even faint scents.

"That's not true. There is no farm and you're not there. She's lying. Badly." The shepherd looked up at the human face gazing blithely down at him. "You're right here. I'm telling Hector." Turning toward his partner, he let out a succession of loud barks. "There. I told him."

"Good job, Ringo." For the first time since he had arrived at the park, Stuart was starting to feel a little bit, just a little bit, at ease. "She's just trying to help me."

The police dog shook his head, rattling his collar. "I don't know, Stuart. Verdampt, this is a tough call. After all, I'm a cop. But—let me get this straight. You can talk to humans now, right?"

Stuart peered down at the shepherd. "Why do you need to know?"

Dropping his customary bravado, Ringo lowered his head and whined softly. "I need a favor from you."

CHAPTER SIX

Something finally drew Ramos's attention away from Jen. She was spouting nonsense, but from all he could tell, it was harmless nonsense. What he was looking at now was of far more interest. Not only because it was so unusual, but because it bordered on the unprofessional.

Ringo was circling the visitor, sniffing at every part of him. Of more interest, and not a little astonishment, Stuart was crouching while Ringo appeared to be whining in his ear. Given the proximity to a complete unknown, Ringo would normally have been more likely to bite off a stranger's ear than burble into it. A bemused (and not a little startled) Ramos scratched himself behind one ear. The day was growing late, it was getting hotter, and the circumstances in which he presently found himself were as confusing as they were unusual.

"What's up with Ringo? I've never seen him like this with a stranger. He's not supposed to interact with any member of the public unless I give him the okay." He peered harder at the ongoing canine interaction. "And why is he whining into that guy —Stuart's—ear? Licking I could *maybe* understand. But whining?"

Jen stepped forward, trying to block the officer's view. "Uhhh, he probably smells *my* Stuart's scent on the jumpsuit." Looking behind her, she fluttered a hand at the unlikely pair. "I, uh, had to lend him something to wear to the park and the track suit was the only thing I had that fit him. He travels light."

Why would anyone come to Newport Beach, Southern California, without appropriate clothing? Ramos found himself wondering. Fortunately for Jen's peace of mind, he was distracted by the hand waving of her three friends. Grinning, he waved back. He was on duty, but there would come a time when he was off duty, and all three of Jen's companions were attractive. Besides, her explanation for what he was seeing made a certain off-kilter sense. What he had originally seen, he had observed from a distance. Now that he had been introduced to visitor Stuart and Jen appeared okay, there seemed little reason to pursue the matter further.

Guitarist Jim chose that moment to wander into view. He was picking up bottles and other trash and depositing them into their appropriate public receptacle. Glass in one, metal in another, paper in a third, unalloyed junk in a fourth. Trotting alongside him was his Boston terrier, Sweetie Peters. She eagerly sniffed every piece of trash as Jim picked it up—until a familiar scent diverted her attention.

Lying down, she put her paws out in front of her. Her tiny tail was generating enough wind to power a small flashlight and she began barking madly. Bending, Jim let go of her leash and urged her on.

"Go ahead, Miss Mami. Go say hi to your friends."

Exploding across the grass, the terrier darted close behind the figure in the pink track suit, grasped another whiff out of the air, did a complete spin, and ended up beside her canine friends, panting hard.

"That," she declared as she gazed at the tall bearded individual squatting beside the police dog, "smells *exactly* like Stuart Louis." She looked over at Marley. "It cannot be Stuart Louis. The look, the posture, and the—the—*humanness*, is all wrong! I mean, just *look* at it—him. He—he's *on two legs*."

"It is him," Marley assured her. "The nose knows. He talks to humans, too. Fluently, it would appear. I have no idea what he's saying to them, but it's plain that they understand him. Crazy days."

Cupcake was watching the unlikely pair. "Can you imagine what we would look like if we transformed like he has? If *he* looks like *that*?"

"You'd probably look like JLo." There was not a hint of sarcasm in Gizmo's voice.

"And you, Gizmo?" Marley wondered. "Who do you think you'd look like?"

"Marc Anthony, of course. Who else?"

Unconcerned about Sweetie Peters, who never strayed far from his presence, Jim continued his honorable trash pickup, singing along to the tune that was playing through his headphones. Distracting by their dogs, who had resumed their relentless barking, they monitored them as well as the bottle collector's progress.

"That park ranger got nice buns," Nina observed admiringly.

"Probably from all the squats he does picking up bottles all day." Wanda's comment was met by laughter from her companions.

While their attention was diverted from Ramos, Stuart chose that moment to divert the officer's attention from them.

"Hector!"

The beat cop tensed slightly. He didn't know this guy. Only that he was, apparently, an old friend of Jen's who happened to have the same name as her dog. Jen's friendship marked him as tolerable in Ramos's book, but not free of suspicion.

"It's 'Officer Ramos,'" he said stiffly.

Stuart apologized. To Ramos it sounded genuine. Almost child-like.

"Sorry. Officer Ramos, Ringo badge number 28897 is suffering with a tooth issue in the rear left molar area. It may be infected, which could spread and do serious damage to this fine animal."

Stuart wasn't sure how Ringo would respond to being called a "fine animal", but it was already clear that his doggo friends could only comprehend the few human words their owners utilized for commands, such as "Sit", "Fetch", "Come here", and a handful of others. He doubted "fine animal" was on anybody's list.

Ramos gave this peculiar Jen-friend the fish eye. "How do you know that?"

Stuart smiled cheerfully. "He told me."

"No, not the tooth thing. For all I know you're a psychic veterinarian. His badge number. That's restricted departmental information. What are you, some kind of dog whisperer?"

"He told me his badge number, too," Stuart explained innocently before turning serious. "It's important that you get him to his vet today. He's in pain and too proud to tell you about it. He's a great dog." Though he could not understand why, it appeared to Stuart that Officer Ramos continued to regard him as something better stashed away in a locked box. "Why do you think he's only been eating canned food and ignoring the dry, no matter what flavor you put in his bowl?"

Ramos was both uncomfortable and perplexed. Taking a firm grasp on Ringo's leash, he led the shepherd away, muttering quietly to his four-legged partner.

"Badge number…how did he know your badge number? And what's this about a sore tooth?"

Ringo responded by barking and growling. Accusingly, Ramos wondered?

Relieved to see the officer go, Jen grabbed Stuart's arm and started walking him back toward her friends. They were now alternating their attention between her and the busy guitarist.

"Do you believe me now?" Stuart inquired softly.

"I do," she mumbled. "I guess I have to. There's no way anyone other than Stuart…."

"That's me!" he declaimed proudly.

"…could have known those things you said. Because Stuart—you—were the only one there when they happened." She looked up at him. That in itself seemed unnatural, because until now she had always looked *down* at him. "You really think my drunken wish came true? Things like this, they just don't happen."

"You're telling me," he whispered back.

She indicated her waiting friends. "Now I have to figure out a way to rationalize everything to them."

"Toss 'em a bone," Stuart suggested.

"Try to make a little more sen…." She paused. "Yeah. Something like that. A diversion." She patted his arm because, thankfully, she couldn't easily reach the top of his head. "Good idea, Stuart."

"I have lots of good ideas," he told her proudly. "For example, that black cat that's always yowling in our yard at night. We could…."

"Not now." Putting on a big smile, she halted near the table, took a bow, and curtsied. She couldn't remember the last time she had curtsied and hoped the gesture came off as sufficiently ironic.

"How was that? Did you like it?"

Wanda frowned back at her. "What do you mean? How did we like what?"

Jen indicated the man on her arm. "Meet my friend from college, Stuart."

"'Stuart'?" Cindy eyed the man in the pink tracksuit with fresh uncertainty.

"Yes. Where do you think I got the name from?" She grinned. "We used to perform together."

Nina sounded sufficiently hornswoggled. "That was all a prank? You punked us?"

"Yeah. Funny, huh?" Jen's voice was tight. "We did music and drama together. We punked everybody, every chance we got. It was good practice for theater. And a break from Shakespeare. How about it? What'd you all think?"

Cindy was shaking her head. "Horrible acting. I knew you were putting on the whole time. Your posture, your mannerisms, all that frantic waving. Obvious fakery."

"Yeah—obvious," Nina added, not wanting to be left out.

Jen would have eagerly agreed, but Jim was quite near now. Having rejoined him, Sweetie Peters trotted alongside. Normally she would have been pawing at the ground, sniffing the grass, barking at her owner. This time, she was dead silent, her attention wholly fixed on the tall figure of—Stuart.

"Be cool," Jen admonished her "college friend". "It's Jim. Remember? The guitar guy?"

Stuart nodded absently, *his* attention wholly fixed (yes) on Sweetie Peters.

Jim adjusted the guitar bag slung across his back so that it fit more cleanly against his shoulders. Or maybe he was just making sure it was out of Jen's range.

"Any luck, Jen? Any word? I've kept an eye out all morning and…."

"Thanks, Jim," she interrupted him. "No need to worry any longer. I just got off the phone with my mother. She took him to the mooers—I mean, the groomers. I forgot. I've been so busy with a new client that I forgot I asked her to look after him today." She stole a glance at Stuart and his grass-stained tracksuit. "He *really* needed a visit to the groomer."

"I could probably use some sprucing up myself," he quipped. "Helping to keep the park clean, you pick up more than bottles. Comes with the territory. Although," he added, eying Stuart, "it's usually not quite so visible. Anyway, that's good news. Friend of yours?"

She nodded. Stuart was now on his knees and Sweetie Peters

was rubbing up against him. Despite the inconveniences posed by a considerable difference in size, he reciprocated as best he could.

"Yeah, old friend from college. He's visiting. We, uh, used to perform together."

Jim nodded. "Interesting. He strikes me as a Method actor."

Pausing in her pushing, the terrier looked up at the pink-clad human. "What do you think you're doing, Stuart Louis?"

He smiled. He would have panted, but he was learning to become a little more discreet in his human habits. "I love when you call me that."

"Have you looked at yourself lately? You're more terror than terrier."

"I know," he whispered. "Walking on two legs. Crazy! I've always been able to walk on two legs. Usually when begging for treats. But it can get tiring." He gestured down at himself. "Not in this body. On the other hand, walking on all fours is out of the question. These legs and hands don't work together for that."

"I don't mean that. That much is obvious. I'm referring to what you're wearing. It's embarrassing."

"Is it? I thought you liked lighter shades."

Also, you're dirty. You know how I like a clean- "

"Clean butt; I know. What's worse than walking on two legs is that I can't taste or smell like I used to. My eyesight isn't as sharp and neither is my hearing. I swear, I don't know how humans get through the day. All their senses are feeble. It's really hard. I mean, everything around me is half of what it normally is. I can't even lick my…."

"Stuart! There's a lady present!"

"Sorry!"

"I just hope this goes away. You know it could never work…"

He stared down at her. "What are you saying, Sweetie Peters?"

"You know what I'm saying, Stuart Louis."

Pivoting, she sprinted off toward a favorite tree. Stuart rose and followed, nearly forgetting to remain upright and not try to run on all fours. A thoughtful Jim contemplated the pair.

"Sweetie really likes your friend." He squinted as Stuart began chasing the terrier around the tree. "I mean, she *really* likes him. I've never seen her take to a complete stranger so completely."

Jen tried to think of something clever to say, but all she could come up with was, "He's a dog person."

"I can see that."

"No, Literally."

He blinked, turning away from his dog and her new friend. "What?"

"Nothing. Just mumbling stupidly. You know me."

"Not really, no." He changed the subject. "So, anyway, I made a few calls and it's true. They're gonna close the park. The News confirmed it this morning. Supposed to be a nice development coming. Sidewalk cafes, trendy shops, like that." His voice fell. "Newport already has acres of sidewalk cafes, trendy shops, and like that. But this is the only dog park."

"Close the park?" Despite the distance and his impacted hearing, Stuart had overheard at least that much. Jim turned to him and managed a smile.

"Hey, I'm Jim."

Stuart eyed him intently. "I know."

Before the other man could reply, Jen was fumbling in her purse for her ringing phone. "I guess it's true, then. I'll call the office and see what my mother knows. She knows everything and everyone." She glanced at her phone. "It's Derek. I gotta grab this." Turning away from the guitarist she spoke toward the phone. "Derek! Hi. Long time no talk. What's up?" His voice came back over the speaker loud enough for Jim and Stuart to overhear.

"Jen, this week is bad for me—unless we can do lunch tomorrow."

"Lunch tomorrow is perfect." She replied without a moment's

hesitation. "See ya then. Give me a call later and we'll pick a place and time." Disconnecting, she turned to Jim and gave him a thumbs-up. "Doing lunch with Derek tomorrow. Plays Baseball. Pro," she added by way of punctuation.

"That's nice." Slipping his headphones back over his ears, he resumed grooving to the music. Giving a gentle tug on Sweetie Peters' leash, he eased her away from Stuart's side. As they walked off, the terrier looked back over her shoulder. Stuart blew her a kiss.

"He's perfect for you," he murmured unexpectedly.

Jen blinked. "Who, Derek?"

Stuart shook his head slowly. "No."

She gaped at him, then at the retreating figure of the guitar player. "Who—*Jim*? C'mon! We've got nothing in common, and after last night I've already got plenty of empty bottles. You're not fooling me Stuart. You just like Sweetie Peters."

He pursed his lips. "I'm telling you, Jen, and I can tell likes when I smell them. He likes you."

"Well it just so happens that I know nothing about him and I don't go for guys about whom I know nothing and for all I know he's nothing but a bottle-collecting vagrant although he does seem awfully clean for a vagrant and he does play guitar and…." Breaking off, she stared at Stuart in horror.

"Oh my god, this can't be happening! I'm getting dating advice from my dog."

❧   ❧   ❧

Sitting on her bed, Jen held the locket tightly. Or maybe, she thought, she should hold it loosely. How had she been holding it the night before? Would pressure make any difference? What about the angle at which she had been holding it? What about the ambient temperature? Had the aircon been running? Was there a breeze in the room? Was she obsessing over irrelevant details?

Did such things actually matter where the impossible fantastical were concerned?

The answer was simple. Since she couldn't remember a single one of those things, she would have to proceed while ignoring them.

Stuart, on the other hand, knew exactly where he had been sitting the previous night, looking on worriedly while Jen willfully degenerated into progressive blottoness. He sat there now, watching her, wondering what she was going to do next and what might happen as a result.

"Just sit still, okay?" she told him. "We have to fix this. Somehow."

"How?" He wagged a non-existent tail.

She rubbed her forehead. "I don't know. Try different things, I guess. Necromancy isn't my area of expertise. You might think it's required in order to get a California realtor's license, but it isn't." She paused, then brightened. "I know. I'll repeat what I said last night, only backwards. Maybe it'll reverse the transformation."

"Okay." Where Jen was involved, Stuart was up for anything. Unless she turned him into a cat. Then they would have a problem.

Readying herself, Jen closed her eyes tightly, pursed her lips, and…sat there. Said nothing. Finally she opened her eyes.

"What did I say last night?"

Stuart considered. He had a better memory for other things. The location of buried bones, the sound of a can opener releasing the delicious aroma of pre-macerated dog food, the scent of a certain bitch—but he made an effort.

"I think it was, something like something about voting control, new business, how mom's always right even when she's wrong…."

She cut him off. "Yeah, yeah, I remember, I got it. Somehow I don't think any of that is relevant. Need to try something more pertinent to the situation." She squinted, took a breath, and recited in a voice that was solemn but not quite sepulchral.

"I wish that my dog—becomes a dog again!"

They both held their breath. The aircon hummed softly. It was not a moment to inspire Poe. Lifting his right leg, Stuart struggled to bend it to scratch behind one ear. The movement might have pleased a yoga instructor but did nothing to validate Jen's demand.

"Let me think," she muttered. After a moment Stuart birthed a suggestion of his own.

"Sing it!"

She made a face. "'Sing it'? Yeah, maybe music will help. Aren't magical spells usually done to music? Can't hurt to try."

Rising, she walked to a closet, opened the door, and began searching. From the top shelf she removed a guitar case glazed with a thin layer of gray dust. Blowing it clean, she finished the job by wiping it with one palm. Stuart let out a sneeze, bent to wipe his nose on the bedspread, quickly thought better of it. Returning to the bed she sat down and cradled the instrument. It snugged neatly against her, as if it hadn't been lying dormant in the closet for many years. Reaching down, she began strumming and singing along with the tune.

"How about...hmm. Turn it around, round, round, turn it around, round round. Go back the way you were before, turn it around, round, round...."

She stopped. The aircon hummed softly. It was not a moment to inspire Dylan. Then Stuart broke into applause.

"That was great! Did you write that? Just now? Wow! "

Her expression was dour. Nothing had changed. Only that she realized how badly out of practice she was. Not that being out of tune either vocally or instrumentally likely had anything to do with the failure of the attempt.

"Uh, nothing. I used to play a little in college, remember." Her eyes widened slightly. "What if," she set the guitar aside, "we change—the picture? The one in the locket? If it's the locket that's even responsible. We don't know that. But the picture changed from one of dog you to one of human you. What if we try to force change it back?"

Rising, she went over to the dresser and removed one of several photos of a certain Boston terrier. Taking scissors from a drawer, she cut the picture down so that it would fit in the locket. Removing the photo of the human Stuart, she replaced it with the freshly trimmed canine portrait. Stuart observed the whole process intently.

"How are you gonna wish this time?"

"How about, "downward dog near or far, meet your body where you are?"

He frowned. "'Downward dog'?"

"I'm kidding. Seriously, now…hmm. Maybe I should just be straightforward about this. Not try to imitate something medieval. I'd probably get the Latin all wrong anyway." Holding the locket shut in one hand she pointed with the other and intoned, "Reverse the drunken wish I made and make him furry once again!"

Squinting at the pointing finger, Stuart held perfectly still and concentrated. It made no difference. Once again, nothing happened.

Well, almost nothing.

Taking a deep, hopeful breath, Jen opened the locket, peered within—and let out a scream. The image was still that of human Stuart. Only this time the pose was different. He was blowing a kiss. Also, he looked a bit shaggier.

"What is it, Jen? What's wrong?"

Rejoining him, she showed him the locket and the new picture. "What the heck, Stuart? New pose?"

He broke out into a wide, innocent grin. "How cool is that?"

"It's not cool. You're still not a dog. You're human Stuart, badly in need of a trim Stuart." Returning to the dresser, she fished her phone out of her purse.

"This is nuts. I better call Arthur." She dialed his cell number.

Rising onto all fours, Stuart executed several circles on the bed before sitting back down again. "What are you gonna tell him?"

"Well, I'll tell him that after our dinner I came home, got really *really* drunk, kinda angry, took his picture out of the locket, replaced it with yours, and made a wish. A wholly inadvertent wish. Then in the morning, when I got up, I thought you had gotten out of the house. And you *had* gotten out of the house, and I went looking for you, and when I finally found you, my dog had become a man. And it's all his fault for not giving me a ring instead of this stupid, stupid, *stupid* locket!"

Drawing back her arm she prepared to fling it across the room, only to catch herself at the last moment. There was no telling what might happen if it slammed into the floor, or the wall opposite. It might kill Stuart. It might kill her. It might scramble whatever enchantment had taken place and turn Stuart back into a dog or her into a poodle. And she had never liked poodles.

Stuart voiced his own opinion. "Great idea! Call him and tell him that."

Yeah, sure, she thought. Nothing like telling your fiancé that your dog has turned into a dude to rekindle a relationship. He'd never come back from San Francisco. That set her to wondering if he ever *did* intend to come back from the City by the Bay. Which led her to ponder other matters of relevance, which offered nothing in the way of reassurance.

As she sat in stasis wondering what to do next, a voice reached her from outside.

"Jen, it's your mother! I got some good news, open up! And this time don't hold Stuart out the window!"

Not much likelihood of that, she thought as she eyed the current six-foot tall iteration of Stuart. She shook herself out of the momentary stupor. "Coming, keep your pants on!" Hanging up the phone before the call was completed, she put it back in her purse, opened the bedroom door, and started out—only to stick her head back in a moment later.

"Stay! Stay, Stuart."

"Do I get a treat when you come back?"

For an instant, just an instant, his reply took her aback. Then she remembered exactly who it was she was talking to.

"Yeah, sure. A treat, right. Stay here until I come for you."

Downstairs, she opened the front door—but not all the way. Just enough to poke her head out. Sylvia frowned at her.

"What are you doing?"

"What are *you* doing?" Jen shot back fretfully. "I'm changing."

"Let me in." Without waiting for permission, Sylvia pushed hard on the door, forcing the issue. Jen stepped back. "I changed your diapers. What's with the sudden reluctance? Frilly red underwear? One could hope."

Before her mother could wander off to anywhere else, Jen led the way to the kitchen. That suited Sylvia just fine, as the small dining table provided an ideal place for her to deposit a folder full of paperwork.

"So since you didn't answer his most recent messages (this delivered in a tone straight from the Arctic), Derek Jones contacted me and I followed up with him. He still wants to meet you for lunch tomorrow to sign papers. You'll find the suggested time and place in your messages from him. Nice restaurant he picked; for a jock the man has taste." She indicated the folder. "Here's your packet. It's all filled out for you. It looks like you did the hard part, getting him on board with Townsend. Congratulations."

"Thanks. I'll get his John Hancock."

Sylvia studied her daughter closely. "You still look frazzled.

Maybe you'd better check to make sure you don't ask him to write 'John Hancock' and that he signs 'Derek Jones'."

Jen replied dry. "Ha ha, it is to laugh."

"That's right, quote Daffy at me." Her tone softened. "So, how did it go with Arthur?" Her gaze dropped to Jen's right hand. "I don't see a ring. That means it went well?"

"That's child abuse." She turned away, fearful of what her mother might see in her face. "I can't even tell you what happened because you wouldn't…."

"Another woman?" her mother interrupted. Her voice rose. "I knew it! Knew it from the beginning, it was *so* obvious."

Jen turned back. "Then why didn't you say anything?"

"What, and interfere in my daughter's life? What do you think I am?" Before Jen could provide one of several dozen possible responses, Sylvia raced onward. "Anyway, speaking of Arthur, I confirmed today that his family is building a new shopping center, and you'll never guess where."

"I heard." She sighed. "The dog park. He never even mentioned it. Jim, a guy who works at the park, told me. I didn't believe it."

"Well, it's true," Sylvia assured her. "Arthur Daly and his family would build a car wash over a cemetery if it meant making a buck. I told you from the first time I met that man that he…."

A very loud sneeze from somewhere upstairs caused her to break off and peer in that direction.

"Gesundheit!" she called out, adding with a quizzical glance at her daughter, "who was that?"

The sound of feet descending the stairs was all that broke the ensuing silence. Entering the kitchen, Stuart walked past both women and headed directly for the cupboard. Opening it, he searched for a moment until he located the box of Milk Bones. Retracing his steps, he paused halfway back to the stairway to regard the two silent women.

"I never understood that. 'Goes in tight' when it actually come out loose." He added a shrug before walking the rest of the way across the kitchen and heading back upstairs. Having followed his progress intently, Sylvia now turned back to her daughter. Had she been in a boardroom she would have coughed lightly.

"Explain?"

"Who is that?" Letting out a nervous laugh, Jen proceeded to improvise, as she had all morning. "That's Stuart. He's an old friend from school."

"You don't have any friends," Sylvia said matter-of-factly.

"Mom." Jen let out an exaggerated sigh. "He's a psychologist."

"Even for a psychologist he has terrible taste in clothes. And his name is Stuart? Like your dog." A sudden thought made her pause and she found herself searching the kitchen. "Where is Stuart? He's always right next to you."

More nervous now but not laughing this time, Jen nodded toward the stairs. "He's upstairs sleeping. The two of us were up all night crying. I mean, I was crying and he was whining. Like, empathy. So I made a call to an old friend and this morning sneezing Stuart came by to help me try and figure out the Arthur thing."

Sylvia raised an eyebrow. "The 'Arthur thing'?"

Jen met her mother's gaze without flinching. "Yeah, the Arthur thing. You coined it, you own it."

The older woman shook her head slowly. "You've lost your mind."

More clumping on the stairs and Stuart reappeared, upbeat as ever. "Jen! Let's go for a walk."

A chance to get out of the house—and get away. "Great idea. Let me grab my shoes." Her gaze switched rapidly from him to her mother. "*I'll be right back.*" She left the room, moving fast.

It left Sylvia alone with Stuart. A risky move on Jen's behalf. She studied the bearded man closely. There was something curious about him. She couldn't quite put a finger on it. A kind of happy-go-lucky innocence. Not that that was necessarily a detriment. On the other hand, his tracksuit smelled as if he had just run from Newport to San Diego. And his breath held a faint odor of—some kind of carbohydrate. Old hotdog buns? Milk Bones? That was crazy. Probably just cold toast. They were not all that dissimilar.

"So you went to school with Jen?"

"All the time. We're best friends. She tells me everything! Always has. Also," he finished proudly, "I'm a real good listener."

Sylvia considered. "Everything, huh?"

"Yep. I know her better than anyone."

"Is that so? You think you know her better than her own mother?"

It was a challenge that would have shut down almost any man. But Stuart wasn't almost any man. In fact, he was hardly almost a man. Instead of a challenge he reacted as if it was just another question.

"Do you know the lyrics to all her songs? I do. She sings them to me all the time. Does she sing them to you? Do you know who her friends are at the park? I do! Her dog friends as well as her people friends. Did you know Arthur didn't propose?"

"Okay, okay, I get it." It was clear this was one friend of her daughter's that, for whatever reason, was not easily intimidated. There had been no malice in his reply; just evident honesty and genuine affection for Jen. "I guess you do know some things I don't. Big deal."

"When she talks, I just listen. I don't interrupt. Because I listen, she tells me everything. I've noticed that few people can or are willing to do that. Most of them just want to talk. Talk, talk, talk, and most of the time they don't seem to say very much. So I sit nearby and listen. Then things just work out." He paused a moment to study Sylvia. "I know you're her mother and that you love her, but do you ever just *listen* to Jen?"

Jen had said that this Stuart was a psychologist. He was

proving it now. He might need a change of clothing, but she could not deny the charm of his bedside manner.

"I do tend to talk more than I listen. Part of it is the nature of my work."

"Don't blame yourself. I got bigger ears than you."

He really did know his stuff, Sylvia had to admit. It was almost as if his perceptiveness was an inborn trait.

"It's that simple, huh?"

"Well, actually," he began, but Jen returned, breathing hard. She hadn't been gone that long and he wondered why she had been in such a hurry to retrieve a pair of shoes.

"Ready, Stu—eh, Stuart?"

He nodded. Rather vigorously, Sylvia thought, but at the moment her attention was more focused on her daughter. Stepping forward, she gave the other woman a firm hug, then released her.

"Honey, do you remember that song you used to sing on the porch? Whenever you were home?"

The question was unexpected, and Jen hardly had room for any more of the unexpected. "You mean, "Poopie on the floor?""

"That's it!" Sylvia beamed. "I love that one."

It was plain that she was in no hurry to leave. Wordlessly, Jen and Stuart continued to stare at her. As the moment stretched into uncomfortability, she finally took the hint.

"Anyway, have a nice walk."

As soon as Sylvia was out the door, Stuart turned to Jen. "Poopie on the floor? I don't know that one."

"I just made it up," she told him proudly. "Not like she would know, anyway."

He was confused, but only for a moment. "So—she was pretending that she remembered a song that never existed?" Jen nodded. "I wonder why she would do something like that?"

"I don't know. Maybe it had something to do with whatever

you guys were talking about when I was upstairs." She peered hard at him.

He replied with hesitation. "One of the things we were talking about was the songs you sing to me. I told her I had heard them all, and I asked if she had."

"Ah." Jen looked past him, down the walkway her mother had taken. "*Now* I understand."

"I don't. Can you explain it to me?"

"Some other time. It's not important. Right now, I have to do something that *is* important."

Picking up her phone she dialed Arthur's number. It rang immediately. Several times. "C'mon, Arthur. Answer the phone!" She held it near her right ear as it continued to ring. At the same time she gave Stuart yet another once-over. "Stuart, you can't keep going around in what's left of my track suit. Let's get you some proper clothes."

He winced suddenly. "Get me to a tree first."

There was a pause following a final ring and she held up her hand to quiet him. There was no Arthur on the line; only his answering service.

"Hi, this is Arthur. I can't take this call because I'm either at the Round Table with Galahad and Lancelot or on my yacht. Leave a message."

Rolling her eyes, Jen hung up before the concluding beep. Standing before her, Stuart was now trembling visibly. "I'm gonna have to show you how to use the bathroom, because you…"

Without waiting for her to finish, he whirled and sprinted for The Tree. He knew where the bathroom was in the house, of course, but was a bit ignorant as to the requisite mechanics. Was it the same for males as for females? He would inquire, but not right now.

Besides, the tree was closer.

CHAPTER SEVEN

School was still in session so the mall was not busy, for which Jen was grateful. Until something could be done about Stuart's grass-stained garb, fewer people meant fewer comments directed his way. That still did not keep her from lowering her head and placing a hand over her eyes whenever she even thought she saw someone who might recognize her. Stuart, of course, could not have cared less. Her sunglasses still rode his nose. Glancing at him occasionally, she wasn't sure if they concealed him at all or if he might have been less conspicuous without them.

At the bottom of the escalator they were riding, a surge of aromatics smacked him in the face like a wet mop and he turned immediately toward the nearby food court. She had to drag him in the other direction toward the Supercuts, and it was hard to do so without a leash. Had she put one on him he doubtless would have allowed her to lead him without effort, but that would have raised the eyebrows of staid passers-by for an entirely different reason.

As soon as he divined the employees' attention in Supercuts, he started struggling. Nothing Jen could say would calm him: he had always hated baths. It didn't matter that she insisted he wasn't going to get a bath. There were hoses, and basins, and water, and what else could that mean except a bath? He knew he was due, but it didn't matter.

She held his hand and stroked his brow with the other while two of the determined barbers managed to hold him in a chair and tilt his head back into the wash basin. When the water started to flow and he seriously began to fight back, she climbed onto the chair and sat on his lap. This flummoxed him so utterly that he (somewhat) relaxed. Their positions were entirely reversed. He was supposed to sit on her lap; not the other way around. While his mind tussled with this conundrum, the employees managed to get his hair reasonably shampooed. A drop of soapy liquid crept into one eye and he yelped, then began to whimper softly.

"It's alright, Stuart. It's just a little soap. Don't be such a baby."

The two barbers exchanged a glance but said nothing. After all, the customer is always right, even if he is a bit whack-a-doodle. His female companion, thankfully, seemed more or less perfectly normal. More or less.

It took considerably longer than average to get the tangles out of his hair and trim down what remained, but when they were finished, both barbers had reason to be proud of the result. Also content, since Jen felt compelled to tip them outrageously. As she and a newly shorn Stuart exited the store, all the employees paused in their work to applaud. So did those customers who had been present when he had been wrestled in. The result was, if not actually miraculously, nothing short of a complete transformation. The man who walked out of the shop beside Jen was—oddly handsome.

Despite his combativeness, Stuart seemed to have lost none of his energy. Jen, on the other hand, was borderline exhausted. But she couldn't give in. There was much more to do. From the neck up, human Stuart now looked more than respectable.

From the neck down, he was Mr. Dumpster. She hoped the track suit, of which she was fond, could be salvaged. Perhaps after a good washing. Or two, or four. Or treatment in a mild acid bath.

Classy mall that it was, the one in Newport Beach was packed with high-end shops. Although she made a good living, to which the incipient Derek Jones sale was going to add, her funds were still limited. Passing all the specialty men's shops, she led him into Bloomingdale's. They had scarcely entered the men's clothing section when they were confronted by an impeccably dressed salesman. His tie, like his complexion, was pink. So overtly flush that it was as if his skin was making a deliberate attempt to flaunt its paleness in the face of the more typical Southern California tan. Taken in toto, the man who greeted them was as flamboyant as a float in the Rose Parade.

"Hi gorgeous," he said to Jen. "I know you. You're the Pet Friendly Realtor." His tone turned mock-accusatory. "*Are* you though. Are you really pet friendly?" If he'd had a monocle, he would have screwed it in tighter.

"I am." Jen saw no reason to elaborate on her reply.

Her borderline curt reply did nothing to dissuade him. She had the feeling that only a small tactical nuclear weapon might do that. "Well, I'm a fashion tiger. My friends call me Bloomie."

"Nice to meet you." She let a beat pass. "'Bloomie.'" *As in blooming idiot*, she mused, but silently. He could be as outrageous as he wished so long as he did his job.

"But you can't call me that unless we're friends," he added solemnly.

Jen was taken aback. Where had the store unearthed this specimen?

"Well are we?" he continued.

She could only shrug. Apparently this was enough for Bloomie. "Just kidding around. Of course we are! I'm playing with you."

Ah, Stuart thought. A word of whose meaning he was certain. "I like to play."

Jen stepped in hurriedly, before Bloomie-boy could discourse on the nature of "play".

"Look, Bloomie, or tiger boy, or whichever moniker you fancy at the moment; I think you missed your calling working in the clothing department. Where you'd really succeed is on a reality show. But that's for future prospects. Right now we need to help Stuart here."

The salesman rested his chin between the thumb and forefinger of his left hand while studying Stuart. "Obviously. Unless of course he plans to join the Cheetah Girls. Ha ha. I do think there's something to work with, though. Fortunately, you have engaged the services of a master. Follow me."

Just trailing behind their guide was enough to make Jen giggle. Stuart struggled to understand her reaction. There was nothing wrong with the salesman's stride. He walked exactly like Cupcake.

"I was thinking...." Three words were all Jen managed to get out before Bloomie shushed her with a dismissive wave of one hand.

"Tch, tch, tch—I got this, girlfriend."

He was nothing if not brisk, Jen decided as they passed rack after shelf of apparel. Finding something he regarded as suitable, he flung shirt after pants after suit toward them. Jen's arms were soon so loaded down with clothing she could hardly hold anything more. Stuart did better. Not that he could carry all that much more, but he was adept at catching the smaller items of attire in his teeth.

When they could hardly see over the mass of clothing, the impatient salesman directed them toward a fitting room.

"Hurry it up, people! I don't have all day. I have other customers, you know. Admittedly, less desperate ones, but still...."

When Jen returned from leaving the pile she had accumulated with Stuart, and after plying him with appropriate instructions, she found their escort waiting for her nearby. Holding a juice drink in each hand, he passed one to her before sitting himself down in one of a pair of ornate faux fin-de-siècle chairs. She marveled at the fact that despite the energy he had expended in collecting clothing he had not a hair out of place nor an unintended crease in his attire.

Before long Stuart emerged. Having followed Jen's instructions to the letter, he was clad in an outfit that was the visual definition of preppiness. The salesman gave it a thumbs-up and a broad smile before Jen shook her head *no*.

The next incarnation consisted of leather jacket, black pants, a chain that led nowhere and enough zippers to outfit a pair of energetic ecdysiasts on the Sunset Strip. It left Jen speechless, from which reaction Bloomie guessed they had another no.

Stuart third's appearance was in a pair of Star Wars pajamas. While this display did not displease the salesman, as a man-about-town outfit it was patently insufficient. As for Jen, she had to turn away. Needing something to help her forget the most recent manifestation of Stuart, she dialed Arthur's number. It rang, and then….

"Hi, this is Arthur. I can't take this call because I'm either at the Round Table or…."

She put the phone away, just in time to see Stuart emerge yet again from the fitting room. Some of the tension that had gripped her faded. He was wearing a blue casual suit over a plain white button-down shirt, no tie. Clean, simple. As she and the salesman looked on, he modeled it in front of a full-length mirror. Striking an occasional pose, he admired himself.

Not bad, she told herself. Not bad at all. More than passable, in fact.

"I like it."

"I love it!" Bloomie concurred.

"Stuart, you look great," Jen confessed.

"Great?" The salesman was mildly offended. "He looks perfect. Now it's your turn. Get in there." He rose. "Give me five minutes."

When he returned, he was loaded down with samples from the Women's Clothing Dept. But not nearly as much as before, since with Jen, unlike with Stuart, he was not starting from zero.

On the third try she emerged wearing an exquisite red summer dress. All that was missing was a breeze to waft her hair ala a really expensive shampoo commercial. Otherwise, it was an impressive presentation.

Stuart had always thought she was beautiful. Now she was even more so.

"Wow, Jen. You look *awesome*."

"You think?" She did a little spin in front of the mirrors, admiring herself.

He nodded, started to loll his tongue, changed his mind. After all, he had yet to see another human doing so. "Much better now that I can see in color."

His comment did not register on the salesman, who was delighted with his effort. "You are stunning! Now all we have left to do is take care of—that!"

When Jen eyed him blankly, he pointed downward. Stuart joined them in looking in the same direction. He failed to understand why either of them should be upset.

After all, it wasn't as if his feet were any dirtier than usual. He wiggled his toes, quite visible where they protruded from a pair of Jen's battered flip-flops, and tried to remember where last he had buried a bone. He thought to ask Jen, but first, she likely wouldn't know, and second, the expression on her face suggested she might be about to puke. Probably not the best time to discuss burying or digging up old, dirty, rotting bones. The best kind.

They found shoes to match his new attire. Donning the clothing gave him surprisingly little trouble. The shoes were another matter. He had never walked in anything except his bare feet and he was having trouble staying vertical. Walking on two legs was hard enough without the added burden of having one's feet enclosed and restricted. He'd always wondered how humans managed it. Now he was having to find out for himself. As long as they were shopping, he considered asking Jen to buy him a new leash, but thought better of it. He was learning to adapt, and had to admit that he had never seen a human wearing a leash. Except maybe that one time on the walkway….

As soon as the final transaction was complete and Jen had her receipt, she leaned into the salesman. "Thanks, Bloomie. I don't think I could have done this without your help." She gave him a heartfelt hug.

"I know." He let out a contented sigh. "I am *so* good at what I do. Fortunately, my innate modesty keeps my ego in check." Pirouetting, he headed back to the sales floor.

Loaded down with bags, the shopper and her charge exited the mall. Eying Stuart, Jen wasn't sure whether to be proud or relieved. He looked—normal. No, she corrected herself. Better than normal. He was downright handsome. Between them, the concentrated efforts of groomers and Bloomie had worked wonders.

One wonder after another, she mused. While she was not sure how she was going to deal with the situation, of one thing she was certain: she could not handle another wonderment.

"So, how do you feel?"

"Seeing the world from up here is strange, Jen. A higher vantage point. Everything looks smaller when you're upright." He winced. "These shoes will get softer, right? My pa—my feet hurt. Can we eat now?"

Just like he's always been, she decided. Never one to linger over a thought. She took his arm. Because it felt right, and because she wanted to be able to hang onto him if he spotted something distracting, like a cat or a hot dog stand.

A shout caused her to look to her right.

"Jen? You look great!"

It was Ramos. Clad in civvies, she didn't place him at first. Stuart also recognized him. She felt him tense slightly.

"Officer Ramos." Stuart's greeting was polite but measured.

Ramos's response was far more enthused as he made no effort to hide his excitement. "It's just Hector, Stuart. I hardly know what to say, so I'll just say I really want to thank you for helping Ringo this morning. I don't know how you knew what was going on with him, but the vet said it was a very bad infection, extensive, and if we had waited another few days it could have started to affect his kidneys. As it is, he only lost the tooth. He's on antibiotics, will be for a while, but the vet said he should be fine." He bit his lower lip. "I don't know how I'd handle losing Ringo. I owe you one."

"That's great to hear, that he's going to be okay," Jen commented. She glanced at the nattily-dressed man on her arm. "Stuart? Do you have anything to say?"

He replied brightly and without hesitation. "Can we set up a play date?"

Ramos blinked. "Say what?"

Jen thought fast. "Uh, Stuart would love to have a play date with Ringo when—when he gets back."

"Sure would." Stuart's incomprehension was exceeded only by his enthusiasm.

Ramos looked uncertain, then relaxed. "Ah. Back from the farm, right? From herding cows?"

"Yep," Jen agreed swiftly, "the farm, still there. With the cows, yes."

Ramos nodded agreeably. "I gotta get going. Errands, some stuff for Ringo. Nice running into you." His gaze shifted. "And thanks again, Stuart."

Stuart started to bark his "you're welcome", thought better of it, and settled for a wave. A gesture he had seen performed by innumerable humans under similar circumstances. Leading led him away in the opposite direction, Jen whispered tersely.

"'Play date', Stuart? Are you crazy? Be careful what you say to people. Just because you can talk doesn't mean you can say the first thing that comes into your mind. No matter how natural it sounds to you, it will mess with peoples' heads. And will end up with them putting us both in the pound." She calmed herself. "Anyway, good job with Ringo. Good for him and good for Hector. Especially since he didn't press you on how you just happened to know there was something bad with Ringo's tooth."

Stuart sounded surprised. "He told me. I told Hector that."

"Yes, I know that, and you know that, but Hector might find that a little odd if you keep pushing it. Even if it is the truth."

"I always tell the truth," Stuart replied proudly. "Always! Didn't you know?" He turned serious. "Dogs don't know how to lie. It's just one more reason why we're such good companions." He shook his head. "I never understood how or why humans do it. Lie, I mean. It hurts. Anyway," he went on, cheerful once more, "there's a much more important question that needs to be answered."

"What might that be?"

"Are you gonna feed me now?"

The food court was crowded and some of the lines were long. Spotting a couple vacating a table, Jen rushed to it and laid claim. It was going to take a moment or two to order and receive their food and there was clearly no chance another table was likely to open up any time soon. She had to make a choice.

"Okay, Stuart. I need you to sit here while I go get us some food. You understand me? Sit here. *Stay*. And keep an eye on our bags...guard them like they are full of Jerky Treats. Good boy. I'll be back as fast as I can."

He was perfectly comfortable being left alone. Jen did it all the time when she went shopping—although he was usually tied. Not that he was inclined to wander off anyway. Not with food finally in the offing. He sat silently, gripping the shopping bags with both hands. He could do this. All he was being asked to do was sit and keep an eye on their purchases. Nothing to it. Even if his stomach was rumbling a bit.

Idly surveying his surroundings, he noticed a red-headed boy seated at the table next to his. The boy was eating—no, luxuriating—in a sizable ice cream cone. Ignoring the boy, Stuart's gaze locked laser-like on the ice cream. Canine motivation number one, food, kicked in. The universe shrank to become one with the vanilla. Having been trained to know that chocolate was not good for dogs, the dark topping was banished. Whipped cream, now…that was another matter. He fought not to salivate and dampen his new shirt.

Unable to avoid the intense stare of the man seated next to him, the boy frowned. "What?" Holding the cone , he offered a taste. "Want some?"

Nodding, Stuart leaned forward slightly. Whereupon the boy, still grinning, jerked it back.

"Sorry." The unpleasant grin widened. "I thought you wanted some." He extended the offering a second time.

Dogs cannot move faster than lightning, but where food is involved it sometimes seems that way.

Lunging forward without letting go of a single shopping bag, Stuart more or less inhaled the entire scoop. At first the former owner was too shocked to respond. Then, upon examining the empty cone he now held, he began to cry. In addition to members of the crowd, the disturbance also drew Jen's attention. Clutching a box of sliders, she increased her pace as she returned to the table. She arrived just ahead of a pair of security guards. This was fortunate, as Stuart's likely explanation might not have entirely satisfied them.

"The boy offered me his ice cream," he explained self-consciously as the guards escorted them from the mall. "I was hungry. I didn't steal it. He *offered*. You know me, Jen. Have I ever turned down food when someone offered it?"

"No, you have not." She stared hard at him. "Did he offer you *all* of it?"

He looked away. "We didn't discuss percentages."

"I'll bet you didn't." She sighed heavily. "Stuart, Stuart, what am I going to do with you?"

He indicated the box of sliders, from which arose an aroma that was overpowering. "Feed me?"

"Is that going to be your solution to *everything*?"

He nodded vigorously. "Pretty much."

Once out at the car she loaded their bags in the back end while Stuart sat in the front passenger seat and consumed (slowly, on her command) the entire box of sliders.

"Hey," one of the mall cops began," aren't you the…um…?"

"No," she replied sarcastically, "I'm not. I get that a lot."

Ordinarily she would have replied without dissembling. But she was tired, Stuart was an ongoing worry, and she just didn't have time for casual chat. Besides which the security guy struck her as a renter, not a potential buyer.

She was more relieved than she could have said when she finally pulled out of the Mall parking lot.

🐾 🐾 🐾

Too tired to do anything with her hair tonight, she reflected later as she stood before the mirror in her bathroom with toothbrush in hand. Had it suddenly turned into a snake it would not have surprised her. That led to a moment of reflection on how one would go about brushing one's teeth with a snake, provided it could be persuaded to keep still.

Danger, Jensen, she told herself silently (well, not entirely silently—she continued to gargle). *That way lies madness.* Finishing her evening ablutions, she called out toward the bedroom as she finished rinsing the decidedly un-reptilian toothbrush.

"Ready for beddy-byes? It feels weird saying that now." But it was what she always said to him before climbing into bed herself.

He did not respond. Normally that would be normal. But he could talk now, so she expected something in the way of a reply.

Flicking off the bathroom lights, she walked into the bedroom to find him fast asleep on the edge of the bed. He was completely wiped out, which did not surprise her since she was maybe one step behind total exhaustion herself. What did surprise, and please, her was that he had managed to undress and then don the Star Wars pajamas she had bought for him all by himself.

I should wake him, she mused as she gazed down at him. The notion of a full-grown man sleeping on her bed caused a natural wariness to engage. Except this was no ordinary man. It was— Stuart. Even if he looked more like an actor than a terrier, it was still just Stuart.

Going to the closet she located a loose blanket, returned, and spread it out over him. Snuffling in his sleep, he kicked out with one leg. His snoring was consistent save for the occasional whine. She wondered what he was chasing in his sleep. A cat, the dog park's insane suicidal squirrel, a car? Did Stuart the man have human or dog dreams? She would have to ask him.

Tomorrow. Everything could wait until tomorrow. She stretched and yawned. Bed loomed. Everything would *have* to wait until tomorrow.

CHAPTER EIGHT

Like any establishment that managed to survive in the Newport area for more than a few years, The Barkery had accumulated a roster of contented regulars both human and hound. Busy but not crowded, it had separate areas for people, small dogs, and larger breeds.

Cindy and her number one employee, Amanda, noticed when Jen and Stuart entered. Not one to miss an attractive member of the opposite sex, it was Amanda who commented on the arrival as she gestured meaningfully in Stuart's direction.

"*Who* is *that?*"

It took Cindy a moment to identify the individual who had arrived with Jen. "Well, it's definitely a better version than the one I saw rolling in the grass yesterday." She was open in her new admiration for Jen's companion. "Maybe he just likes dressing weird sometimes. Some guys do. He and Jen were pranking us anyway, so I guess the outfit he was wearing was part of the gag." On the counter nearby, Cupcake was standing on her hind legs, barking, and waving the front ones.

"What's got into her?" Amanda wondered aloud. "She's been relaxed all morning. Now she's going bonkers." She tapped her lips with the tip of an index finger as her attention shifted back to the latest arrivals. "He's *cute.*"

Cindy removed her apron, then scooped the excited Pomeranian up off the counter and went to greet Jen and her friend.

"Hi guys. Welcome to The Barkery."

"Hi Cindy." Jen indicated her companion. "This is an old college friend, Stuart."

Amanda looked confused. "Stuart, like your dog?"

"Jen also calls me Stuie Louie." As he smiled brightly, Amanda edged a little closer.

"You're funny."

Cindy's expression continued to reflect her uncertainty. "Have you been here before?"

"Sure! I've been here many, man…."

"He's passed by many times," Jen said hurriedly.

With her owner unable to restrain the wriggling, twisting Pomeranian any longer, Cindy looked on as the excited Cupcake leaped into Stuart's arms and began licking his face enthusiastically.

"Look at that." Cindy was plainly flummoxed. "Cupcake never does that. She nips; she doesn't lick."

"Nope," Amanda agreed. "Never seen her do that before." Her voice dropped to a murmur. "Can't say I blame her. Nothing wrong with a little lick now and then." Though she did everything possible to lock eyes with Stuart, he ignored her.

"She's quite the hostess, Cupcake is." Jen sounded lame even to herself.

"Cupcake wants to show me the doggie lounge," announced the object of the Pomeranian's affection.

"I'm sure she does," said Cindy. "It's Yappy Hour; everything's half price." She chuckled. "Don't worry—she's not on commission. Unless you consider an extra cookie snack a commission"

Amanda took another step forward, her tone suggestive of activities that would fall outside the realm of puppy play. "C'mon, I can show you." Reaching out, she moved to take Cupcake from Stuart's arms. The Pomeranian promptly let out a snarl and lunged as if to bite her. Not just give a playful nip, either. Taken aback, Amanda left the dog to Stuart's care while nudging for him to come with her.

"Follow me." To herself she added under her breath, "Little bitch".

Leaving Cindy and Jen engaged in conversation, Amanda led her visitor to the small dog area.

"As you can see, here we have facilities that exemplify the best possible…." She broke off, gawking.

Continuing to ignore her, Stuart ceased petting Cupcake and set her down gently in the play area. Perfectly normal pet owner behavior. What followed was not. Ignoring any possible danger to his new clothes from urine or other stains on the floor, he promptly laid down beside her and started making circles in the air with one hand. Cupcake straightaway started following his movements, spinning in circles and occasionally leaping over his outstretched arm.

Observing the activity, other dogs trotted over to join in. Every single one of them. Soon Stuart was surrounded by a veritable canine circus, with every member of every breed following his directions and leads, all eager to join in and please the newcomer.

As the dogs lined up to participate, their owners gathered outside the play area. Phones emerged and began recording. Whispers of amazement filled the room.

"Choo Choo never did that before," declared one customer in response to a poodle doing repeated backflips. "I never taught her that." She checked her phone to make sure it was recording. "My husband needs to see this."

The man next to her could hardly keep his attention on his

phone long enough to make certain it was recording, so enthralled was he by the demonstration taking place before him.

"See that Maltese; the one with the slightly darkened face? I could never get my Rusty to sit, let alone do *that*!" In response to the gestures and murmurings of the man lying on the floor inside the play area, the puffy pooch in question was jumping back and forth over Cupcake. Ordinarily, she would have bit the crap out of any dog attempting such a trick. Amanda was now doubly amazed.

"Who is this guy?"

"He's not a dog whisperer," someone else declared. "He's a dog shouter!"

When Stuart finally emerged from the play area to take a seat, everyone within range clustered around him. Though he understood their questions perfectly, he answered none of them. His attention was on the dog named Choo choo who had climbed onto his lap. As the crowd yammered at him, he listened intently when Choo stepped up to whine into his ear. At least, to everyone else present it sounded like a whine.

The dog hopped down and Stuart handed him to his owner. "Choo Choo forgives you and wants you to pick up a few codfish cupcakes. They're half price right now," he added encouragingly.

Out front, Cindy was grilling her friend. "So what's the deal, Jen? You never told me what happened with Arthur and I hear Stuart—your Stuart—is on vacation at 'Aunt Sally's farm'?" As Jen ignored the implication, Cindy changed the subject. "So Arthur didn't even mention the shopping center that's going to do away with the dog park?"

Jen turned away slightly so that her friend couldn't see the pain in her face. "Not a word. It's just another business deal to him."

At a loss how to respond to her friend's obvious distress, Cindy offered up a small cupcake-laden tray. Jen waved it away. Was she getting fat? Would it matter? Why should she care if that's what Arthur might be thinking? Why should she care about anything he might be thinking?

They were interrupted as a breathless Amanda arrived, glancing rapidly from one woman to the other.

"You have to come see what's going on!"

Cindy made a face. "Somebody wants a refund for something?"

"No, no." Waving her off, Amanda turned her full attention to Jen. "It's your friend, Stuart. This guy's *amazing*. He's talking to Choo Choo and then his owner goes ahead and buys a dozen codfish cupcakes. I know Bob and he *never* buys codfish cupcakes. It's crazy. So hot."

The two women exchanged a glance, followed Amanda into the small dog lounge. They had to push their way through the assembled crowd of owners to get close enough to see that Stuart was relaxing in a chair with one of the dogs on his lap. That in itself was not particularly remarkable. What did cause their jaws to drop was the sight of nearly all the other dogs lined up neatly nearby, sitting quietly at attention awaiting their turn, like so many children at Christmas waiting for their turn with a Mall Santa.

The exception was a trio who had parked themselves in front of a doll-sized counter where Cupcake the Pomeranian held sway.

"So you're saying," a fuzz-faced schnauzer snorted, "one day he just woke up human? Kinda hard to believe."

"So are certain pet food company's claims that their product contains no filler." Cupcake had assumed the air of One Who Knows All. "That's exactly what he told me. And now he can speak dog *and* human."

A dewy-eyed dachshund eyed her in wonderment. "Is he stuck being a human for the rest of his life? Will he ever be a dog again?"

"I don't know," Cupcake replied honestly. "*He* doesn't know.

All we know about his situation is that nobody knows anything. Right now that's the gold standard, dog."

Prim, proper, and pampered, the third supplicant, a miniature poodle sporting a bejeweled collar, coughed for attention. "Ahem." Cupcake turned to her.

"May I help you?"

"Yes. Can I please get two sausage covered bacon brownies?"

"For here or to go?"

The poodle looked at the growing mob of humans; surging, squabbling, and above all, stinking. "To go, please."

Cupcake let out a short bark. "I'll put them on the counter and your human can pay when you leave."

More little dog owners line up as Stuart receives Mitzi, a Yorkie with her hair in rubber bands not unlike Baby Spice. Mitzi whispers her deepest concerns into the ear of the dogman. Her owner eagerly awaits the prognosis. "More attention?" he balks as Stuart reveals what Mitzi just told him.

"That's what she said. Since the new baby arrived, she doesn't feel like part of the family anymore." Taken aback Mitzi's dad assures her his family wouldn't be complete without her. Once again Mitzi whispers into Stuart's ear, the crowd goes pin drop silent. Stuart reveals her latest request, "She also wants to be pushed around in a stroller, like the baby."

By this time the line outside The Barkery had grown long enough to stretch around the corner. People with pets were having a difficult time controlling their animals as well as themselves. Perhaps mistaking what was taking place but not wanting to miss out on anything exceptional, one aspirant stood with a cat in walking harness. The cat was not happy.

Crossing the street while ignoring the honking of numerous irate drivers, a boy let his pit bull lead the way. Once safely across, he fought his way through the waiting crowd to the front of the line.

"Excuse me! Come on, Butch. Excuse me, please! We have an appointment!"

At the front of the line, an older man cradled his pinscher safely away from the pit and growled at the new arrival. "That so? Who you got an appointment with?"

"The groomer." Unintimidated, the boy eyed the accuser man to man. "You know how hard it is to find a groomer who'll work on a pit bull?"

"Oh." Taken aback by the unexpectedly reasonable reply, the man apologized. "Sorry. Go on in, son."

"Right, thanks. Come on, Butch."

It took the man another thirty seconds to remember that The Barkery did not do grooming, but by that time the boy and his dog were already inside.

Spotting his arrival, Cindy stepped away from Jen to intercept. Her tone was kindly but firm. "Honey, we have a lot of small dogs in here right now. Your doggie is a little too big to mix with everybody else."

Bravado dissolved into tears. "Please, miss, please! I ran twelve blocks and through traffic for Butch to meet the dogman, please?"

Looking on, Jen could only marvel at how fast events were moving. So now Stuart was "the dogman". The fact that the description was more accurate than the boy knew did nothing to mute her bewilderment at it all.

Well, they didn't call her the pet "friendly" realtor for nothing.

Bending over, she reached out to pet Butch. The powerful, heavyset skull came toward her—and then he was licking her face. It was all about ownership and treatment, she knew; not the breed. As the boy looked on hopefully, she glanced up at Cindy. Her friend's expression softened.

"Alright, c'mon. But hold Butch close, okay? And no matter what, you don't let go of his leash."

The boy nodded vigorously. "Yes, miss. Don't worry."

"I have to." Turning, Cindy led them toward the small dog play area. "Goes with the job."

She did not have to ask people to step aside. Butch managed that all by himself. Any dogs not being carried likewise scooted out of the way without having to be told. It was like the canine parting of the Red Sea, although Butch was no Moses.

The new arrivals did not slow their advance. As the crowd looked on with a mixture of expectation and apprehension, Butch walked right up to Stuart. Though his owner kept a tight grip on the pit's leash, few in the crowd felt he could control his dog if the animal decided to go berserker.

Standing up on stocky hind legs, the pit put his face close to Stuart's and—they hugged. The pit's tail was going like a metronome. A sound floated out over the now nearly silent cluster of onlookers. The pit was whimpering into Stuart's ear, and the man now anointed the Dogman was crying.

Nobody said a word. Until Stuart spoke. Not to Jen, not to the boy, not to anyone in the crowd.

"I know, I know," he whispered to the pit. "It's okay, buddy. You're not a bad boy. It's okay. Nothing's your fault."

Closing the short distance between them, the boy began stroking Butch along his back. "He's always sad. He cries at night."

Still hugging the whimpering pit, Stuart looked over at his human. "Someone told Butch he's bad because he's a pit bull. It's not his nature and he can't help his breed. He can't do anything about it. He says he's never ever tried to hurt anyone, not even when some of the other kids in your neighborhood throw things at him. He just wants to be him. He's kept chained in the yard?"

"That's my dad," the boy explained. "He doesn't want him in the house. He says pit bulls are all dangerous and aggressive."

"What does your mother say?"

"She's the one who brought Butch home." The boy's gaze dropped and he hesitated a moment. "She left my dad and I a year ago. I think maybe sometimes she brought me Butch to keep me company because she knew she was going away."

Stuart listened quietly. He could not offer anything in the way of advice where human interactions were concerned, but dogs….

"You love Butch, right?"

"I love Butch, yes. He's my best friend."

By now Cindy and Jen had moved closer, listening. They were as silent and astonished as the rest of the crowd.

"Then let your dad know he should love Butch as much as you do. You love Butch and Butch loves you, and if nothing else your dad should love him for that reason alone. Tell your dad that not all pit bulls are aggressive." He gazed down at the traumatized pit, who stared back up with a happy, stupid expression on his face. "Part of it is just the name. If the breed was called Poofy Bits instead of pit bulls, people would react differently to them. Every dog is an individual just like humans and deserve to be loved as much as you love Butch." He put out a hand, Butch put out a paw, and they shook.

"When you tell your dad Butch is the most loving and loyal friend you've ever had, he will let him in the house. Butch will take care of his end. Trust me. Be strong, Joey. You'll grow up and Butch will grow with you and one day everything in your life will be better."

"I will, I'll do that. Thanks, dogman!" He gave a gentle tug on the leash and Butch reluctantly backed away from Stuart. "Hey? How'd you know my name?"

Stuart did not reply, just waved goodbye. To Butch, not to the boy. Butch let out a quick bark, soft enough so as not to unsettle the still uneasy among the crowd. It was anyway mostly lost in the applause that filled the room. An amazed Cindy looked to Jen for a comment, a clarification, something to explain what she had just seen. All Jen could do was shrug and join in the applause. There was, after all, nothing she could say. Nothing, at least, that would not result in her being hauled off for extensive medical examination.

It was something of a surprise to encounter Derek and his dog Avery when she stepped outside to get away from the crowd and catch a breath of fresh air.

"Fancy meeting you here," she said. *Oh Jen*, she told herself, *your wit is legendary*. But as is usually the case it was too late to think of something else to say. She did remember to smile.

He smiled back. He had a very nice smile, she decided. Open and honest, not fake professional. "I might say the same. I didn't know you worked here. I thought you sold real estate."

"On occasion." *There*," she thought, *that was a little better*. A little. "What are you doing here?"

He looked past her and into the store. "A friend called. Said there's this insanely good dog psychic here today. You know ballplayers. We're superstitious about everything. So I thought I'd drive over and see what's going on." He grinned down at the golden retriever by his side. "I don't buy into it myself, but who knows? Maybe Avery would like to get his paw read."

A glance showed Stuart making his way toward the doorway, politely declining request after request by owners to minister to their dogs. Seeing that the session, or whatever it was, was over for the day, those who had been waiting in line began to disperse. In general, they were more than a little disappointed. The cat was not.

"Here he comes," Jen said. "I'll introduce you."

"Excuse me." Stuart was almost pleading. "I have to get back to Jen."

The last disappointed petitioners dropped away as Jen grabbed him. Leaning in, she whispered in his ear. "This is a client. Derek Jones. Be extra nice because…."

Before she could finish, the retriever had jumped up to plant his tongue on Stuart's face, causing Jen to stumble slightly.

Catching her before she could fall, Jones steadied her, helped her recover her balance.

"Thanks." He was, she reflected, in considerably better physical condition than Arthur. Or anyone else she had ever dated.

There was no need for her to caution Stuart because he was as open and cheery with this new human as he was with everyone.

"Hi, Derek Jones."

"Ha!" The ballplayer eyed the retriever. "Did Avery tell you that?"

"No." Stuart looked to his right. "Jen did. Just now."

"Of course. What was I thinking? So good to meet you, man. I hear you talk to dogs? We've got a couple on our team who need a lot of work." He chuckled in spite of himself.

Utterly oblivious to the reference, Stuart replied brightly, "I hear you can throw a ball pretty far. Avery says that's his favorite thing and he misses the orange one."

The ballplayer's grin vanished. "Avery said that?"

"He wants to know where it is," Stuart added before Jen could intervene. Beside him, the retriever began to bark and bounce excitedly. Turning away from the visiting human, Stuart engaged the other dog in play. At least, Jen reflected, he didn't drop to all fours. They were safe—for the moment.

Forcing himself back to reality, Derek turned to Jen. "Can we do that lunch meeting today at my place? I know I mentioned that restaurant, but I promise there'll be actual food and it'll save my schedule. Which I blew coming down here today. Not that I'm sorry I did." He looked over to where Stuart and Avery were chasing each other in circles. "Interesting character for sure, your bud."

"Noon works," she replied readily. "Stuart is visiting. He's an old friend from college."

"Not a problem. Bring him. Avery'll be delighted."

"And you?" She eyed him questioningly.

"I never met a dog I didn't like, and I think the feeling's mutual."

"Okay." She turned back toward The Barkery. "Let me finish up here with everyone and we'll see you at noon." She started toward the store, beckoning to Stuart. He joined her a bit reluctantly.

Derek waved as they departed. "Nice meeting you, Stuart. See you guys in a bit!"

Stuart winked back at him, momentarily throwing the ballplayer off-stride. He shrugged it off. What else could you expect from a dog psychic? At the same time, Avery let out a sharp bark. The guy certainly had something, Derek admitted. Though he chose not to speculate on what that something might be.

Leaving proved a tad more difficult than arriving. The crowd had grown and now a couple of news trucks were blocking part of the street. Nothing much of interest happened in the L.A. basin that didn't make it onto the news within half an hour of revelation.

Not everyone had left and the space outside the store was still packed with customers. They ignored Jen in favor of bombarding Stuart with questions. Is what I'm feeding Trixie really the best choice for her? My Rufus gets filthy but hates baths: what can I do? Savonarola hates his name: is it too late to change it to Savvy?

Ever polite, Stuart did his best to supply an answer to every query. As long as Jen was nearby he was happy to oblige. Besides, right now she was on the phone. Despite the distance between them he had no trouble overhearing.

"Hi, this is Arthur. I can't take this call because I'm either at the Round Table with Galahad and Lancelot or on my yacht. Leave a…."

For a moment he thought that Jen was going to throw her phone into one of the sample doggie bathtubs stacked behind the main counter. This struck him as uncharacteristic. Apparently, she relented, because she put her phone back in her purse. Jammed it back in, actually. Then she was at his side once more. For some reason she seemed suddenly unhappy.

"Let's get out of here," she muttered as she searched for a path clear of the crowd.

"But all these people—" he protested.

"They'll get over it. Maybe," she said sarcastically, "we can sign you an advice column. Meanwhile, say goodbye to all your fans. We have a lunch appointment, with Derek."

That was all it took. "Lunch! Okay!" Displaying exceptional physical dexterity, he hopped up onto a bench as effortlessly as any gymnast. "It was nice meeting you all today! Remember to brush your teeth before you go to sleep, and remember to brush your dog's teeth, too. Or at least make sure they get regular dental chews." Barks and claps punctuated his words. "For a good, tasty brand, I can personally recommend…."

Grabbing an arm, Jen pulled him off the bench.

In a hurry to get to her car, she nearly bumped into guitarist Jim. It left her flustered and embarrassed. He was going to think that unyielding physical contact was her preferred method of greeting. Stuart ignored him, having eyes only for the petite terrier leashed at his side.

"Jen!" he exclaimed.

"Jim!" she mumbled.

"Sweetie Peters!" Stuart cried joyfully.

"Ruff!" the terrier added.

Formal greetings having been satisfactorily concluded, it was Jim who spoke first. "Everyone is talking about you guys. It's all over the media. Professional as well as social. What's going on here?" Distracted, he noticed that a news anchor from CBS was chatting with a figure he recognized. "Look, there's Derek Jones, from the Angels." He remembered their earlier conversation.

"The lunch date you told me about? It's with *that* Derek Jones? That's a home run, Jen."

She smiled. No point in denying it. "Yes, it's him."

With Jen engaged with the guitarist there was no one to counsel Stuart to not get down on his knees in front of the Boston terrier. She took a couple of steps back, closer to Jim's feet.

"Don't embarrass me in front of everyone, Stuart Louis." Looking around, she saw other dogs at her level staring in their direction. "Little bitches will gossip. You know: yap, yap, yap."

Flustered, he sat back on his heels. "I would never do that to you, Sweetie Peters."

"Maybe not intentionally, but how do you know what you might do in your present form? Humans have a whole culture devoted to embarrassing one another. When are you getting back on all fours?" She looked him over. "You don't look too bad this way. For a human. But you're more bare-skinned than a greyhound and you've got no tail. I'll never understand how humans can really express emotion without a tail." For emphasis she wagged her own. "The whole park is talking."

"It sucks, I know," he told her. "It's getting easier, but I still feel like I'm going to fall down every time I take a step. As for missing tail-wagging, from what I've seen humans are very sparing with it, and when they do it, context is really important or you can get into serious trouble. I'm doing everything I can. I promise."

Nearby, the news reporter that had encountered Derek Jones and Avery, had corralled them for an interview. Jones, that is. She would have learned a lot more had she been able to interview Avery. With a cameraman at the ready, the producer standing beside him held up five fingers indicating that they were on air. Immediately the reporter's expression morphed from thoughtful to that frozen rictus of happiness all television reporters are required to master.

"I'm Maria Sanchez and we are live at The Barkery in

Newport with Angels' shortstop Derek Jones." She turned from the camera to her interviewee. "What's going on, Derek?"

"Well, we're off to a good start this season. Won a few games, well-positioned to move up in the standings. Our next seven games are at home, so we're all looking forward to that. I'd like to kick my average up about ten points, but I've hit a few home runs so…."

She waved him off. "No, no, not that. I don't mean what's up with baseball. I mean here, at The Barkery". She nodded in the direction of the store and the crowd that was still mulling around out front. "I understand there is a dog whisperer inside right now."

"Not inside." He turned toward the store. "I think he's outside now and…."

She cut him off again, bloviated with faux excitement. "Did your dog talk to him?"

Having done dozens of interviews over the years, Derek had learned patience. Instead of chiding the reporter for interrupting, much less electing not to talk baseball, he simply pointed.

"Yeah, Avery here just talked to him." The retriever crowded close around his owner's legs. "He's right over there with Jen Jensen. You know—the pet friendly realtor?"

The reporter's professional smile remained lacquered on her face, but the rest of her expression was blank.

Jen, however, noticed her new client talking with the reporter. When he pointed in her direction she knew it was time to go. The thought of Stuart being interviewed on live TV conjured up possibilities to which she knew she would not be able to appropriately respond.

Noticing her stare, Jim looked in the same direction and saw only the ballplayer being interviewed by a reporter. "Everything alright, Jen?"

"Uh, the park, your guitar, dogs, big real estate deal, we really gotta go, just call me later. I'll explain, maybe, kinda, if I can, so you don't think I'm crazy." Aware that how she was speaking and what she was saying might be perceived as contradicting her last comment, she gave up. "We'll fix, don't worry, bye Jim." Putting a hand on her companion's shoulder, she gave a gentle squeeze. "C'mon, Stuart. Time to go."

He straightened, his attention still on the terrier in front of him but now far below eye level. "Goodbye, Sweetie Peters. See you later." The response was a polite bark.

In the process of frantically trying to reposition her camera team, Sanchez brushed off her exasperated interviewee as effortlessly as one of the surfers in the nearby water dropping into a barrel.

"What?" he reproved her. "Don't you want to talk about baseball? Did you see the catch I made of that line driver last week against the Marlins? Why are you talking to me, anyway?"

She wasn't. Not any longer, anyway. She was gesturing to her producer, who initiated a second five-finger countdown as Jen and Stuart escaped through the far side of the crowd.

"I'm Maria Sanchez, CBS 2." Shading her eyes with one hand while she gripped the mic with the other she struggled to see over the crowd. "Where'd they go?"

Knowing that calling out "where'd they go?" was unsatisfactory content for live TV, the producer signaled to his team in the nearby truck while miming a cutting motion across his throat. The transmission went dead, along with Sanchez's hopes for a mid-afternoon scoop.

Looking back and seeing that for the moment at least they were clear of both the crowd and the news crew, Jen broke into a jog. Stuart said nothing but matched her stride for stride. He loved it when they could go for a little run.

He panted as they ran, but only out of habit.

CHAPTER NINE

J en felt certain that Derek Jones' house was going to be an easy sell. The asking price was fair, it was in a great neighborhood, and it was in like-new condition—probably because the owner hadn't utilized half the rooms. Its internal layout made it suitable for an executive's home or a sizable family. She felt fortunate to have the listing. As if that weren't enough, the owner was…

Charming, she told herself. Just charming. Leave it at that. Don't go down that road. Not now. There were other issues that had to be dealt with first. Her mother. Arthur. She glanced sideways at the good-looking chap striding along beside her. Her —dog. Brother, did she have issues.

As they approached the main entrance Stuart made admiring sounds.

"I told you it was huge." Even as she was monitoring him her professional eye was making fresh mental notes of every section of fence, every stalk of landscaping. "I think he's decided it's much bigger than anything he needs. And he's got two birds. I don't know why. Maybe they remind him of the roar of the crowd. Or maybe he just likes birds."

"Birds?" Stuart's expression was child-like. "Real birds?"

Having come out to greet them, Derek had overheard. "Holly and Molly. I put them upstairs. They were in a very loud mood today."

"'Today'?" Jen eyed him archly. "What were they doing the last time I was here? Whispering secrets?"

"You'd have to ask them." His gaze shifted to her companion. "Or maybe Stuart here could ask them. Or does he only do dogs?"

Jen tensed slightly. Thankfully, Stuart didn't respond. He was too busy sniffing the air emanating from the house. Interesting aromas arose from within. Derek noticed, and the distraction was enough for him to change the subject.

"I made us a Niçoise salad for lunch. I hope you like tuna."

"*You* made?" *Don't go there*, Jen reminded herself. Still, the fact that he had fixed lunch by himself instead of ordering in checked another box on her list of desirable male qualities. He might not have actually cooked anything, but it was still a step in the right direction. Not to mention the fact that he could correctly pronounce "Niçoise".

"Sounds delicious," she told him.

Stuart felt rather different about the midday meal prospects. Plainly grossed out, he leaned over to whisper to Jen as Derek led them into the house. He had learned enough to know not to say out loud what he was thinking. Most of the time, anyway.

"I *thought* I smelled tuna. That's cat food. Cat food on top of rabbit food. I can't eat that."

She nudged him in the ribs. "Shhh, be quiet."

Though doubtful, where an instruction from Jen was concerned he always complied. Feeling of his side where she had tapped him, he followed her in.

Bounding past Derek, Avery all but leaped into Stuart's arms. His owner might have seen the retriever lick his visitor's face enthusiastically. He likely did not see Stuart return the licking.

"Hey buddy." Letting the retriever down easily, Stuart stroked the top of his head. "Nice place you got here!"

"It's okay," Avery replied. "Gets lonely when Derek is playing in away games. Come play outside, Stuart!"

As Derek led them to the table where lunch would be served, Jen was unpacking a sheaf of papers from her oversized purse. "I have the paperwork with me. Just take a couple of minutes to go over the last details and add signatures."

He shrugged. "Don't worry about that right now. There's plenty of time. Let's eat first. Just take a second to set the table." Observing that his dog was trying to be everywhere at once he added, "Let me take Avery outside. He has a bad habit of begging at the table, especially when I've got company."

Taking hold of the retriever's collar, Derek led him toward a back door. Avery complied, following the lead, but whining softly as he looked back. Moving to a rear window, Stuart stared as Derek released the retriever into the ample yard. He was as anxious to play as was his longer-haired counterpart.

Coming up beside him, Jen whispered anxiously. "I have to get this done, Stuart." She gestured back toward the table. "I need to get those papers signed. Please control your instincts."

"Oh, all right." He turned away from the window. "Humans and their papers."

Returning after releasing Avery, their host proceeded to set the table and make a second trip to the nearby kitchen, returning with a large glass bowl mounded high with greens and speckled with flakes of yellowtail. Jen took a seat while Stuart carefully imitated her movements.

"Help yourselves." Derek sat down at the other side of the table. "My mother taught me how to make this salad. God bless her soul."

Jen's expression fell. "I'm so sorry. Did she recently pass?"

"No." As he replied to Jen's question, Derek served himself. "That would be 'God rest her soul'. Just 'God bless her soul'." Using the salad tongs she placed a large helping on her plate. "Got it." The last time Jen had been this nervous at a meal had been in a certain Italian restaurant. While the circumstances were very different this time, she was still searching for an important resolution. "Glad to hear she's still alive. Amen." When the man seated next to her made no move to do the same she said quickly, "Let me pick out some good stuff for you, Stuart." As she doled out a serving she tried to put some emphasis on the tuna without taking it all. It didn't matter. He ignored the green mass on his plate completely.

Letting his fork rest on his plate, Derek added some pepper from a grinder to his salad. "So…Stuart. It seems you have quite the gift, or so everyone is saying. Reading dog thoughts, is it?"

Stuart replied without looking at him. His attention was focused on Avery, who was gamboling happily out in the yard. Having fun while he, Stuart, was trapped inside a house with prattling humans and disgusting plates of cat-rabbit food.

"No. I just talk to them like I talk to you. I talk to my friends just like you would talk to your friends. How else is someone supposed to talk to someone else? Now it's my turn: I have a question."

"Shoot." Derek forked up half a tomato.

"It's a really important question."

"You have my full attention." Lettuce followed tomato.

"How far can you throw a ball?"

Jen rose quickly, and not entirely to break the tension. "Excuse me, guys. I need to use the lady's room?"

"This isn't a gender-specific household." Turning in his chair, he pointed. "It's just down the side hall a little ways and off to the right." "I know where it is and there's five of them. I'm listing this place!" Derek laughed, "Touché!"

She then gave Stuart a look. He knew that look. It was stern but loving. A look that said simply, "Behave!" As was their custom, he sat quietly, waiting for her to return while gazing after her. His posture was correct and his attitude expectant.

Both did little for conversation. After waiting for what he considered to be a polite, if not excessive, interval, Derek finally cleared his throat to induce his guest to turn and face him once more.

"So. You and Jen went to college together?"

Stuart replied by bobbing his head up and down, remembering at the last moment not to let his tongue loll out and to one side.

"Sometimes. We sang a lot together."

He would have said more but his train of thought was derailed by Avery's barking, which was strong enough to reach into the dining area from outside. Derek, of course, heard nothing *but* barking. Stuart heard….

"Stuart! Come out and play! C'mon!"

This time his guest's indifference tried Derek's patience. "Um, Stuart?"

With an effort Stuart turned back to his host. Avery's beckoning kept ringing in his mind.

"You guys are very close, huh?"

"No. We just met today." Once again his attention shifted to the back yard.

"Not you and Avery. You and Jen—Ms. Jensen."

"Oh yes, very close. It's always been that way between us, a long time now. She tells me everything and I mostly listen. I'm a good listener. I remember one time at school she farted and blamed it on me."

This not being quite the response he had expected nor one he wished to explore in depth, Derek changed the subject once more. He gestured at his guest's plate.

"Stuart, you're not hungry? I see you haven't touched your salad. I mean, I'm no chef, but I'm told I throw together a pretty good bunch of greens. If you'd like something else, I can see what's in the pantry that I could break out for you quickly."

"The issue's not your salad."

Why won't he look at me? Derek wondered. He wiped at his mouth and chin. Nothing dripping or hanging, so what was it, then?

"Did you eat a big breakfast or something?"

"No. I'd just rather go outside and play with Avery."

The guy really was dog-crazy, Derek thought. *Was he hiding something, or was he just really, really, laid-back?* "Sure, go ahead. And while you're at it, ask him where he hid my favorite slippers."

Whereas inquiries about lunch had failed to garner his guest's attention, this did.

"I already told you, when we were outside The Barkery. He misses his orange ball. Give it back to him I bet you get your slippers back."

Derek frowned. It took him a moment to remember. "That scruffy old ball in the trunk of my car?"

"Is that where it is?"

"That thing's half chewed-up. I bought him a new one. Two new ones."

"He likes the old one. Its shape is familiar, its taste is familiar, and it's texture is familiar. He's just like you that way."

"I don't understand what you mean. In what way am I like that?"

"Avery likes his old ball. You like your old slippers. No wonder you're friends. You have the same tastes. People and dogs often do. You want your old slippers? Get him the old ball."

"I can't believe I'm doing this." Derek muttered to himself as he stood. He raised his voice to reply to Stuart. "Hang on. I'll be right back. I need to get the car fob."

Shaking his head, Stuart watched him go. "They think they're so smart. They know how to talk, but they don't know how to listen. They pretend they do, but they don't, not really. Mostly they just like to listen to themselves. No wonder they fight all the time. Always over unimportant things. So many "things", when they don't really need anything more than a dog."

"What are you whining about?" Though she had been as fast as possible in the bathroom, Jen saw that it had not been fast enough. She searched the dining area. "Where's Derek?"

"He went to get a ball from his car."

Uh-oh. Ball. Car. Stuart.

"Listen, Stu, I have some important business to conclude here. Not only is it important to me, it could be important for you. I'd like to upgrade your food, but that costs and…." She stopped, started over. "Please don't…."

She cut herself off as Derek returned. Not knowing exactly what had transpired between him and Stuart, she anticipated a brief explanation. Instead, he threw her a quick smile before addressing his other guest.

"I got it." He tossed the ball up and down in one hand. It was indeed, Stuart noted, well masticated. Even from the other side of the table he could smell Avery on it despite how long it had languished in the car trunk.

"Give it to him."

"That's it? No commands, no pointing in a certain direction?"

"Nope. That's all."

Hopeful but disbelieving, Derek headed for a back door and went out into the yard. Watching him go, Jen still held onto the hope that he would sign the necessary papers. Certain other more nebulous hopes began to wilt.

"What is he doing?"

His attention on Avery, Stuart replied absently. "He wants his slippers back."

Immediately espying the ball, Avery went into his best impala imitation, jumping and spinning and pronking while barking enthusiastically. As Jen and Stuart watched from inside, Derek threw it clear across the yard. Fur flying, Avery exploded after it.

Their host's smile went from ear to ear as he returned to the dining area.

"Should I get the paperwork going?" Jen tried not to sound desperate. A little pleading was okay, but not outright despondency. "We can do it while we finish our salads." She eyed her companion accusingly. "Stuart, you haven't touched yours. It's not polite to refuse f…."

Their host interrupted her. "It's okay, Jen. I haven't seen Avery this excited about anything since I don't know when."

Great, she told herself. Now the *both* of them were ignoring her and staring out into the backyard. As if after the debacle with Arthur her confidence needed another hit.

Derek was tracking Avery as he spun and dashed like a maniac: tossing the ball into the air and catching it, throwing it into the landscaping so he could dig it out, and pushing it across the grass with his nose.

"Man, he loves that ball!" Derek turned to the equally intent Stuart, who replied without looking at his host.

"The nose knows," he responded simply.

"That's for sure. But what about my slippers?" Leaning closer to the glass, he searched the yard. "Hey, where'd he go?"

There followed a brief pause during which Stuart said nothing; only raised his eyebrows and gestured for his host to look behind him. There was a distant plastic *slap*. The kind of muted noise that might be produced by, say, the flap of a doggie door opening and closing.

Head down, the retriever rejoined them. There was a pair of slippers in his mouth. They were muddy and battered and maybe a little bit chewed, but still intact. Dropping them to the floor, a patently abashed Avery backed slowly away.

For a moment, Derek had no words. Plopping himself back into his chair, salad and everything else forgotten, he kept shifting his gaze from retriever to slippers and back again. A glance indicated that after a professional cleaning, the footwear should be just fine.

"Dude," he finally mumbled, "how did you know that? He was actually mad at me. He would never bite me, or run off. I took his ball away, so he took my slippers away. I didn't know dogs could feel spite."

"You'd be surprised what dogs can feel," Stuart told him. "If humans knew what dogs could really feel they might treat them better. Although I have to admit that some of us do just fine." He threw Jen the most soulful look imaginable.

Coming over to him, Derek enveloped him in a heartfelt bro hug. Looking over the bigger man's shoulder, Stuart flashed the retriever a wink. Avery winked back. Derek didn't see it, but Jen did, and threw her arms upward.

"I am *so* lost right now."

Releasing Stuart, Derek smiled at her. "Then let's try and recenter you. Where are those papers?"

She gaped at him. Behind him, Stuart winked again. Off to the side of the table and also behind Derek, Avery also winked again. Instinctively tempted to wink back, Jen managed to forgo the response and instead start removing the oversized clip from the sheaf of real estate forms.

Her hands were shaking so much it took her two tries.

Later, when everything had been properly signed and co-signed and stamped, Derek accompanied her outside to help her install her broker's sign in the front yard. It gleamed proudly in the Southern California sun, her name nearly as prominent a part of the declaration as TOWNSEND REALTY. Had her mother been present she might have broken out into a little jig. Jen was glad she was not there.

Tools dangling from one hand, she gazed up at Derek. There were several things she wanted to say. Instead, she opted to go wholly Business Mode. In doing so she knew she was either being very professional or very stupid.

"Thanks for lunch. I enjoyed it even if it wasn't to Stuart's taste. He can be like that with food sometimes."

"That's okay," her host replied. "Not everybody's big on salads, not even in SoCal. I guess he's just more the carnivorous type."

"You have no idea. Let's set the broker caravan to show the house for next weekend and then we can start marketing on Monday." She smiled. "It's a fine property and I'm sure it will sell quickly. Especially since your asking price is so reasonable."

He shrugged. "Professional ballplayers move around a lot. For many of us a house is not a home until we're in our forties, sometimes later. Just the way it is." He saw that she was peering past him. "You looking for something, Jen?"

"Yes." She raised her voice. "Stuart!"

A head appeared from around a corner of the house. Perfectly coiffured earlier in the day, it was now thoroughly messed and full of grass, as was its matching beard. The second head that appeared belonged to Derek's retriever, Avery. Both trotted over to rejoin their humans.

"Are we leaving?" Stuart made no attempt to hide his disappointment. Reaching up, he alternately brushed and scratched at the verdure that had become entwined with his hair and beard.

"Yep." She looked at Derek. "All forms executed and ready to be filed."

"But why?" Stuart wondered.

Please, she thought. *Don't start whining.*

"Really glad you came along, Stuart." Derek stuck out a hand. Having seen humans perform the ritual hundreds of times, there was no lag in Stuart's response as he took the proffered hand and shook it.

"See you, Jen." Derek turned toward Avery. "Hey buddy, wanna go throw the long ball at the park today?"

The retriever started to spin in frantic, happy circles. Stuart managed half a spin before Jen's hand clamped down on his arm and brought him to a dead stop.

"Let's go!" Man and dog ran back toward the house. Knowing better, Stuart made no attempt to follow. Or maybe it was because Jen still had an iron grip on his wrist.

Together they walked back to her car. Or rather, she led him. Once Derek and Avery had disappeared back into the house and she and Stuart were back in the car, she felt she could let go of him. He did not try to open the door or worse, bolt out the window.

Sitting there with a purse full of signed papers at her side and her name on the For Sale sign outside the big house, she knew she ought to be happy. That she was *not* had to do with real emotions and not real estate. The car was ready to go; she wasn't. Instead, she lingered, staring straight ahead. Stuart rested in the passenger seat, silent and patient until he could stand it no longer.

"What's wrong, Jen?"

She looked down at her lap. "I still haven't been able to reach Arthur. I listened to his stupid recording over and over and I left a lot of messages. Maybe he just doesn't wanna talk to me?"

"Doesn't want to talk to you?" Stuart was genuinely surprised. "Everybody wants to talk to you!"

She turned to him. Both her tone and expression were full of melancholy. She was not going to cry, though a part of her wanted to.

"*You're* the one that everyone wants to talk to, Stuart." A touch of irony colored her voice. "Everyone and their dog. Not me."

It was quiet in the car again. Jen sat enveloped in gloom while Stuart, as usual, empathized and tried to think of a way to make her feel better. That was, after all, his job.

"Stick your head out the window."

She came back from wherever it was she had been moping to look over at him. "Huh? Say what?"

"Do it. When we get moving." His ears twitched and it looked almost normal. "It's great!"

She shook her head. "Uh uh. I haven't got time for silliness, Stuart."

"Everyone has time for silliness. They'd better. If you don't have time once in a while for a little silliness, then you don't have time for anything worthwhile at all." Cocking his head to one side he flashed her the best sad puppy eyes he could muster. "Please?"

The elderly woman fetching her bills from her mailbox found the peace and quiet of her neighborhood suddenly interrupted as a small but rapidly accelerating car came hurtling down the street toward her. She stood watching, mail in hand, as it shot past. Their heads out their respective windows, the occupants of the car were screaming at the tops of their lungs. Both were human if one slightly less so. As the car careened past, Jen turned her face toward the paralyzed mail recipient and howled. She did as good a job of it as her hirsute male passenger.

Head still out the window, she looked back inside at Stuart. "You're crazy!"

His response was instructive. "Ahhooooo…!"

He broke off, transitioning from animated to somber in the space of a second. "Stop the car, stop the car!"

Alarmed, she hit the brakes and pulled over to one side of the street. "What? What's the matter?"

He still had his head out the window as he replied. "I hear a dog crying."

Pulling herself back in, she searched the street ahead, then the sidewalks. "What dog?"

Stuart strained to hear better. "It sounds like a Labrador in pain." Pushing the passenger side door open, he hopped out. Jen gaped at him in wonder.

"You can even tell the *breed*?"

Instead of replying he tilted back his head and sniffed the air, then pointed. "That house there." He started off in its direction.

"Hey!" She scrambled to catch up to him. "It doesn't matter what you heard, or what you think you heard. You can't just go walking up to somebody's home and…." She broke off as she caught a glimpse of their destination.

"I know who this is," he said, confirming what she had already realized. Loud barking echoed from within.

"I know this house, too," she admitted. "It's…."

The door opened abruptly, to reveal a pleasant middle-aged woman of Jen's occasional acquaintance. She and Sarah Axelrod were not the closest of friends. Different ages and frequently different interests, but they got along well enough.

"Jenny! What a surprise. What brings you here today?"

A golden-hued streak, all rippling fur and long tongue, shot past her to spring directly into Stuart's chest. Both of them went down, the lab on top of Jen's companion. Neither seemed to mind. As if to confirm it, as soon as they separated Stuart jumped on the Labrador.

His owner was less pleased. "Oh, Mozart! Get off him. That's not nice boy etiquette."

The two concerned humans heard only barking. The two dogs heard each other.

"I heard about it but I didn't believe it." As they wrestled, the lab was looking his friend up and down. "How did you do it?"

"Calm down, Mozzy. I don't know. Jen doesn't know. So— nobody knows. I heard you crying. Are you okay? I made Jen stop so I could find out."

Leaning in, the lab licked his friend's right ear. "Stuart, you gotta get me outta here. It's these singing lessons. This kid is killing my ears!"

They separated. As he stood, Stuart brushed himself off. Even as a dog he knew that humans did not like their companions tracking grass and dirt into their homes.

"I'll see what I can do."

Entering the house, they encountered a red-haired boy torturing a piano while trying to accompany it with a song. Vocally, his as-yet immature tone fell somewhere between the sound of Jen's garbage disposal when it encountered a stubborn deposit and the explosive reaction of a prowling cat Stuart had once surprised from behind the previous Halloween, when Jen had dressed him in a cute doggie devil costume. The kid was so off-key his wails were out in the yard somewhere. The pre-adolescent din made him flinch. He could only imagine what hours of it must be doing to poor Mozart. Heedless of offending their hostess, he put his fingers in his ears. It was a small temporary advantage the lab did not have.

Without commenting on the qualitative positioning of Stuart's fingers, Sarah spoke to Jen. "Is this your friend I saw on the news today?" She regarded Stuart uncertainly. He certainly didn't look special, but still…. "Can he really talk to dogs?"

"Yes, Sarah, he can. As much as anyone with his, uh, unique background can." Looking to her left, she made introductions. "Meet Stuart." *You've met him before, she thought, but elaboration would only result in disbelief.*

He was forced to remove his fingers from his ears in order to hear what the two women were saying.

"I'm sorry, Stuart, for Mozart jumping all over you like that. He's usually much more restrained with visitors."

"I know. It's okay. We're friends." He looked down at the suffering Labrador. Mozart currently was lying on the floor, moaning. "Can you stop the kid?"

She blinked, unsure she had heard correctly. "What was that?"

Looking up from the tormented lab, Stuart met her gaze directly. "Stop the kid. Mozart needs a break. The, um, 'music', is killing his ears."

"Ah. Well, not all dogs like classical. A break? Yes, that's a great idea. It's about time for one anyway." She turned toward the downscaled demon seated at the piano. "Elliot, sweetheart, would you like to take a few minutes? That's a good boy."

Sliding off the bench, the boy turned to find Stuart staring at him. It was all the subject of the youthful gaze could do not to growl.

"I saw you at The Barkery today. Everyone said you were amazing."

"Amazing? Really?" Sarah did everything but applaud. "That's fantastic!"

Pushing out his lower lip, his gaze still fixed on Stuart, the red-head responded without looking at her. "I thought you sucked. Not impressed."

Any notion of applause vanished from the piano teacher's horrified thoughts. "Elliot!"

The boy's tone turned mocking. "Oh, Choo Choo and Mitzi, poor babies. Does daddy have a stroller for the little baby?"

This time Stuart did growl. But very, very softly and mostly under his breath, so that not even Jen heard it. "I remember you! The ice cream kid."

"Yeah, I *had* ice cream." Elliot did everything short of physically challenging the much bigger adult. "And you ate it."

Stuart took a step toward him, remembered his new size, and managed to restrain himself. Though his intent was only to deliver a warning nip he doubted Jen or Sarah would understand, far less be sympathetic.

"I did," he shot back. "It was great. Got anymore?"

The boy sat back on the piano bench and crossed his arms, deliberately disrespecting both Stuart and the instrument. "Not for you."

Having trouble following the exchange, a bewildered Jen decided to ask for clarification. "What are you guys fighting about?"

Looking up at her, Elliot pointed an accusatory finger at Stuart. "He ate my ice cream."

This explanation struck her as unaccountably funny. She started to giggle. She could not recall the last time she had broken out in uncontrollable giggles and made a valiant effort to suppress them; an effort that was only partly successful.

"Mmph—did you, Stuart?" Her voice turned little-girlish even as she intended to chide him. "Did you eat this little boy's ice cream?"

The image that formed in her mind could not be suppressed. One instant she envisioned Stuart Louis in terrier form gobbling down a kid's ice cream. That in itself threatened to see her burst out in unrestrained hilarity. The next, in her mind's eye she saw full-blown human Stuart acting in exactly the same fashion. At that point she lost it completely and half collapsed in laughter. Stuart joining in made it all the harder to calm the situation down. Meanwhile Elliot remained seated, arms still crossed, fuming silently as only a spoiled child his age could do.

Baffled, and feeling certain that she must be missing something significant including the joke, Sarah tried to de-escalate the confrontation.

"Why don't you play something for us, Jen? I haven't heard you play in a while."

"Not her!" Unfolding his arms, Elliot jabbed a finger at Stuart. "I wanna hear the ice cream thief play piano. Can you?" he said challengingly. "*I* can. I bet you can't."

"I can play better than you," Stuart shot back.

Even as Jen struggled to stop laughing, a part of her knew it was a losing battle. She barely managed to croak out a comment.

"Stuart is—*mmff*—Stuart is classically trained. He can play Rachmaninoff. He can play George Crumb's *Mundis Canis*. Sliding off the bench, Elliot made way. "Go on then. There's the piano."

"Go on—Stuart." Though she kept a hand over her mouth it wasn't enough to muffle her nonstop chortling. "Show them."

There was a twinkle in his eye as he adjusted the piano bench. Carefully, he positioned his knees on it, cracked his knuckles to warm up, fluttered his fingers as he prepared. Jen's hand slipped up, from covering her mouth to cover her eyes. She was doing her best to stifle her laughter. If anything, she was having less luck than before.

Stuart cleared his throat. Save for Jen's half suppressed laughing it was dead silent in the room. With great care, Stuart raised his hands—and brought them down.

The piano shook under the impact, and not melodically.

Kneeling on the bench, Stuart pounded the keys wildly as he threw back his head and bayed at the ceiling. He was immediately joined in his recital by the deeper if more frantic cries of Mozart, who alternated howling with equally deafening percussive barks. Sarah's jaw fell nearly to the neat pile carpet. Elliot, devoid of an immediate response, did not know whether to taunt, scream, or start howling himself.

No such indecision afflicted Jen. Her laughter, barely contained for the preceding minutes, now spilled out afresh. It complimented the piano pounding, howling, and barking nicely. She let the acoustic chaos rattle and bang for another minute before wrapping her arms around Stuart and pulling him off the bench and away from the piano. He was panting with excitement.

"That was great, Stuart! Not only Crumb would've been proud, but Springsteen too!"

"You think so?" "I know." She smiled affectionately at him. As they looked at each other, Mozart—high on the energy that had briefly filled the room—continued to bark and spin. Moving to him, Sarah did her best to quiet her dog.

"Can't we all calm down? Stuart, that was—I don't know that piece."

Elliot was shaking his head energetically. "That was not Rachmaninoff. That was stupid! So was the crummy!"

Stuart ignored him. He pretty much shut out the world whenever Jen had her arms around him. At such moments, shape and form seemed utterly unimportant.

"Play one of *your* songs for me," he asked quietly. "Please?"

There was desperation in Sarah's voice as she fought to control her pet, who continued to struggle against her. *Couldn't she share in his joy?* The Lab sighed. <u>Humans</u>—especially the females. Simply no inclination to break out in uncontrolled howls.

"Yes, Jen," Sarah implored. "Play us something."

She couldn't turn down two requests. After a moment's pause, she sat down nearby and began to sing.

Stuart, you're the one who brightens up my day.
Stuart, you're the wind that blows dark clouds away.
Only you, can make my heart beat like a drum.
For only you, I sing this song
To only you, my heart belongs.

For the first time since his transformation, Stuart found himself trembling. He had yelled, run, questioned, snapped, growled, stolen ice cream, watered trees, tongue-lolled and eye locked—but this was the first time he had shed a tear. It was a remarkable sensation. Sitting down beside Jen, he leaned up against her and joined in. No barking this time. No howling. Having accompanied her while she sang this song before, he knew the words very well. But now, for the first time, they came out properly.

"Each night, I thank the moon and stars above,
For your loyalty and love."

He went silent, letting Jen finish alone.

"Stuart Louis, you're the one."

A delighted Sarah broke out in applause. Nearby, Elliot let out a grunt and turned away. All this lovey-dovey stuff was making him sick and he wished he had some ice cream.

Inclining her head toward Stuart, Jen met his gaze. It was one she recognized immediately. So intimate was the connection that she was not troubled by the fact that the eyes meeting hers were human.

"If I had to stay two-legged for the rest of my life," he murmured, "just so I can tell you how much I love you, it would be worth it."

Elliot couldn't stand it any longer. Rising from the piano bench, he walked over to tap Stuart on the shoulder. "I hate to ruin this Kumbaya moment, but I'm paying for this lesson time with my own allowance. Do you mind?"

Sarah escorted her guests to the front door. As they reached it, Stuart looked back to where an impatient Elliot stood waiting for them to be gone. Ordinarily, following a visit to one of her friends he would just let Jen lead him outside. But as long as he was stuck being a people, he figured he might as well take advantage of it.

"Kid," he called back to Elliot, "you don't have enough money."

For once, he reflected as he trailed Jen out the door, something sounded better in human than in dog.

He waited until Sarah and Jen had said their goodbyes. Moving to follow, he paused long enough to whisper to their somewhat frazzled host.

"Sarah, your student is hurting Mozart's ears." He nodded back the way they had come. "Not just this kid. All of them."

She eyed him uncertainly. "Is that so?"

He nodded vigorously. "Mozzy is not capable of telling you in words what bothers him. All dogs have sensitive hearing. It depends on what's being played and how loud. Mozzy *likes* Mozart, but not when it's being banged out off-key." He smiled. "Look for signs. He'll let you know."

She considered the stranger's strange words. "I guess maybe you're right. How did I not see that? I supposed it's because I hear bad music so often that I automatically tune it out." She winced slightly. "To tell you the truth, some of it kills my ears, too. I can't imagine what it does to his. And he doesn't have these."

She removed the ear plugs she had been wearing. At her feet, Mozart wagged his tail and gazed up at her. Then he snorted on her shoes.

Canine punctuation.

CHAPTER TEN

Jen heard her phone going insane inside the house even before she unlocked the front door and they entered. It rang and wouldn't stop ringing. Which made no sense. Why would her land line home phone be ringing off the hook when the one that was always in her purse stay silent? Pulling it out, she checked the screen and got her answer. Dead battery. She moved quickly to grab the phone in the front living area from its charger.

"Stuart," she told him, "if you're hungry there's some cold pizza in the fridge." *Messages*, she told herself. Start with the voice messages first. As she worked the phone, Stuart headed for the kitchen.

Opening the refrigerator was easier with hands. So was digging around inside. Ignoring the container that held the third of a pizza that would have been perfectly at home in the ruins of Pompeii, he began sorting through packets of lunch meat. Packages were also easier to search with hands, he mused, though not necessarily easier to open.

The first recording on the phone belonged, unsurprisingly, to her mother. "Jen, we got thirty-seven calls for you today. I just got into the office. Where are you? Why haven't you been answering your phone? Call me."

A beep was followed by the next message. "Hi," a voice began with professional chirpiness, "I'm Maria Sanchez with CBS 2. We were at…."

If only out of latent masochism Jen would have listened to it all, except that the playback was automatically paused for an incoming call. The phone identified it as originating from ….

ARTHUR DALY

For an instant she froze. Regaining her composure, she accepted the call and before anyone on the other end could say word one, she snapped into the phone.

"Arthur! Where the hell are you? Why don't you answer? I've been calling you all day! I tried different times, I left messages, I…."

"Take it easy. I was out on a boat with no reception. I just got signal and have twenty calls from you and from my mother. She says you were on TV with some baseball player? What the hell is up with *that*?"

Entering the room, Stuart paused politely, a package of lunch meat in hand. He held it out to Jen who, being neither hungry nor curious, ignored both it and him. At the moment she was too busy dealing with an entirely different kind of bologna.

"What are you talking about?" It took her a moment to realize where he was coming from. "Oh, for goodness sake, Arthur! I listed his house. It's nothing but business." Honestly, she thought to herself, sometimes the man was impossible. He had nothing to worry about.

He certainly didn't, because at that very same moment, Arthur Daly was standing on the bridge of a fairly sizable yacht flanked by an assistant and two very attractive younger women as it motored into a San Francisco Bay marina,

None of which kept him from speaking accusingly into his own phone. "Oh yeah? And what about that dog whisperer? Mother says he never left your side."

"Who? Cesar Milan?"

"Yeah, that's him," Arthur replied sarcastically.

Becoming impatient now, Stuart inserted the lunch meat package more forcefully into Jen's field of vision. Irritated, she nudged him aside as she kept her grip on the phone.

"It's Arthur," she whispered to him. "Be quiet." Louder and to the phone she said, "Look, Arthur: we have to talk."

Stuart would not be denied. Moving in close once more, he pointed insistently to the expiration date stamped on the package. "Jen, can I still eat this? The date is bad. Is it too old? I don't want to get sick. You know what happens when I get sick. I can't help it where I get sick." He pouted. "You don't like me when I get sick. Especially when I get sick on the bed, or in your shoes." He held the package up higher and raised his voice to make certain she was hearing him. "Maybe you should just dump this old ham."

When she didn't respond he tossed it to one side and, frustrated, headed back to the kitchen. Turning away from him, she covered her phone with her free hand. On the other end Arthur was confused and fuming.

"Who was that? Who's calling me an old ham?"

"Relax." Jen rolled her eyes. "It's just an old friend from college."

"That's great, Jen," came the taut reply. "I'm gone one day and —wait. You don't have any friends."

Claim, accusation, or joke, his comment was absurd no matter how you took it. She decided to play it diplomatically. "Well, I have *one*, anyway. And he loves my locket with your picture in it. He wants to get one for his mother. Where'd you say you got it?"

In the kitchen a hungry Stuart was pawing through the fridge in search of something, anything, edible. Something packed in foil caught his attention. Picking it up and unrolling it he discovered a turkey leg spotted with fungi. Mold, not mushrooms. He wrinkled his nose at it and raised his voice, shouting toward the living room.

"Jen, why do you hang onto this old turkey?"

"I heard that!" The reply crackled over the phone Jen was holding. "'Old turkey'? I don't care if this guy *is* your friend, nobody calls me a turkey, old or otherwise!" Behind him on the yacht, the assistant had turned tactfully so he could not see her face and was gazing at a brace of seagulls. The two girls broke out in giggles.

"Arthur, we're breaking up."

"What?" He tried to make sense of her increasingly garbled words. "Did you say we're breaking up?"

Most of what he spewed into the phone dissolved into static and the rest was incomprehensible nonsense. After a couple of moments of electronic uncertainty, the connection went completely dead. Jen frowned at the phone.

"That sucks. We almost had him."

On the boat, Arthur turned to the young pair behind him.

"What are you two laughing at?"

Turning, they headed toward the stern.

"What an old ham," one murmured.

"Definitely a turkey," agreed her companion.

Arthur didn't have to hear what they said. Their attitude told him all he needed to know. Unlike the girls his assistant was unable to flee, much less giggle. Though she very badly wanted to do so.

"Sandy, get me on the next flight to L.A. Allow enough time for me to get back to the hotel, get my stuff together, and get to the airport with some time, but cut it close."

"Yes sir." Out came the assistant's iPad, on went her fingers.

Meanwhile Arthur leaned on the nearby railing and addressed the ocean, which could not have cared less. While seagulls cawed and wavelets slapped against the side of the boat, he muttered darkly to himself.

"No one breaks up with Arthur Daly."

Back in Newport, Jen had no sooner put the phone down than it warbled for attention again. Picking it up, she all but yelled into it.

"Arthur! Your phone sucks!"

The voice that replied was calm, controlled, almost subdued. "Jen? This is Jim?"

She slumped. *Was she doomed to forever embarrass herself with this man?* "Jim? Thank god it's you. Arthur's phone sucks. It keeps dropping out. He claims it's because he's on a boat but I don't know that I buy that. You'd think with all his money he could afford a decent carrier, right?"

Jim replied, a little less subdued this time. "I don't know this Arthur."

"Oh, land developer guy, longtime associate. We've had some dealings with each other. Anyways. How are ya? You're calling about the guitar, right? I can write you a check or if you want cash, I can maybe get to the bank this afternoon and we can meet…."

He interrupted her. "I'm not concerned about that right now, Jen. I already got a new one."

It threw her a little bit. Jim had not struck her as someone with access to ready cash, and a replacement instrument of the same quality as the one she had wrecked would not come cheap.

"A new one? Already?"

"Don't worry about it. Right now I'm more concerned about the park. There's gonna be a Town Hall meeting at the hair salon across from the parking lot. You should come. Your input would be valuable."

"That's news to me. Of course I'll be there. What day and time?"

"In fifteen minutes."

She choked. "Fifteen minutes? You mean like, in fifteen minutes today?"

"That's right." He proceed to pass on as many pertinent details as he had been able to gather. She listened intently.

Seated at the kitchen table, Stuart had discovered that in addition to acquiring many other human traits he was now able to operate her computer. This did not shock him. Not given how many hours he had spent sitting patiently at her side watching her engage with work and play on the same machine. Having fingers, he reflected, made all the difference.

At the moment he was on the order page of Petco.com., talking to himself as his human digits worked the keys.

"A box of bully sticks." Using the mouse, he moved on to another image. "Oh yeah, those fish skins are delicious, let's have a box of those, too." He did not pause to consider anything other than his appetite. "Let's do four boxes of bison jerky: that will last a day or two, and also…."

"STUART!"

He closed the laptop and hurried to the front room. Jen was hunting down her purse. "Stuart, Jim just called. Something important, real important, has come up. We gotta go now!"

Immediately he set aside all thoughts of the laptop, the prospective food order, and everything else. When Jen said they had to do something, that took primacy over anything and everything else. Even when he didn't have a clue what she was on about.

"Where are we going?"

"To the salon. The one by the park." She headed for the front door.

"The park!" His delight was unrestrained.

She held the door open for him. "It's not what you think. This isn't a trip *to* the park. This is a trip *about* the park."

He puzzled over that as she shut the door behind them.

🐾   🐾   🐾

The parking area was crowded, more so than usual, but providentially someone pulled out right in front of the salon and she was able to grab the space. Shutting off the car she turned to her passenger. His hair was mussed more than normal because he had hung his head out the window for the entire duration of the drive from her house. She stared at him hard, her tone serious.

"Okay, Stuart. I need you to stay *right here*." She cracked the door. "I'll go inside for a minute and scope it out. There may be some not so nice people here who think I'm part of the problem. Townsend people." Her expression twisted. "Hard as it is to imagine, they may have some supporters. I'll come get you soon. Just stay in the car."

He looked doubtful. "But everyone knows you shouldn't leave a dog in a car."

From the look she gave him he realized that rationale wasn't going to fly. Worth a try, though, he thought.

"I will stay right here," he said stiffly. "I will not go anywhere."

"Good boy." Leaning over, she kissed him on the head. Then she lowered the windows, made sure she took her purse, and exited, heading for the salon.

As soon as she was inside, he started hunting. The glove box volunteered only gum and a stray Quest bar. He could have consumed the latter, especially since he knew it was unlikely to adversely affect his human form, but it had chocolate chips in it. He had been trained from puppyhood that chocolate was dangerous to dogs and even though he was now human he was unable to overcome his conditioning (except, he remembered, when ice cream was involved). Exploring beneath his seat and the driver's produced some loose change, a pair of old sunglasses, a flash drive whose contents were a mystery to him, and a lot of beach sand, but nothing remotely edible. His foraging having failed, he slumped back in his seat.

"I should've brought a bone to work on," he muttered to himself. They had left the house in such a hurry that the notion of taking food along had not occurred to him.

The salon was spacious and modern, providing enough room for multiple stations to operate simultaneously. A number of women were having their hair done while another was receiving a manicure. In the back, the space where beauty demos were given had been taken over by the group putting on the town hall. A crowd was clustered around the makeshift stage, which was currently empty. Making her way through the people and the chatter, Jen spotted Wanda and Nina and pushed her way toward them.

"Wanda, is this your deal?"

The other woman shook her head. "Hell no. I just work here. I was prepping my station and the next thing you know all these people are coming in." She looked past Jen. "Here's Cindy. Maybe she knows something."

The new arrival looked at Wanda, then Jen. "You guys set this up?"

"I just asked Wanda the same question." Jen pondered. "So okay, not us. Then who?"

Wanda pointed toward the small stage. "I think we're about to find out."

A woman none of them recognized stepped up onto the platform and took up a stance behind the portable podium. She gave the mic a tap and the resultant thump went out over the crowd. At that moment Jen recognized her. They had met before on a couple of occasions involving business, but it had been a while ago. Different coiffure, different attire, faded memory. Jen still felt she should have remembered the speaker.

"Thank you everyone for coming to this Town Hall meeting. I'm council woman Martha Martinez. As some of you may already know, we are facing the potential loss of our beloved dog park."

It was all true, then, Jen thought. As if any further confirmation was needed. She just hadn't wanted to believe it. That was what often happened in instances such as this. Nobody wanted to believe that the worst was going to happen, until it was too late. It was a good thing, she reflected, that she had left Stuart in the car. He would not have been able to remain silent during the meeting. And she could not have blamed him. It was going to be hard for her to restrain herself. Looking back toward the entrance she was relieved not to see him. Whatever happened in here, at least he was behaving himself in the car.

No food scraps. No bones. No treats, not even TV. Stuart was already bored beyond measure. At least in his four-legged guise he could have hopped easily from front seat to the rear and back again and had some exercise. But enmeshed as he was in his bipedal form he could not even do that. Not as long as he was confined within the car. But he had promised Jen to remain where he was, and a promise in any form was a promise to be kept. No matter what.

Then he saw the cat.

It was sauntering along among the other cars. He slipped instinctively into full watch mode; all senses alert, muscles tense, eyes roving. Dropping down off the roof of a Honda, the feline vanished among tires and bumpers.

When it reappeared, it was on the hood of Jen's car.

Lurching forward, Stuart slammed a hand against the inside of the windshield. The cat reacted quickly but calmly, once more disappearing out of sight. Stuart's gaze flicked from side to side, scanning. Simultaneously he sniffed at the air, but caught nothing on the breeze. Cat was gone.

Cat reappeared; legs spread, flattening itself against the

windshield and peering inside. Its eyes were yellow, wide, challenging. Its expression was contemptuous.

Going ballistic, Stuart leaped out of the car. Or would have save for the fact that he didn't quite fit through the open passenger side window. Remembering what he was now, he fumbled a moment with the handle to open the door. By the time he was able to exit, the cat was long gone. The faint resonance of risible meow hung in the air.

Quietly enraged, he hunted for his tormentor, peering beneath parked vehicles, even searching a nearby trash can. No cat. Only the memory of its disrespect.

Movement caught his eye. It was Marley, using a paw to signal to Stuart from the other side of a Totally Clips front window. As soon as he was sure he had caught Stuart's eye, the Puli vanished. Stuart headed in his direction.

Marley reappeared, as per his paw-waving instructions, at the back door to the salon, which was standing open. He was not alone. Cupcake and Gizmo were there as well. The odd sensation of a tear forming at the corner of one eye brought an elated Stuart up short.

"Hey guys! It's so good to see you."

"Same back atchoo, Stu." Plunking himself down on his butt, Gizmo used a hind leg to scratch behind one ear. "We've missed you at the park."

He smiled. "How's Freddie?"

"Fast and crazy as ever," Cupcake told him. "You were awesome today! The news lady came into The Barkery and wanted to put you on TV, but nobody could find you."

"I was with Jen. Is that good? Being on TV, I mean. Humans seem willing to do anything to get on TV. When humans are willing to do anything for something, it makes me suspicious."

"Then you need to get over it." Marley was as serious as Stuart had ever seen him. "You getting on TV could help save the park."

Switching sides and legs, Gizmo continued scratching. "I

talked with some East Side chihuahuas who are afraid that if the dog park here closes, fancy little uptown dogs might move in on their turf. Of course, me and the guys would have them for breakfast. First Lhasa Apso that tried something like that would be upside-down in a minute. But we can't challenge their owners."

Cupcake took a step forward. "Stuart, you are the only one who can save the park. The humans will argue and debate and bark about 'quality of life' and throw stupid numbers around like they always do, but you're the only one who can speak for *us*."

"Yeah, bro," Marley put in. "Cupcake's all right on this one, know what I'm sayin'?"

"You're the only one who can talk human to them," Gizmo added. "It would make more sense in Dog, but no matter how well or loudly we took our stance, all we'd get in return is 'Shut up, you!'." He looked disgusted. "As if 'you' was a proper name."

Inside the salon, the councilwoman was concluding her talk. She had been energetic and earnest—but she had not sounded very hopeful.

"So I would like to thank you all as we gather to try and save our park. We have much to try to do and, sadly, not much time in which to do it. For reasons I could go into. Instead, let me introduce you to someone else who has made it his business to step forward and offer his support in this matter." Applause filled the confined space as a man from the audience advanced to the podium. The councilwoman made room for him.

"Let me introduce you to Jim. He is very involved in the effort to save the park. In fact, it was he who made this meeting possible and on such short notice."

In response to this, someone shouted from the crowd.

"Too short? You're telling me! I found out five minutes ago!" Cries of support and agreement rang out from the assembled. They settled down when it became apparent that the man standing next to Martinez was ready to speak.

"Hi, everyone." He glanced to his left. "Thanks, Martha." For a moment he was silent, surveying the crowd and waiting for the last of the attendees" understandable anxiety to die down. "Many of you don't know me and may think I'm relatively new to the park. Well, I grew up in Newport and played at the park with Gatsby, my first Boston Terrier, back when I was a kid. I've been living elsewhere for a while, but now that I've moved back, Sweetie Peters and I are there daily. She takes me to the park (a few of the listeners chuckled in agreement) because I can do my job there and be around what I love most: dogs.

"It's not just a 'dog park'. Everyone here knows that. It's *our* park. I would've brought Sweetie with me to give you her opinion but right now she's at home, resting. This whole ordeal has made her a bit nervous. Isn't it interesting how our pets somehow know what's going on? When we're happy or sad, when we're relaxed or on edge? We have hundreds of locations in Southern California especially designated as places for *us* to rest and relax. Dogs have only a few. Somehow, we have to get that across to those who would remove one more locale from that already short list. Somehow." He paused to let his words linger.

"So I prepared some petitions for us to sign," he continued, "asking that the removal of the park at least be delayed until appropriate land and usage studies can be completed. Because those are lacking from the relevant rezoning request. I know; I checked. I hope you will sign them tonight even though I'm afraid we may not beat the clock in time and Townsend/Daly will come level the park before we can mount a proper legal fight. If we can present cease and desist petitions with enough signatures quickly enough—well, all we can do is try."

While she was surveying the crowd, one face caught Nina's attention. She nudged Jen in the ribs and gestured. "Here comes your friend."

Coming from the back of the salon, Stuart had no trouble finding his way. Nor was he alone. Three dogs trailed in his wake. Though leashless they advanced with dignity, heads high, tails under control. Not a single inappropriate bark was heard.

"Oh no," Jen murmured. "I told him to stay in the…."

"Wherever you told him to wait," Cindy said, "it looks like he has something important on his mind. And I think he's going to say it."

CHAPTER ELEVEN

I t was far too late to do anything, Jen saw. At least not without causing a ruckus. Stuart was already on stage and Jim was ceding the floor. If she had spotted him earlier….

She shut her eyes. There was no telling what he might say and if it proved to be outrageous, no certainty that she would be able to explain it away. She could only stand with her friends and hope.

Looking out over the audience, Stuart beamed. "Hello all dog owners and non-dog owners." Frowning at his choice of words, he looked uncertainly at Jim. "Non-dog owners okay?" When Jim gave him a smile and a thumbs-up, he relaxed and continued.

"I am here to tell you Jim is right. Like many of you here, he loves the park. I don't think that love is dependent on whether you have a dog or not. The park is a special place, a unique place, and if it goes away there won't be a replacement. All of us will be parkless." Everyone in the audience was listening intently. They knew who he was. Or thought they did.

"Parkless, and dogless. If you don't have a dog we can get you one. There are plenty of furry hearts looking for a home. That's what this is all about: heart."

The crowd applauded. To Stuart it seemed genuine, and he believed he knew enough about humans to tell when they were being honest or when they were lying.

"Then, because you love your new best friend so much, you will want to take them to the park. Right? Because your heart and their heart will both be in the same place."

From back of the crowd and nearer to the front of the salon, a woman having her hair done had been trying to listen but was having trouble making out Stuart's words.

"Where is all this going? What are you saying? That we need to own a dog?"

"Mrs. Wildhorn," Stuart called back, "take your hair dryer off. I'm explaining why we all need to sign Jim's petition or there is going to be no more dog park."

This time she heard his every word clearly. If there was one thing Stuart had always possessed, it was a strong set of lungs. Nor was he finished.

"Your dogs deserve to have a park. *You* deserve to have a dog park. They need a good, safe, clean place to pee and chase squirrels. So do you." Everyone laughed at this—but it was good natured laughter. The crowd was with him. He could sense it.

"The dog park has been a part of Newport for a long time. It's what we love, and it's what we need. Not another shopping center. We already have plenty of shopping centers." Looking back, he addressed the three dogs seated politely behind him. "How was that?"

All three nodded in unison. Fully engaged in its own passionate debate, it was doubtful if anyone in the crowd noticed. Satisfied with his friends' approval, he turned back to the assembly.

"Anyone here besides me care about this? Enough to do something about it? Sign the petition!"

Pushing back the hair dryer beneath which she had been sitting, the woman next to Mrs. Wildhorn rose to speak. She had foil in her hair and interrupting the work of the dryer would not be good for the final results, but her enthusiasm got the better of her.

"My Fifi here really loves the park. I care!" Seated on a cushion in a chair beside the dryer, the eponymous poodle let out a series of high-pitched barks that reached Stuart and the trio sitting behind him.

"Pensez-vous que je devrais aller avec des ongles rouges ou roses?"

Utterly baffled, the three looked to Stuart for support. If anything, he was more confused than his friends.

"I have no idea what she just said." Turning back to the audience he inquired loudly, "Jen?"

"Uh-oh," Wanda murmured to the subject of the query. "You know they gonna be on you in three, two, one…."

Following Stuart's gaze, the befoiled lady picked out Jen in the audience. "Isn't that Jen Jensen, the Pet Friendly Realtor? She must have a vested interest in the dog park. She should be able to do something, right?"

"Told ya." Turning away, Wanda lowered her gaze.

"Aren't you with Townsend Realty?" The woman was suddenly uncertain.

"She is," Stuart exclaimed even as Jen was making frantic shushing gestures in his direction. "And real good at it!"

Continuing inexorably, the foil lady might as well have suddenly turned into a minion of Satan himself. "And isn't your fiancé with Daly Enterprises? Arthur Daly?"

Jaunty as ever, Stuart responded. "No, he didn't propose."

Out in the crowd, Jen covered her face with her hands. She was too numb now even to try and silence Stuart. Sensing she was on a roll, though of what kind she was not certain, the speaker addressed her directly.

"I heard around that you're like dating him for eleven years, and you knew nothing about this plan to take out the park and

put a shopping mall on the site? That's kind of hard to believe."
Muttering in the crowd showed that her accusation was not a
solitary one.

Jen straightened and raised her voice as she addressed the
crowd. "First of all, the 'pet friendly' thing: that was my mother's
idea. Something to set me apart from other realtors, she said.
Me? I never liked it. Secondly, Townsend is just a place I work
and I have no control there. I'm not an executive or anything
and as such I'm not privy to company decisions. I just list and
sell houses. I'm not involved with the commercial property end
of the business at all. So not only do I have no say in such
matters, I don't know what's going on with them, either. And
lastly," she concluded, her words biting, "it was seven years, not
eleven."

Someone in the crowd blurted out, "Another woman?"

"No!" The subject of the town hall meeting seemed to have
strayed very far from its rationale. "Why don't you all just get
your hair done and shut up!"

The murmurings continued, but restrained now. In the back,
a bald gentleman looked quite forlorn.

Cindy rose from her seat. "Everyone, listen up. How many of
you saw The Barkery today on channel 2?"

Cindy's interjection was sufficiently off-base to induce Nina
to rise and push her friend aside. There was a purpose to
everyone being in the salon and it wasn't to promote Cindy's
business: something she would put in Cindy's face, but at a later
time.

"Ay ya sientate!" Nina turned to the assembly. "Remember
what we're all here for. Stuart is right. Our dogs will be pissed if
Jen's boyfriend who is not her fiancé builds a shopping center
over our park! It has to be stopped!"

Vaguely aware that she might have overstepped the bounds of
propriety even for Southern California, the lady with the foil in
her hair struggled to offer support.

"Well, if anyone can talk to their boyfriend who is not yet her fiancé after seven years it's Jen Jensen!"

"Yes!" yelled someone in the crowd, "Jen Jensen, the pet friendly realtor!"

"You can do it, Jen!" someone else shouted.

"Do it for all of us," another exclaimed. "For us, and for our dogs!"

"She can't," a man near the center declared, "because I bet she's still in tight with Arthur Daly—even if he hasn't proposed."

As the crowd fell to arguing among themselves, Jen could contain herself no longer. This wasn't how things were supposed to go. Instead of an orderly group of people prepared to organize, the crowd had become a mob whose primary interest now seemed to be focused on her private life. Pushing her way to the front, she stepped up on the stage to pull Stuart aside.

"I told you to wait in the car," she hissed. "Why can't you behave?"

He shrank away from her. If he'd had a tail, it would have been tucked between his legs.

"But Jen," he pleaded, "I had to do something to help save the park, right?" He gestured weakly toward the chattering, arguing audience. "They wanted me to say something."

"*About the park.*" She was beyond exasperated. With the chaos in The Barkery, with Arthur, with her life, and now with Stuart. "Not about *me*. Not about my work, and certainly not about my relationship with Arthur. That's private stuff. You don't just go spouting to a bunch of strangers about someone's personal relationships. Maybe *dogs* do it, but humans don't. You're just making things worse." She nodded toward the crowd.

"Now people are mad at me. Or suspicious, or amused, or—I don't know what. But none of it is good. So please just stop." She hesitated for an instant. "Or go away."

"Away? But Jen, I…."

"You're not obeying me, Stuart. That part of you has changed.

You're not like a dog anymore. You're becoming like...." She halted.

He tried to meet her gaze. "Becoming like? Like what?"

She raised her eyes to his. "You know what I'm thinking."

"No." He was open and innocent. As ever. "I only know what dogs think. Like what?"

She was a little too angry just then to think clearly. She was *mad* right now; mad at pretty much everything, and the only one she could take it out on was Stuart. His eyes widened as she all but growled at him.

"Oh no! Please don't say it, Jen."

Too late. The image and the word had already formed in her mind.

"A *cat!*"

He stumbled away from her. "*Noooo!*"

Whirling, he stumbled toward his three friends. Still sitting patiently behind him, they observed his agitated demeanor with puzzlement. Cocking his head to one side, Marley regarded his friend uncertainly.

"Did you just get called a *cat?*"

A distraught Stuart glared down at him. "Not funny, Marley. Jen hates me now."

With that, and for the first time using his long human legs to express displeasure, he stepped *over* a startled Marley and headed for the rear of the salon.

Slightly off-kilter as usual, Gizmo looked around in evident surprise. "A mi si me gusto—I think it went great!" By this time a shaken Cupcake had fled to Cindy's arms. Marley regarded the chihuahua sternly.

"It's not that you miss a few things, Gizmo. Somehow you manage to miss *everything.*"

The smaller dog looked around, openly bewildered. "Que? What did I miss? Whaaaat?"

Upset, whimpering, and not a little scared, Stuart stumbled

out the back door of the salon and took off running down the service alley. He had not gotten far when he heard a voice. It was low, slow, and a had a bit of a slink to it, like a lounge singer after a couple of drinks.

"It's just not going your way, is it?"

The words brought Stuart up short. Panting, he looked around, checked behind him, squinted down the length of the alley, but saw nothing. Proving that he had not gone crazy, the voice spoke again.

"So you think you can save the dog park? What a shame."

"Who said that?"

As far as he could tell, he was the only one in the alley. Was this something that affected humans when they were alone? Mysterious voices spoke to them out of thin air? Jen had never mentioned such a thing. But if it were something that only afflicted humans, why should she mention it to a dog? He missed that innocence. He missed being him.

"It's me," the voice declared afresh.

His fruitless searching continued. "I hear you, but I don't see you."

"Of course you don't. You never see me. It's perfectly natural, and yet it's not. It shouldn't be, but it is. It's the unfortunate nature of things. That's Nature for you. Unfortunate."

"I'm not sure I understand what you're saying. Why don't I see you?"

"Let's see now. Hmm." The voice paused to consider. "Maybe because I'm never at the dog park? Or never anywhere where you are?"

For the moment, the unreal conversation allowed him to overlook his distress, to forget why he was in the alley in the first place.

"How come? Everybody goes to the dog park. Everybody loves the dog park." He continued seeking the source of the voice.

"You're half right," the voice informed him. "Everybody loves the park. Some of us are less crazy about the dog part."

A very slight noise, as of something scratching on metal, caused him to turn sharply. Lying atop a nearby trash dumpster was a large, gray, partially striped, discontented—cat.

"A cat?" Stuart blurted redundantly. "You're a cat."

"Ah," the feline murmured, "one is but helpless in the face of a dog's inimitable powers of observation. You're in my backyard now." The cat considered the human figure standing before it. "You don't look so good for a human, and worse for a dog. Looks like you might need a little help."

Stuart took a step toward the dumpster. The cat tensed but held its position. "I should chase you, you know. Nothing personal. It's just how it is."

"Chase away." The cat was unperturbed. As if to further tempt Stuart, it began cleaning its ears, licking one paw and then bringing it down over first the right ear, then the left. "You'd never catch me. You'd have a hard time catching a house cat. Out here in the real world one has to move fast and smart. I'd be gone before you got in gear. Like the squirrels you never catch."

Stuart replied excitedly. "You know Freddy?"

The cat looked up from its grooming, mildly interested. "Squirrel?" Stuart nodded. "Resident of the dog park?" Stuart's head bobbed up and down a second time.

The cat returned to cleaning itself. "Then why would I know it? I just said I never visit the dog park. You have a short memory. For a dog, that can be useful. For a cat—fatal. I don't know your Freddy, but I do know squirrels, and I know you will never catch one. But you try. You try so hard. Right?"

Stuart's initial excitement at the mention of Freddy's name had faded. "I do," he confessed. "Freddy is faster than me."

"Also quicker," observed the feline. "But not faster or quicker than a cat. I can attest to that," he added ominously. "Trying to save the dog park? It's a waste of time. We cats know when we're wasting time. That's why we sleep away most of it and when we are awake, make the most of it. You dogs have not learned that yet."

Stuart's head hurt. Being a dog was so much easier than being a human. So much less to think about. So much less to worry about.

"I'm still having trouble understanding you. What are you trying to say?"

Rising to all fours, the cat stretched and yawned, showing claws and teeth. "I'm saying that you're wasting your time, dog. You can't save the park. You can't catch a squirrel. You can't even be a dog anymore." Walking over to the side of the dumpster, it pointed with one paw to a dirty window. "Look at yourself."

As if hypnotized, Stuart stumbled over the window. There was more than enough light in the alley for him to see his reflection. Heedless of the accumulated grime, he used the palm of one hand to wipe the glass clean. The result was a sharper but not more reassuring likeness.

"Is that what a dog looks like?" From atop the dumpster, the cat's voice was reproving. "Trust me. You're no longer a dog and you don't make a very convincing human. Best if you just run far, far away."

Insulted by Jen. Judged by a cat. Stuart was sure he could not fall any farther. His defeat was total, his depression all-consuming.

"Where—where would I go?"

The cat exhaled, a scornful *pfft*. "Anywhere for you is better than here. A failure is the same no matter where he is. Just go."

Moving slowly, a downcast Stuart resumed his trek down the alley.

"GO!" the cat urged him. Jolted by the feline shout, unsure what to do or where to run, he broke into a sprint.

Settling itself down on its hindquarters, the cat serenely resumed licking its paws while muttering to himself.

"Stupid dog. You can tell them to do anything."

As the crowd filed out of the salon, still jabbering among themselves, Jen and her friends brought up the rear.

"I don't care what anyone thinks." Nina was defiant. "I *like* Stuart."

"Yeah, me too," Wanda confessed. "He's either dumber than we think or smarter than we think."

"Maybe," Nina added, "We're making him out to be something he's not. Maybe we should just let him be—Stuart."

Cindy had been searching through the crowd and had checked the area around the stage. Now she looked over at Jen. "I don't see him anymore. He was up there with our dogs, now he's not. Where'd he go? You should bring him by The Barkery again."

Jen was fed up. Tired, frustrated, and less than happy with the women who were supposed to be her friends.

"Oh yeah? For what, Cindy? A follow-up news story? That'd be great for publicity for the business, right?" Taken aback by the vehemence of Jen's response, Cindy retreated. Leaning in, Wanda whispered to Cindy. "She's pissed. I don't blame her. The meeting didn't go the way it should have." Taking the other woman's arm, Wanda guided her away. "Let's all of us just leave her alone for a while. Let her get her head together."

Nina nodded agreement and together the three of them collected their dogs and departed the salon.

As they joined the remainder of the crowd in exiting, Jim came over. He had been observing quietly. Now that Jen's friends had left he felt a little more comfortable in her presence.

"I feel bad now that I asked you to come to this." She managed a wan smile in response. "I'm really sorry, Jen." He looked past her, toward the stage and the rear of the salon. "Stuart took off?"

She was only half listening to him. Her thoughts were churning and her emotions were all over the place. "I had a gut feeling when I got here, something was going to happen. It just wasn't anything I anticipated." She shook her head. "It was worse.

That woman who spoke about me…." She caught herself, started over. "I asked Stuart to not come inside. No—I *told* him not to come inside. Guess it doesn't matter what I say. Everyone gets crazy around him."

"I'm not sure 'crazy' is the right description," Jim said. "Maybe 'fascinated' is a better word. Or enthralled—I don't know. There's certainly something unique about him. Something special. You can sense it."

"Bologna," Jen remarked. His expression contorted.

"What?

"Bologna." Her voice skated on sarcasm. "That's what you're sensing."

He hesitated and nearly laughed, but the look on her face stopped him. She was not happy.

"Whatever other qualities he might have, no one can deny that he has a gift with animals," he continued. "I was hoping he could give me some advice." Now it was his turn to look downcast. "Sweetie is not eating. I called the vet and they can't see her til Monday.

"I'm sorry to hear that. Poor Sweetie Peters. Good girl. I hope you can solve the problem. Meanwhile, I better go find Stuart so I can apologize for getting mad at him. I just lost it there for a moment. It was that woman, and having my personal stuff broadcast in public, and not in a flattering manner. That coupled with what Stuart said and—well, I usually have better control of myself." Look, again I'm sorry for what happened here. Hope everything works out for you with Arthur." "Look, Arthur is a long story and I hope you don't think I was aware of his…" Jim interrupts, "No need to explain, I understand. I should get going." She gathered her emotions. "About Sweetie: I'll ask him about her for you."

🐾　🐾　🐾

Stuart could do several things well. One of them was run. But even his reserves were not infinite. By the time he reached the dog park he was out of breath. It was one of only two places where he felt completely safe. The other was Home, but that was too far away and besides, Jen might be there, waiting to berate him again. Her words had hurt him like a stick.

Looking for a friend, any friend, he spotted Hector and Ringo. Watching them play only added to the pain he was feeling. It should be him and Jen. Jen throwing the toy and him joyfully fetching it. Not the policeman and his canine partner.

Hector had a good arm, and the stick he threw landed nearby. It was tracked and followed seconds later by the big German Shepherd. Snatching it up in his jaws, Ringo turned to rejoin his fellow officer when he noticed Stuart. Trotting over, he dropped the stick between them.

"Hey, buddy, how y'doin'? You here for that butt sniff now?"

The man towering over him dropped his gaze. "I'm not feeling well, Ringo."

The shepherd was immediately sympathetic. "Something's bothering you, Stuart. I can recognize human expressions and interpret their meanings. Part of the job. What is it? Maybe I can help."

Hector's voice reached them. "Hey Ringo, you okay over there?" Then he recognized Jen's friend from college. The one who had told him about the shepherd's infected tooth. He relaxed. If there was another human he didn't worry about Ringo interacting with, it was the kindly if decidedly peculiar dog whisperer.

"I think I'm wasting my time trying to save the park for the dogs." He met the shepherd's stare. "You have Hector and the whole police training area to play in. Small dogs need a special area or they get into trouble." He hesitated. "Me, for example. I know I'm in trouble. I could let it all go, forget about it. But I know the others are depending on me. Sweetie Peters is depending on me."

"Must be tough." Ringo didn't know what to say, but he could offer emotional support.

"It's almost as hard as trying to catch Freddy."

Ringo turned thoughtful. "Freddy, the squirrel?"

A morose Stuart eyed his friend. "You know another Freddy?"

"Actually, yes. Bloodhound. Works Narcotics. But another squirrel with that name, no. You don't understand, Stuart. You don't 'catch' a squirrel."

Stuart looked puzzled. "No?"

"No. You *trap* a squirrel. If you want to chase him, for fun, that's your business. But you won't catch him." Ringo sat back on his haunches. "You'll never see me run after that varmint."

"Hmm. So you're saying I can trap Freddy and I don't have to be faster?"

"No. You have to be smarter, not faster. I graduated from Police Dog Academy. I know a lot of things, Stuart, and among them is when to engage in a pursuit, when to call for backup, and most relevant to your question, how to set up and execute a trap. 'Don't be dumb and get some'," he recited.

Stuart pondered what the shepherd had said. It took a moment for revelation to arrive. "I get it now. Stupid cat!"

Ringo's head swung from side to side as he scanned the immediate vicinity. "What cat? A cat I can chase."

Crouching, Stuart took the shepherd's right paw and shook it gently. "Ringo, we're even. I officially pass on the butt sniff. You just gave me a great idea. Thanks!" Straightening, he turned and hurried off, out of the park and through traffic, to disappear across the street accompanied by the percussive bleating of several car horns. Ringo watched him go.

"I hope he isn't planning to trap Freddy," he muttered to himself. "That stupid squirrel is a protected park animal. Friend or no friend, I'd have to run him in for that." Shaking his head made his collar slip slightly. He'd have to get Hector to adjust it. Being a cop meant always looking one's best in public.

Hector was whistling to him now. He started back, remembered, and turned. It wouldn't do to forget the stick.

🐾   🐾   🐾

The outer office was busy. But then, as successful as it was, Townsend Realty was always busy. Newly empowered by his conversation with Ringo, Stuart entered and started searching. Glass shelves were filled with awards recognizing sales and other similar accomplishments. Many of them were for Jen's mother, Sylvia. But he hadn't come to gawk at awards for her or anyone else.

Finishing with the person on the other end of a call, the receptionist put down her phone to regard the newcomer. "Can I help you, sir? Do you have an appointment?"

"I'm here to see Sylvia. Jen's mom."

The receptionist offered a pleasant smile. "Lots of people come here to see Sylvia Jensen. Once again, I have to ask you, sir, if you have an appointment."

Stuart struggled to control himself. "I'm an old friend of Jen, her daughter."

"That's nice. How 'old'?"

"College." He tried to think of something else. "I'm living at her house."

That caught the woman by surprise. "Oh. Okay, then. Is this about Jen? Is something wrong?"

"I need to speak to her mother."

The receptionist deliberated, then rose from behind her desk. "Come with me, Mr...?"

"Stuart. Don't worry. Sylvia knows me."

Sylvia did indeed know him; enough to sit in uncharacteristic silence in her office as he unburdened himself of his thoughts and feelings.

"So," she said finally, "what is your deal? First you have the nerve to tell me how I should handle my own daughter. Then you turn the dog café upside down on live local news. And now you want to tell me what?" She leaned back in her executive chair, crossed her arms, and waited. Her expression reminded Stuart of a berserk wolf hybrid he had once seen challenged by a bulldog. One growl from the hybrid had seen the bulldog fleeing to whimper behind its owner's legs.

He was not intimidated. For one thing, Ringo's advice had stiffened his resolve. For another, he was not here to buy a house.

"I know you, Sylvia. You are a wonderful mother. I also know that you always get what you want."

Mollified, she relaxed a little. "Carry on."

Encouraged at not being rejected out of hand, the words spilled out of him in a flood. "I also know how much you love Jen. I know you would do anything to make her happy. *Anything*. As long as it was in your power to do so. I can tell you with complete confidence that she would be devastated if the dog park became a bunch of stores. Even if one of them was a Petco.

Sylvia blinked at him. "'Devastated'? That's a pretty strong conclusion, Stuart."

He nodded in agreement. "It could throw her into a depression she might never escape."

This observation caused Sylvia to uncross her arms and sit up straight. "Huh? What on Earth are you talking about? Where do you get this 'depression' stuff?"

"I know Jen. I know her moods, what she likes, what repels her. She has a personal investment in that dog park that goes way beyond just taking m—taking her wonderful, remarkable, handsome dog Stuart there for a stroll. She goes every day. It relaxes her, she meets with her friends, and it helps her to tackle the day's work. The park isn't just grass and pooper scoopers: it's therapy. For humans as well as for dogs. Take that away and both will suffer. Including Jen. Especially Jen." Mimicking the woman seated before him, he leaned back and crossed his arms.

"Pick a side, Sylvia Jensen. Dog park or shopping center. One more business deal or your daughter's happiness. We won't even talk about the trauma it would mete out to her precious, unique, exceptional Boston Terrier."

Confused and atypically uncertain, she studied him closely. "Look, Stuart. I like you and all. You make a persuasive case. But your opinion of my daughter's emotional health is a bit beyond my understanding. It all seems a bit overwrought. But you're the psychologist, or so Jen said. So give it to me straight. I need to be certain where Jen stands on all of this, and then I'll have a better idea where I need to stand."

"Of course." At that moment he had enough confidence to hang out a shingle: "Stuart Terrier – Accredited Psychologist— People and Dogs (no cats!)". Leaning toward her, he lowered his voice to a conspiratorial whisper. "For one thing, I have a plan."

In response, she uncrossed her arms and leaned across her desk toward him, her tone only mildly sardonic. "Do tell."

Jen arrived moments later, sucking air and looking around wildly. The receptionist pointed in the direction of Sylvia's work area.

"She's in her office." As Jen rushed in that direction the receptionist added a heads-up. "She's not alone."

Jen burst in without bothering to announce herself, only to have her worst fears realized. Stuart was there. With her mother. And yet, something was not quite right. Sylvia seemed unusually —relaxed. Calm, almost. A condition as rare in her mother as empathy. Her elbows on the desk, she was resting her chin atop her interlocked fingers and gazing appreciatively at Stuart.

"So, how much do you charge for a therapy session?"

"Stuart, there you are! I've been looking all over for you. I…."

Fearful, he had jumped up on his chair and nearly fell,

forgetting for a moment that his center of gravity was considerably higher than usual. Sylvia gestured at her daughter, whose initial panic at encountering Stuart in her mother's office was beginning to subside. Whatever had occurred prior to her arrival, it did not seem to have sparked even a small crisis.

"Jen, we have to talk. Sit down."

Grabbing an empty chair, Jen brought it forward. Complying in his usual manner, Stuart waited until Jen sat and then matched her movement perfectly. Sylvia nodded toward the doorway.

"Stuart, please give me a minute alone with my daughter."

Nodding vigorously, he rose and went to the nearest corner. Halting, he faced the wall and put his hands behind him. Jen hurried to correct the situation.

"Stuart, go wait for me in the lobby. I'll be right there. And stay there this time." Obediently, he rose to exit. "And don't talk to the receptionist," she added quickly.

He departed without a word, relieved that Jen had spoken to him, if not exactly warmly, without yelling. Maybe she wasn't mad anymore. Or at least, less mad. Out in the lobby he walked stiffly past the receptionist. Engaged in her own work, she didn't even glance his way. He thought to make casual conversation, except that Jen had warned him not to. Besides, every time he tried to make conversation with other humans, things always seemed to take an awkward turn.

They were not alone in the lobby. Another Townsend employee was hanging a new picture on the wall among a dozen or so other renderings of important company developments. It was a detailed computer image of a shopping center. Stuart didn't recognize the buildings, but despite the drastic changes to the image and thanks to a certain tree that was featured prominently in the render, he immediately recognized the property on which it sat.

Freddy's tree. The only tree that was left in the picture.

He started to whimper softly to himself. The rendering had

rendered his second favorite place in the whole world cold and dead. One tree remaining. No open grassy sward, no bushes, no play tunnels or hoops. Just concrete and glass.

A hand came down lightly on his shoulder and he nearly jumped. It was Jen, but the Jen he loved; not the one who had yelled at him back in the salon. She wore a determined expression that bordered on anger. The anger was not directed at him: he sensed that immediately. He almost leaned close to lick her—but there were other humans present and he felt they would not understand. He was learning the ways of people, even if he did not want to.

Her words were unexpected and encouraging. "Stuart, we won't let them take the park away." She looked back toward Sylvia's office. "Mom will help. She can't do it by herself, but she can do some things. She says we have to find Arthur's parents." Turning, she headed for the door, knowing that he would heel.

He smiled, happy to follow. Sylvia had listened to him, Jen had listened to Sylvia, and progress had been made.

His plan was in motion.

CHAPTER TWELVE

The building was sleek, glass-paneled, and full-on Southern California modern, exhibiting about as much old California influence as a fast food taco. It was much bigger and far more impressive than the offices of Townsend Realty. Grateful for the end of their shift, dozens of employees were filing out into the parking lot.

Exiting her car, Jen and Stuart headed for the building as employees flowed around them. No one thought to question their presence. There was security inside the building, but Daly Enterprises was not NASA. It was assumed that anyone entering likely had a good reason for doing so.

Jen slowed anyway as they neared the impressive structure. How *were* they going to get in farther than the lobby? Increasingly tentative, she looked over at Stuart.

"So the plan is we go in and tell Arthur's parents to cancel the deal? That's it?"

He nodded in agreement. "I've always thought the best plan was the simplest and most straightforward."

She looked dubious. "Maybe that works with poodles. I'm not so sure it will go over well with the senior Dalys. They're never gonna listen to us. We'll probably get laughed out of their office —if we can even get in to see them. I wish Arthur were here."

A very large vehicle was slowing off to their right. Stuart recognized it as a limousine because he had seen a few parked at the Townsend offices and had managed, once, to surreptitiously mark it. As Jen continued to study the main entrance, he watched as a figure emerge from the sidewalk side of the car.

"That was good, Jen. Very good!" He could hardly conceal his admiration.

She frowned at him. "What are you talking about?"

He pointed to where Arthur Daly was now walking up the access steps.

Stuart smiled. "Now just wish me back like that. Back to myself. If you can bring him back just like that, surely you can change me back too…."

"It's Arthur!" she exclaimed. "Why is he here? He's supposed to be in San Francisco."

"Isn't it obvious?" Excited, he followed her into the building. "Didn't you just…?"

Only paying part attention to him because she was focused now on Arthur, she mumbled, "What are you talking about, Stuart?"

"Didn't you just wish him here?"

She ignored him as all three entered the lobby at nearly the same time. Arthur immediately spotted Jen and they locked eyes. If anything, his surprise exceeded hers.

"Jen! What are you doing here?"

She headed straight for him. "I could ask you the same. I thought you were in San Francisco?"

He did not quite stammer. "I—just got back. I came as soon as I could catch a flight." He gave Stuart a quick once over, not impressed but definitely curious. "Is he with you?"

"Of course I'm with her," the object of Daly's interest replied blithely. "I've always been with her."

Arthur stared a moment, frowned, and tried to digest the reply. "Excuse me?"

Jen stepped in. "I guess that's true. But it's not what you're thinking." His attention swung back to her and it was plain that he was Not Pleased. "It's hard to explain, Arthur. *Really* hard to explain."

"Try me," he said curtly.

"I will, I will. Some day." Her expression, if not her words, pleaded for time. "I honestly want to...."

She broke off as an older couple emerged from the elevator and came toward them. There was no mistaking Arthur's parents. Mr. Daly carried himself with confidence and dignity. Mrs. Daly carried a white Persian cat. Or rather, she carried a huge mass of perfectly coiffed white fur within which the body of Persian cat appeared to reside. From a distance, its true catness was obscured and it looked instead like the world's largest dandelion puffball.

As they approached, Daly peré was his characteristically serious self. His wife stroked infinite depths of fur as she greeted her son.

"Arthur, dear, you're back so soon? I thought you had important business that was going to keep you in San Francisco for a while." She affected mock concern. "I trust everything is going okay up there in the fog?"

"The business is fine, mother." His irritation was evident. "I'll go back: this was just a first, quick trip." He gestured to his left. "You remember Jen?"

She took a step toward Mrs. Daly. As she did so a hiss, soft but cautionary, emerged from within the mass of white fur.

Neither woman extended a hand toward the other. "Hello, Mrs. Daly. Nice to see you. It's been a while."

"Jen. Of course." The Persian hissed again. So did Mrs. Daly, but no one could hear her.

At the same time, the cat in her arms took notice of Stuart.

This time its hissing was more than cautionary. More of a schizophrenic suggestion of a forthcoming attack crossed with abject fear. Concerned, Mrs. Daly hastened to reassure her precious.

"Calm down, Muffy. It's only Arthur's little music friend from college." Jen bridled but said nothing. Fortunately, she was not one to grind her teeth.

"Don't be silly, dear," her husband huffed. "It's Arthur's old girlfriend, the pet realtor."

Don't grind your teeth, Jen continued to counsel herself. Don't say what you're thinking, either. Was Arthur's would-be oligarch of a father saying that she had been a girlfriend for eons, or that she was just old? A double insult, to which she could not diplomatically reply.

While she pondered a non-lethal response, the Persian had scrambled from her owner's arms and up one bicep to take up residence on Mrs. Daly's shoulders. It sat there like a white fur stole with all of its feline alarms going off simultaneously. Fussing with it, Mrs. Daly entreated her son.

"Arthur, be a dear and get Muffy off my neck."

Stepping behind her, he carefully detached Muffy from mother. The task was made challenging by the Persian's reluctance to let go.

Only when Jen thought to glance at Stuart did she notice him making a series of quick, distorted faces at the cat. She gave him a sharp nudge. He responded with a look of complete innocence that she did not buy for a second.

"I'm just playing a little," he told her innocently.

"Not *now*, Stuart," she whispered.

Not having a clue what to make of this byplay, or perhaps simply indifferent, Arthur's father eyed him sternly. "Son, the bank analyst's report is on your desk." His tone was dry. "Do try to review it."

Jen nudged Arthur with her elbow and he flinched.

"Indeed, dad. First thing Monday. Glad to be home," he added unctuously as he handed the squirming cat back to his mother.

"Good to see you too, dear." Mrs. Daly eyed Jen the way she would an extra place setting at a table. "Maybe we can all have dinner together one night. You must tell me how the pet real estate business is going." She struggled anew with the Persian. "Muffy! Calm down. What is the matter with you? There are no dogs here."

As soon as they were out of earshot Jen whirled on Arthur. "Did you hear what she called me? Your 'little music friend from college'." As if we haven't been dating for years."

He scrutinized the still active lobby. It wouldn't do to have his dirty laundry exposed in front of employees. "Not here." He gestured and turned. "In my office."

Quite an office it was, too. Large, with a good view, and expensive modern furniture. You know…the kind designed to look cheap, but branded. The electronically-controlled window screens cost more than many employees' entire houseful of furniture. It was all designed to make the office-holder look important and knowledgeable. In this it usually succeeded—but not now. There was a time when such things would have been important to Jen, but she had grown beyond that.

"She's just never gonna like me, huh?" she was saying as they entered and Arthur closed the door behind her. "Anyway, enough about your mother." *Anything is enough about your mother*, she thought to herself. "Why haven't you responded to any of my messages? I sent you plenty."

For once, his indignation was halfway justified. "I tried calling you back after you broke up with me, but I was on a boat and dropped my phone in the water on the way back to the dock. So since I couldn't get ahold of you that way, I booked the first flight back."

"Why were you on a boat?" Jen began. "I thought this trip was all about work and…wait a minute. I broke up with you? When?"

"I smell perfume on him, Jen, and it's not yours." Stuart did not quite growl the observation. But he wanted to.

"Now, look." Arthur addressed Stuart sternly, as if prepared to deliver one of his laudatory lectures on himself, the subject on which he possessed the most expertise. "I was sitting on a plane for two hours next to a…." He paused, blinked. "Who are you, again?"

"Stuart." *He had better be nice to Jen, or I'll bite him. No matter what she says.*

Arthur looked from him to her. "Are you guys dating?"

"Oh god, no. " Jen assured him.

"I have a girlfriend." Stuart volunteered this information with a touch of pride.

Jen smiled, then lowered both her gaze and her voice. "Stuart, please let me talk with Arthur alone. Just for a little while, I promise. Can you wait outside?"

I'd still like to bite him, Stuart thought to himself. But he knew that no matter how much such an action could be justified, it would upset Jen. He'd already had her upset at him once today and he did not wish for a reprise. So he complied with her command.

Arthur confronted her as soon as the door shut behind her … whoever this guy "Stuart" was. "Explain the baseball player mother saw you with on TV."

Mother Daly again, Jen thought to herself. It was plain that she didn't spend *all* her time with that spoiled cotton ball of a cat. "I wasn't *with*. I was just there. Derek is a client, and a very valued one. He just listed his five million dollar home with me. He's an Angel."

Arthur was not satisfied. "An 'angel', huh? That's a bit of a friendly description for someone who's just a client."

She rolled her eyes and sighed. "Oh, for the love of… he's a shortstop for the California Angels, Arthur."

He digested this, then brightened. "Derek *Jones*? Oh! He's a great player. Maybe not an all-Star, but good enough to start. If he'd just get his average up another ten points…wait a minute." His expression darkened. "What about this guy Stuart?"

Having been told by Jen to step outside, Stuart had done exactly that. After lingering outside Daly's office, boredom had set in and he had gone—well, further outside. Unable to resist a perfectly manicured, healthy lawn, he was enjoying it to the fullest. Presently, by rolling around on it.

Spotting him through the office window, Jen had a moment of panic as Arthur rose from his chair. Fearing he would see Stuart and subsequently question his, and possibly her, sanity, she moved to grab him by the shoulders and push him back against his desk. That way she could keep him facing her and more importantly, from looking outside.

"Old college friend," she explained, finally responding to his query. "Never mind. There's nothing there. We used to sing together now and then. I know what you're thinking, and you're barking up the wrong tree." As he started to turn she gripped him harder. He looked at her in surprise, not entirely unhappy with her proximity or sudden aggressiveness. Seeing the look in his eyes she backed off a little, lest he get the wrong idea. Or was it the wrong idea? Everything that had happened, everything that was happening, was leaving her confused and on edge.

Focus on the dog park, she told herself. Something concrete. Something real. But other matters intruded. Matters of a much more personal nature. Reaching toward her neck, she carefully lifted the locket away from her skin.

"Before I forget, do you remember where you bought this lovely locket you gave me? It's not your grandmother's or anything like that, right? If it's a family heirloom I want to be extra careful with it."

He dismissed the gift with a glance and a shrug. "No. I got it at a quaint little antique shop across town. Why? Was your 'friend'

Stuart asking about it? Why should he care? Does he want to replace my picture in the locket with one of his?"

That was so on the mark she nearly choked. "Quite the opposite actually. I mean, he thought maybe it would be a cute gift for *his* grandmother. If I gave it to him. Which I'm not gonna do. Because, like for one reason, I don't think his grandmother is alive."

She nearly choked again: this time on laughter.

Arthur was not amused. "Grandmother? I remember you saying it was his mother."

"I'm not sure she's alive, either…mphh…mother, grandmother —Arthur, do you think I remember? It's just a small thing, no big deal. Of course, if you can't recall the details of the purchase I can always…."

"Okay, relax," he said. "I think I have the card from the place. If not, I can check the credit card receipt."

She released him. Walking around behind the desk, he opened the top drawer and pulled out a handful of cards. Several were expired, a couple he shuffled so they were on top of the stack, another pair he made sure she did not see before finally locating the one for which he was searching.

"Ah, here it is. 'Antiques and Angels'. Charming little place. The kind you're more likely to find occupying a stall in Porte de Clingancourt in Paris, not in Newport. Sweet old woman runs it. Very spiritual and tuned in. A delight to listen to. I spent considerably more time in there than I intended. Even learned a few things. She asked me about my life, how it was going, and what I wanted the locket for. None of her business, of course, but she was so kindly and obviously wanting to be of assistance that I found myself talking to her until I completely lost track of time. Had to buy the locket and hurry to make my next appointment."

Jen listened to all this with skepticism and a couple of degrees of separation. It did not sound like the Arthur she knew.

"Antiques and Angels? Look at you, getting spiritual in your old age."

As usual, he completely missed when she was being sarcastic. "Ya know, Jen," he mused, "sometimes I question Existence. I look at the universe and ponder how many lifetimes we've already had…."

She let him ramble on for a bit, lost in the magnificence of his own imagined profundity, which in reality was nothing more than the usual pre-digested New Age poppycock run through a faux philosophical blender until he thought it was original with him. She was far more distracted by the sight of Stuart outside, running circles and jumping for joy out on the grass as the sprinklers came on.

"You do?" the small portion of her that was still paying attention to him mumbled.

"Yeah. I even bought this crystal."

Reaching down to one side of the desk he struggled for a moment before he managed to wrestle a massive cluster of quartz crystals off the floor and onto the (fortunately sturdy) piece of office furniture. Despite the distraction outside she found herself genuinely impressed.

"Wow, that's huge!" Stalling for time she added, "Where'd you get it?"

"Another shop near the antique dealer." His forehead wrinkled. "I don't know what was with me that day. I usually don't buy stuff like this. The locket, I mean, and this crystal." He ran a hand up and down one gleaming hexagonal shape. "It's from Arkansas, they told me."

"Never been to Arkansas." She watched Stuart as he gamboled through the spray from the sprinklers. He had stopped running and was now trying to bite one of the streams. "If it would help the situation with the dog park, I'd buy one myself. What *about* the dog park, Arthur? I don't understand why you didn't tell me anything about the deal. You know how much that park means to me, and to my friends. It's not like I never talk about it. You can't claim you were unaware."

He thought carefully before replying. "I couldn't say anything to you. I wanted to, but I couldn't. I had to sign a non-disclosure agreement until funding loans cleared." He smiled. "I was going to tell you any time now. I just didn't think, as far as you and I were concerned, that it mattered that much."

She pursed her lips and nodded. Her response was flat. Controlled now. "Seriously?" She added, "I get it. It's just 'business', right? No need to be involved on a personal level."

He nodded, pleased that he had reconnected with her. "I'm glad you understand. It could have been—awkward—otherwise."

"Oh, I do understand, I do. What I don't understand is how I spent seven years with you. Not just with you, but onto you, into you, and every which way with you."

While he tried to comprehend fully what she was saying, she glanced out the window yet again. The sprinklers were still running and so was Stuart. He was now thoroughly soaked: happily so. As she looked on he took a dive toward the nearest sprinkler, mouth agape and arms outspread, like a big bird flying through a rainstorm, and she was reminded yet again of What Was Important. Turning back to a plainly baffled Arthur, she offered him a wan smile that doubled as a farewell.

"Well, I'd love to stay and chat about priorities, yours as well as mine, but I have a park to save."

With that she exited, her retreating back having to serve in lieu of a kiss, handshake, or by-your-leave. Brooding, he watched her go. Having caught her several times looking out the window, he now did so himself, only to find a singular soaked figure gazing back at him. It was that fellow Stuart. A very wet Stuart, smiling and waving at him. Absently, Arthur waved back.

"Hmm. From college, huh?" Within a mind that could be more than a little calculating, wheels were turning across several lines of thinking, and none of them led to any place particularly nice.

❧ ❧ ❧

Stuart was used to the bathroom in Jen's house. It was a fun place to investigate, often full of fascinating and intriguing smells, especially when she was putting on assorted washes and soaps and perfumes. At such times he was free to run around, sniff, and explore so long as he did not do two things: put his feet up on her and drink out of the toilet. In his present body he would not dare to do the former and as regards the latter it did not matter, since the seat was down. He would not have indulged in any case since he was confident Jen's reaction would have been more extreme even than if he had been in his natural form.

While he would have been more comfortable without any clothes on he sort of understood why she was making him wear some even while in the bathroom, though the bathrobe he had on was too tight for his male torso. At the moment, she was drying his hair with a blow dryer. He didn't like it. In point of fact he had never liked the damn thing. It was noisy and hurt his ears and the steady gust of hot hair felt unnatural. In his canine book, as far as irritating home appliances were concerned, the blow dryer came in second only to the vacuum cleaner. In this, at least, he and cats were in accord.

Having had about enough of being tormented by the fiendish device, he grabbed it away and pointed it at her. *See how you like it*, he thought. Actually, he told himself, that was a pretty stupid thought, since she pointed it at herself all the time. Laughing, she put up both hands to shield herself from the warm blast. It was quickly apparent she wasn't laughing at him.

"Arthur was so serious!" Though her merriment wound down, an occasional muffled chuckle still interrupted her speech. "I almost busted out laughing watching you rolling around in the sprinklers and snapping at the spray. Why would you roll around on wet grass like that?"

He set the blower aside, suddenly serious. "Isn't it obvious? I miss being a dog, Jen. I miss running through sprinklers and tearing up cardboard boxes. I miss consistent food, and being able to go to the bathroom when and where I wish—well, mostly where I wish—and not having to be formal and wonder if I'm using the right words." His earnestness threatened to overwhelm her. "I miss being *me*. Humans are so certain that being human is the best way there is to be when they don't have the slightest notion what it's like to be something else. Well, I can tell you from my personal experience that it's not all you think it is. It's pretty good having a dog's life—especially if you are one."

"I'm sorry, Stu," she replied, somber now. "We're gonna fix this I promise." She paused a moment, then perked up. "Speaking of that, the good news is that I got the contact information for the place where Arthur bought the locket. It doesn't mean that anything will come of it, but the least we can do is talk to the lady who sold it to him and see if she knows anything. What do you think?"

He didn't hesitate. "Can we go now?"

She was apologetic. "The card says they close at five, so we've missed it for today. But for sure first thing tomorrow. Assuming the shop is as small as Arthur hinted, I don't imagine there'll be anyone there except the owner and maybe an assistant. So we should be able to…." Her words melted into an uncontrollable yawn.

He eyed her with concern. "Tired?"

She contracted from the stretch that concluded the yawn. "Why should I be tired? Just because today was the craziest day of my life? I'm beyond tired, Stu. But I can't relax now. We've got to keep hammering on this, we have to save the park and most importantly, get you back to normal, Stuie Louie. " She was unable to stifle a second yawn.

"Oh, and I spoke with Jim. Now that he knows I was… am dating Arthur, he probably thinks I knew about the dog park all along and thinks the worst of me." Are you starting to care about what Jim thinks? I told ya he was the right guy for you! "You're saying that again? You are so about Sweetie Peters that you would want me to marry Jim." *Marry?* Stuarts eyes widened. By the way, he also mentioned Sweetie is not eating her food." "Not eating?" He didn't have to ponder long. "She's sad. We don't eat when we miss someone. Especially someone close to us. We can whimper, we can howl, but we can't really cry. So we stop eating." He looked evenly at her. "I didn't eat when you went to Mexico with Nina for her sister's wedding."

"Really?" Jen didn't try to hide her surprise. "Mom didn't tell me that. Was it because you missed me? Aw, that's so sweet and sad, Stuart."

"It was only partly because I missed you. It was also because Sylvia didn't go to Petco like you told her to and buy what I usually eat. Instead, she bought some cheap kibble somewhere. I wouldn't eat it. Neither would you, but you have a lot more choices than I do.

She looked abashed and he opted to change the subject to a more important matter.

"Can you call Jim and put me on the phone with Sweetie Peters? I'll talk to her and maybe that'll help."

🐾   🐾   🐾

Usually it was Sweetie who was begging. This time it was Jim. She was lying on her bed sadder than he had ever seen her. Worse, he didn't know why. Physically she seemed normal. There was nothing wrong with her legs or anything else. At least, nothing visible. Normally a happy, vivacious dog, now she was just lying around as if drugged. And she wouldn't eat, no matter how much he pleaded with her.

At the moment he was on his knees holding a food-filled spoon. It was salmon, her favorite. He would have offered her filet mignon if he'd had any but he doubted she'd eat that, either.

But canned salmon dog food never failed to tempt her. Until now.

"Come on, Sweetheart. What is it? What's wrong? Tummy upset? Did you eat something nasty that Dad didn't see?" He pushed the spoon a little closer to her face. All she did was turn further away. "I don't want to have to take you to the vet. If you don't eat there, they'll have to force feed you, and I don't want to think of that. Please eat something Sweetie…."

The phone rang. Rising, he went to a nearby table, picked up the phone and answered. Given the present difficult circumstances he would not have responded, but the screen showed that it was Jen on the other end.

"Can I talk to Sweetie Peters?"

"Stuart?" Jim replied. "Yes, can you put Sweetie on the phone. Jen told me she hasn't been eating." "I'm about to worry myself to death. I'm here trying to get her to eat something. I even alluded to having to take her to the vet. That's a word she knows and usually it sends her scampering under my bed or the kitchen table or something. This time she didn't even move."

Impatient Stuart, "Can I talk to her now?" " Of course! Let me get her." "Sweetie." came the male voice from the other end of the connection.

"Hang on Stuart, I'll put you on speaker"

Switching his phone to speaker mode, he set it down upright next to the terrier on the bed. "Sweetie, you have a call."

What followed sounded to Jim like a person doing the best dog imitation he'd ever heard. The series of barks, whines, grumblings and growls made absolutely no sense to him, but as soon as the exchange commenced, Sweetie Peters raised her head and lifted her ears. What really threw Jim was that the voice on the other end of the connection sounded more like a dog than she did in her replies. Maybe, he thought, it had something to do with pitch. Or maybe he was so worried he was just going a little crazy.

No such confusion afflicted the terrier, who understood perfectly what the doggie voice on the phone was saying.

"Sweetie Peters, it's Stuart!"

She sat up and replied, all anxious barks and whines and woofs. "Stuart Louis, is that really you?"

"It sure is! I miss you mon chérie!"

"Is that French? You are so romantic. Although you sound kinda funny."

"It's this stupid human throat. It doesn't make quite the right sounds. But I think that is dog French, yes. Gizmo says it all the time to female dogs at the park." He started to choke up. His human throat was capable of that, anyway.

"I heard you're not feeling well?"

I'm very sad about the dog park. I've only been there a few times myself but more often recently because my human likes to work there."

"I understand, Sweetie. But we won't let them take our park."

"How?" she replied. "If the park goes away my human won't have a place to work where we can see each other. Also, I met the most perfect Boston, the dog of my dreams, and the next day he was short two legs. How is that going to 'work out'?"

"I don't know," he confessed. "I just feel that it will, somehow. Trust me when I tell you that you are the reason my heart beats. Being stuck in this stupid upright body doesn't change that. Now please eat something because Jim is very worried about you. He needs you. I need you." "I'll try." "Goodnight, Sweetie. Dream of warm days and hamstrung squirrels." "Goodnight Stuart Louis."

There was silence at the other end. Picking up the phone, Jim wondered what to do next. Before he could even respond, Sweetie Peters had started eating from the dish of dog food he had set beside her. And not just eating. She was attacking the salmon pâté, her face deep in the bowl. He stared in wonderment, then remembered the phone.

Stuart 's job was finished. He handed the phone over to Jen,

"Jim?" "Jen, I'm amazed. I don't know what he said, it sounded like an injured puppy to me, but whatever it was, it worked! She's eating. I love this guy, whoever he is. Tell him that. And tell him thank you." I will. Jim, about the guitar— "Never mind that. This means way, way more to me than that. I have forty of them, anyway, goodnight Jen."

Via the phone, her voice was full of disbelief. "Forty? What does anybody need with forty guitars?"

But wholly engrossed in watching Sweetie Peters devour her dinner, he had already hung up.

CHAPTER THIRTEEN

I t was a dark and not stormy night (this was Southern California, after all). But it *was* a bit foggy in Newport as cool sea air moved in over land that had been heated during the day. There was a kiss of condensation on the window behind the table where Jen's home office was located. Light came from overhead and even brighter light from the laptop whose screen faced away from the window. A figure sat facing the computer, working the keys slowly and carefully. It was not Jen. It was also drooling. Definitely not Jen.

Stuart gazed hungrily at the computer as he worked through an assortment of screens. He was clumsy at it both because he was still not entirely comfortable manipulating objects with his fingers and because working on the internet was something he knew only from watching Jen. But he had a good memory and sharp eyesight, both of which allowed him to recall entries for passwords and related keystrokes. As he worked he murmured to himself.

"Bacon and beef! Let's see—how many?" He read slowly to ensure he was understanding the human words on the screen.

"Sixty-four in a box? This is too good to be true!" He squinted at the screen. "Free delivery, woof!"

The touch of a finger added an order to the electronic shopping cart. The number within the little image of a cart changed to thirty. Nearby was a total for the multiple orders: $596.

He frowned at the screen. "What do you mean, two day delivery? No way. Can't wait that long. I need a snack *now*." He was on the verge of checking out the button that promised Expedited Delivery when a pop-up ad caught his eye. He read slowly.

"Win a year's supply of beef and chicken jerky. Just come to any Petco near you. Bring I.D. to enter. 4 Petco locations near you. Click here!"

He didn't hesitate, clicking on the indicated circle immediately. It took him to:

YELP – 4 PETCO LOCATIONS

Yet again his non-existent tail set to wagging as he threw up his hands in delight. "Finally! A human device that's easy to understand. It's on Yelp street!" Rising from the chair, he hurried in the direction of the bedroom. "Jen—gotta get Jen. Got to enter the contest." Envisioning a year's supply of jerky, he started to salivate again. He couldn't help himself.

He burst into the bedroom, her name on his lips. It stayed there as he saw that she was sound asleep on the bed. He wanted to wake her; desperately wanted to wake her. But without startling her. She didn't like it when he did that.

Leaning over, he gently stroked her shoulder with his right hand, performing the gesture exactly as he would have in his proper guise. Only the pressure was different. When she did not respond, he added a soft whine. That usually worked. This time he could also whisper her name, and did so.

She let out a snort that would not have embarrassed a prize porker and rolled over, away from him. Drawing back from the bed, his mind filled with visions of beef jerky falling like attenuated dark raindrops, he considered what to do next. There were other things he could try, other ways of waking her that he knew would work. Peeing on the bed was definitely out. So was bringing in his water dish and dumping it on her head. He could bark in her ear, but the one time he had done that to wake her it had not ended well.

Wait a minute, he thought. Why did he even need Jen? He knew his way around the general neighborhood. Those places he hadn't walked he had ridden in the car with Jen, his head stuck out the passenger-side window, taking in everything they passed. He remembered the nearest Petco store: both its appearance and its smells. Surely he could find it on his own? All he needed was a little help, and he felt certain he could find that. Total strangers had always been ready and happy to interact with him.

"Where's my I.D.?" he muttered softly. His words didn't rouse Jen, but he had moved on beyond waking her. Turning to go, he hesitated, then walked back to the bed. Carefully, he gripped the edge of her blanket and pulled it high, covering her up to her neck. He knew exactly how to do it—because she had done exactly the same thing for him, so many times.

Downstairs, he started for the front door, then paused, mumbling to himself. "Where's my I.D.?" If there was one thing he knew for certain, it was never to leave the house without his I.D. Grabbing it off the hook by the front door, he left quietly, making sure to shut the door firmly behind him.

While it did not take him long to make his way to the nearest commercial district, no Petco store was immediately evident. He wandered a bit, checking one storefront after another without success. He felt no compunction about asking for directions.

Any other healthy male of his apparent age and appearance would have employed a different opening line with the two gorgeous girls walking toward him. Stuart queried them without hesitation.

"Hi. Do you know where the Petco is?"

They kept on walking past him, without answering. His question did throw them off, however.

"Petco?" one wondered aloud. "Is that, like a college?"

Her companion frowned. "Like a prep school?"

They were still debating as Stuart approached an older couple. "Hi. I'm looking for the Petco."

They both gave him the once over. While his appearance and demeanor might have caused comment someplace like Topeka, he fit perfectly in Newport Beach. The man pointed west.

"That way. It's a bit of a hike from here."

"Great." Stuart looked in the indicated direction. "Is it the one on Yelp?"

"Don't be silly, young man." The woman smiled at him. "They're all on Yelp."

"Really? Thank you!" He hugged her before she had a chance to wave him off, then turned to her husband. The older man raised his hands defensively, but by then Stuart was heading up the street. Shaking her head, the woman commented to her spouse.

"Milton, did you ever think the day would come when we would know more about the internet than some hippie boy?" They shared a laugh at the notion.

Stuart loved to run, but it was much more difficult on two legs and he soon found himself out of breath. There had to be a better way.

Not far ahead and off to his right, people were pulling up to a nightclub and dropping off their cars. First one valet then another ran up to take keys from owners. Stuart headed in their direction. Breathing hard and unsure what to do next, he wandered into the middle of the lineup just as a white Jaguar pulled in. Exiting his vehicle, the burly, well-dressed owner spotted an out-of-breath Stuart and, not unreasonably, assumed he was one of the club valets. Also, there were friends waiting for him on the inside and he was late and in a hurry. So much of a hurry that it never crossed his mind Stuart was anything but what he seemed.

"Working hard tonight, kid. You know, when I was sixteen I worked three years parking cars in a spread-out venue like this. It kept me in shape. Builds your wind." He tossed the keys toward Stuart, who caught them reflexively.

"Park it close by and I'll take care of ya." He nodded toward the club, from which loud music was seeping. "I'll be awhile."

Wide-eyed and innocent, Stuart looked from the keys to their owner. "Thanks. It's just what I need."

"Yeah." The owner of the Jag adjusted his jacket and headed for the club entrance. "Everybody needs a good workout."

Stuart had no trouble quickly climbing into the car and sliding behind the wheel, but he took his time studying the instrumentation.

"Jen does it like this," he said to himself. "Always has her left hand on the steering wheel. Right hand works everything else." He reached toward the side of the steering column. "Turn this key in here." Rewarded with the rumble of the engine starting up, he contemplated his next action. "Push this here to put it on the little 'D', and then step on this flat thing down on the floor."

With an ear-pleasing *vroom*, the Jag shot off into the night. That it missed the curb, the next car in line waiting to be parked, a fire hydrant, two power poles, and an outraged cat, was due more to good luck than any incipient driving skills on Stuart's part. This was confirmed when the speedometer passed a hundred. A cacophony of horns accompanied the Jag's wild acceleration as it occurred to Stuart he might be going just a teensy bit too fast.

"Ahhhh!...Jen makes it look so easy!"

Eyes wide, both hands clamped on the wheel, he remembered the function of the other pedal and stomped the brake. Demonstrating the car's excellent responsiveness, it immediately did two consecutive three-sixties before coming to a stop with the brake pedal pressed all the way to the floor.

Breathing hard, he slowly released the brake. The car began to move again. Merging with the traffic allowed him to maintain an appropriate speed without having to study any signs. Without any clear idea of where he was going, he experimented with an assortment of controls. Music came on, was turned off. While he usually enjoyed music in a car he didn't need any distractions. Another switch lowered the driver's side window. Hey, once you got control of it, driving a car was fun! He stuck his head out the window, tongue lolling as he delighted in the feel of the wind on his face.

What was even better was that all the other cars got out of his way as he swerved from lane to lane. Sometimes, he thought, humans could be really polite. He let out a howl of pleasure.

Sitting in his cruiser in the Starbuck's parking lot, the officer of the law stared over the muffin he had been noshing as the Jaguar zoomed off the street, onto the sidewalk, and back out onto the street, scattering a strolling couple but fortunately not hitting anyone. The cop was not a rookie and this was Southern California, but it had still been a while since he had seen anything quite so shameless. Usually when such brazen incidents occurred they were reported to him over the radio. They didn't happen in your face. There was no way, he knew, that the driver of the Jag could have failed to see the police cruiser sitting right there at the front of the lot. It made him so angry he dropped his muffin on the floor, which made him even angrier.

Focused on staying in at least one of the lanes on the boulevard, Stuart merrily ignored the flashing lights behind him, just as he ignored the spotlight that was being shined in his direction.

"This is officer Jackson, PC two-seventeen on Ocean Blvd. heading north," the flabbergasted cop was saying into his radio pickup. "Requesting backup. We have a three-oh-two in progress." He paused a moment as he adjusted the spotlight. "I've got a light right on the driver and he's just ignoring me. It's like he doesn't even know I'm here. Either he's wasted or indifferent; I can't tell which. He's not running—yet. Just cruising, but all over the place and at speed. We need to get this guy off the street *now*."

🐾 　 🐾 　 🐾

So quiet. So peaceful. Rolling over, Jen slung her right arm across her body. Fingertips struck the end table and the contact was enough to cause her eyes to flutter. Yawning, she began to wake up. It was dead quiet in the bedroom. The individual who usually greeted her upon awakening did not show himself. Neither in his original form nor in his present two-legged one.

"Stuart? Stuart, are you under the bed?" She sat up and turned on the light. No hint of movement disturbed the bedroom and nothing called back to her from from under the bed or downstairs. "*Stuart*!"

There was no response.

🐾 　 🐾 　 🐾

The howling was remarkable for its persistence and intensity. As an imitation it was uncannily accurate. Had it been rolled out on a talent show it likely would have taken first prize. But there were no prizes in jail. And the audience of prisoners was less than appreciative. A number of them had retreated to the far side of the large holding cell, their hands pressed over their ears. The only prisoner capable of putting a quick stop to the aural outrage did not. Instead, this massive, tattooed, bald-headed specimen stood off to one side sobbing softly to himself. The howling sounded exactly like the pet mastiff he had lost to disease only a

ALAN DEAN FOSTER

few months ago, although the present iteration was considerably higher pitched.

"Holy…." The guard increased his pace as he neared the cell. "Who's making that racket? Is this a jail or a damn kennel? Shut up, whoever you are!" He called out before reaching the cell and discovering the source of the canid lamentation. "Stuart Louis! You have one call."

Stuart shut down before the guard could identify him as the unrepentant howler. When the jailer opened the holding cell and a now silent Stuart exited, his departure was greeted with a round of relieved applause from the other prisoners.

"Is it Jen?" Stuart asked anxiously. He was trembling. "I hope so. I'm so scared." The guard did not reply.

Outside the holding area, the jailer picked up a large plastic zip bag. It contained the few personal effects that had been found on the prisoner. Among them was Stuart's dog collar. Holding it up to the light, the sergeant squinted to read the inscribed phone number on one of the metal tags.

"That's my collar," Stuart offered helpfully.

The guard nodded without looking at him.

"My owner gave it to me," the prisoner added.

"Uh-huh." The sergeant favored him with a sour expression. "Is that supposed to shock me? This is Southern California. You'd be surprised how many of these I've seen. Or maybe you wouldn't." Picking up a phone, he began dialing the number off the tag.

Having dressed hurriedly, her hair still unkempt, Jen was searching the house. She checked all Stuart's usual hiding places, to no avail. Nor did he respond to her repeated calls. It was while engaged in a careful search of the kitchen that she happened to notice that his collar was missing from the coat rack. Confused, she walked toward it. There was no sign of the collar on any of the hooks, nor on the floor. She was about to search the pantry when the phone rang.

Ordinarily she would not have answered an unknown number on her home phone. However, the screen displayed the callback as "Newport Police Dept.". She might have ignored that as well, given the likelihood that it was some kind of spam call. Except—Stuart was missing. Blood drained from her face. In his present form, anything could happen to Stuart. Or Stuart could happen to anything. Regardless, a missing Stuart plus police department was under any circumstances not a promising combination.

"Hello? This is Jen Jensen. Who am I speaking with? Is this really the police department?"

"Miss Jensen," came the no-nonsense reply, "this is Sergeant Miranda with the Newport Police. We have a Stuart Louis here at our central holding facility."

"Oh my god." She put a hand to her lips. "Is he okay? Is he in some kind of trouble?"

"'Some kind', yes, you could say that. We're holding him because he is involved with the theft of a vehicle, reckless driving, speeding, evading an officer of the law, driving on a sidewalk, and not having proper identification. Not to mention not being in possession of a driver's license and disturbing the peace inside a public facility. He requested that you be his one call."

It being too much to take in at one time, Jen found herself stuck on the initial accusation. "Stolen car? How? He doesn't drive. He doesn't know *how* to drive."

"Funny," came the reply. "That's what arresting officer Jackson said."

She started looking around for her purse and car keys. "I'll be right there."

"Ma'm," the sergeant explained firmly, "there's no need to come. You won't be able to receive him this evening. Or likely in the morning, for that matter. Grand theft auto is not a game. Well, it is a game, but we're talking the real thing here. It's a

213

felony and he will have to see a judge first thing tomorrow. It will be out of my hands then and everything will be decided in court." His tone darkened. "Frankly, given the number of charges levied against him, I wouldn't be overly optimistic as to the outcome."

"There are, uh, extenuating circumstances," she mumbled.

"That's good, ma'm. I'm sure the judge will take them, whatever they are, into account."

"He's okay, right? He's not hurt or anything?"

"Physically, he's fine," the officer told her. "He wasn't in an accident or a collision, and fortunately he didn't hurt anybody. From the report I read that seems to be something of a minor miracle. But he *is* howling."

"Howling?" Jen continued without thinking. "That's normal. Thank you, officer. I'll be there in the morning."

Wait, Miranda told himself. "Normal"? With a shrug he prepared to return to the prisoner to the holding cell. As he had observed earlier, this was Southern California.

Hanging up, Jen looked into the bedroom mirror. The face that stared back at her was more than a little nonplussed as she mumbled to herself.

"My dog…is in jail."

Back in the cell Stuart sat hunched down in a corner, head thrown back as he howled mournfully at the ceiling. It was pitiable. It was strung out. And it was very, very loud. As before, the other prisoners kept their distance. Several of them were big enough to break the howling man in half, but they were wary. Nobody knew what the guy was on. It might be some variant of meth or worse, flakka. Heavy dosing on junk like that could give a guy superhuman strength and the ability to ignore pain. Better, they decided, to let him howl away harmlessly in his corner until he ran down. Stuart's condition was the subject of much discussion among his fellow internees.

"Man," one muttered as he stared guardedly at Stuart, "what kinda drugs is this guy *on?*"

Pacing the cell floor, another prisoner crossed in front of them, nodding in Stuart's direction. "I recognize the sound. It's similar to one I heard as a young boy on the rez. He's calling out to his wolf pack." The speaker gives a dead stare to his cell mate.

🐾   🐾   🐾

There was plenty of parking in the police station lot. Pulling in to a spot, Jen checked the car's clock. If she had timed it right they should just be opening to the public. Sure enough, as she mounted the steps to the entrance, someone flipped a sign in the window to "Open". Entering, she walked quickly to the reception counter and the cop seated behind it.

"I'm here to see Officer Ramos."

"Just a minute, ma'm." The uniformed woman checked to make sure the subject of the visitor's inquiry had signed in before offering Jen directions. She gave a hasty nod of thanks before hurrying off down the indicated corridor.

"Jen?" Hector Ramos looked up from his computer to direct his guest to a chair on the opposite side of his desk. She settled into it gratefully.

"How is he?" He did not have to ask "who".

"He's fine. He eventually quit howling when mealtime came around." Ramos frowned. "Does he always eat nothing but meat? The evening report said he didn't touch the bread roll, vegetables, or potatoes."

"He's big on protein," Jen replied quickly. "Thanks for seeing me. Is there anything you can do to help him out of this? This is all a big misunderstanding."

Ramos's expression was grim. "Jen, I'm afraid there's not a whole lot I can do. The charges against him…." He broke off, began again. "For starters, he had no identification on him. When the arresting officer asked for his license, he gave him a dog collar. With a *dog* tag license on it."

215

Jen feigned surprised. "He did?"

"He did." Leaning forward slightly, Ramos studied his visitor's face. "What's particularly interesting, at least to me, is that the collar had your dog Stuart's tags attached to it."

Jen's reaction reached new heights of simulated astonishment. "Nooo…."

"Yes. How did you think Sergent Miranda got your number when he called?" He lowered his voice. "Speaking of your dog Stuart, Jen, where is he? Still on the farm? Maybe we should take a ride out to that farm today and see him? Make sure he's as 'okay' as the Stuart we have in here?"

It was too much for Jen. She had faked it as long as she could. She broke down in front of her host. Another officer passing in the hall glanced in, caught a look from Ramos, and moved on.

Jen eventually got ahold of herself, wiping at her eyes. "Hector. Didn't he help Ringo?"

Ramos looked pained. The present situation was no less uncomfortable for him than it was for his visitor. "Yes he did, and I will never forget that. But regardless of how I feel there's only so much I can do for…."

Jackson, the officer who had taken Stuart into custody the previous night, burst into the office. He spared a quick glance for Jen before sputtering to his colleague.

"Ramos, you gotta come see this. I'm seeing it and I still don't believe it. Nobody believes it."

"Believes what?" Ramos was taken aback by his fellow officer's barefaced amazement.

"Just come and see." Jackson took note of Jen, added uncertainly. "She's here for him?" Ramos nodded. "Then I guess she might as well come too."

Together, she and Hector followed Officer Jackson deeper into the jail complex until they reached a security door. It was standing ajar. Further in, a number of officers had crowded in front of an individual holding cell. Several were straining to see over the tops of their taller colleagues. Jackson pushed between them while Ramos and Jen followed.

Intended to contain and restrain one or two prisoners, the cell in question presently held five individuals. Four of them were canid: thick-bodied, muscular specimens any one of which when unleashed were capable of intimidating even hardened criminals. Acting as a pack they would effortlessly have struck fear into the hearts of any number of evildoers. At the moment they were not striking fear into anyone, least of all the person crouching before them. To a one, they were sitting on their haunches, tongues lolling, as they followed the human's every move. Expecting screams of pain and the sound of ripping flesh, the assembled cops could only look on in astonishment.

"Ranger, you should say you're sorry to Ringo." Less than a yard away from jaws that could crunch bone, Stuart was wagging an admonishing finger at the shepherd in question. Instead of biting the waving finger, the police dog whimpered. "You know that was *his* milk bone. You ate yours *and* you ate his. You guys are on the same team. Is that how a friend treats a friend?"

Pushing out his front paws, the German shepherd laid down and folded his paws over his eyes. Stuart whispered something no one else could hear, then raised his voice.

"It's okay. He forgives you." He reached out to the police dog. "Come here and give me a hug."

Rising, the shepherd approached Stuart and raised up. While the prisoner hugged him back, Ringo's counterpart gave the human face a couple of quick licks. In front of them, the other three dogs barked happily in unison. Outside the cell, a bevy of blue chattered excitedly among themselves. One lanky corporal turned to the man next to him.

"If I ever left Ranger alone with a perp like that and I wasn't around to countermand, he'd rip him apart."

"Same thing with Samson," declared another officer. "He

won't let anybody but me so much as touch him." His voice rose. "Jeezus, look at that!"

Having induced Ranger and Ringo to make up, Stuart was now rolling around on the floor with all four dogs, the only apparent danger he was in that of being licked to death. One of them grabbed his leg between its jaws and tugged gently, play-biting. Outside the cell, his human partner could only gape at the interaction. Police dogs simply didn't 'play bite'. But that was exactly what was happening.

Putting an arm around Jen's shoulders, Ramos gently guided her away from the cell and its flabbergasted audience. Getting her off to one side, he kept his voice down.

"There's obviously something you're not telling me, Jen." He gestured back in the direction of the cell. "What's going on in there makes no sense. It's absolutely unprecedented. I was watching you while you were watching it. Anyone whose friend turned up in a cell with four unrestrained police dogs should be freaking out. You didn't panic, you didn't let out a shout. You didn't even look surprised." Folding his arms, he eyed her sternly. "What's going on here, Jen?"

She couldn't meet his gaze. "I wish I could tell you, Hector, but you'd never believe me."

Ramos lowered his voice even more. "Forget about the fact that his only ID was Stuart's dog collar. Watching him interact with the dogs in the park and now with that quartet of canine cops in there, I've managed to forget that none of this makes any sense. But—the world is full of things that don't make any sense. Cops know that better than most people. That doesn't make them less real." He paused a moment. "That's Stuart in there, isn't it? *Your* Stuart. He nodded at the crowd packed in front of the cell. "There's no Stuart out on a farm is there?.

She hesitated. Was Ramos being straight with her? Or was he fishing for confirmation of the unbelievable? If she answered in the affirmative, would she find herself in a cell next to Stuart's?

Wrapped up nice and tight in a white shirt with the fasteners in back?

Shoot, she told herself. At this point what did she have to lose? If Ramos was being honest, it would be a relief to know that she was not the only one aware of what was going on.

"He's got me convinced," she told him bluntly.

He shook his head. "Crazy. It's always crazy in here, but this is way, way beyond normal crazy. If there is such a thing as normal crazy."

"What about Stuart?"

Ramos looked apologetic. "At most, I can get you a day or two if you can manage bail. Release him into your custody. You'll have to sign for him."

She almost smiled. "I've been signing for him his whole life."

"Right. I'll handle the paperwork." He started to lead her out, halted abruptly. "Don't leave town. Either of you."

"If we run," she replied good-naturedly, "I promise I won't let him drive."

Ramos did not laugh.

Filling out the necessary forms took half an hour. She and Stuart drew some strange looks as they exited the station but no one stopped or questioned them. Ramos had been as good as his word. Glancing down at her purse Jen saw that one end of Stuart's collar was sticking out and she hurried to cram it down out of sight.

"Why did you pull me out?" He was complaining as they made their way down the steps outside the station entrance. To look at him or hear him you would have thought nothing untoward had happened. "I was having a great time with those big guys. Did you see the Rott called Samson begging me to chew on his neck?"

"Yes Stuart." Her tone was as dry as the Namib. "It was cute. All of it, so cute. You stole a car, ran from the law, ended up in jail without proper identification, and now you want to play with police dogs. What a swell time. I'm so sorry I wasn't around to enjoy all of it."

Her sarcasm flew past him like one of the seagulls that visited the park. "You're right Jen, but you did wish all this on me." There was sudden determination in his voice. "You gotta get back to being me." Jen agreed readily, adding with determination, "Let's go get your fur back."

CHAPTER FOURTEEN

Though packed to overflowing with items ripe with charm, it was easy to miss the antique shop's comparatively narrow storefront. It was situated in a bit of an alcove inside the mall and the sign above was modest for a business where so many tended to the garish. Leading Stuart inside, Jen made a show of inspecting some of the hundreds of baubles and trinkets that crowded glassed-in cabinets, tabletops covered with lace, and shelves of every size and composition. Jewelry gleamed while the faces of wooden dolls competed for attention with carved gargoyles. Squeezed in among stores selling overpriced sneakers and designer sunglasses, the place was a cornucopia of wonders.

It was also, she noted, very reasonably priced. This made sense. Why would anyone who dealt in miracles need to resort to price gouging?

"Wow. Look at this." Reaching onto a table she picked up an angel that had evidently been cut from a single transparent quartz crystal and showed it to Stuart. "Somebody carved this, I guess." She rubbed a finger across the vitreous surface of one wing. "Must have taken forever. This stuff is *hard*." She put it carefully back in its place on the table and moved on.

The next time she looked back, he had it in his mouth. Exasperated, she took it away from him. She was always taking potential toys away from him, and the potentially tooth-cracking quartz angel was most definitely not a toy.

"What is it with you and putting stuff in your mouth?" She shook the sculpture at him. "This will break your teeth!"

It took her a moment to register that he was not looking at her but at something behind her. Turning sharply, she found herself staring at Mrs. Walley, from the park. The woman's unexpected appearance and proximity gave her a start.

"Mrs. Walley! You scared me!"

"Hello, Jen." Kindly as ever, the younger woman thought. "I'm sorry. I didn't mean to come up on you like that." She proffered a motherly smile. "People say I float. That's just a euphemism, of course. They mean to suggest that I walk softly."

Jen collected herself. She and Stuart were not here to swap pleasantries. "We sure bump into each other a lot. What brings you here today?"

A knowing smile this time. Mrs. Walley struck Jen as something of a cross between a cuddly godmother and one of the biker chicks she occasionally encountered on Pacific Coast Highway.

"Well, I've owned this little shop for quite some time now. I spend a lot more time here since Harold left us." She heaved a matronly sigh, then added a four-letter word that did much to undo the effect of the sigh. "He helped me with the inventory and such but the store was never really his thing."

Jen was sufficiently startled by the unexpected revelation that she neglected to inquire as to what Harold's thing might have been.

"This is your place? I've never seen it before."

"Really dear?" Picking up a feather duster from the lap of a bentwood rocker she began dusting hither and yon, trying to keep the hithers clean without disturbing the yons. "It's been right here all the time, right under your nose. Of course, the outside is a bit nondescript until you're right on top of it, so if you were walking fast, or on the other side of the walkway, or hypnotized by a stupid phone like so many of your generation, I suppose it would be easy enough to miss."

Favoring her young visitor with a cherubic smile, she walked over to a counter and unscrewed a wide-mouthed jar. Also sitting on the counter was Angel, her Lhasa Apso. As soon as her owner began fiddling with the jar, the dog ambled over to sit nearby, dog out and tail metronoming.

Handing the cookie to the Lhasa, Mrs. Walley looked to Jen's companion. "Stuart, would you like a treat?"

Jen found herself nodding. "So you know."

"Know what, dear?" The teasing tone in her voice was all Jen needed for confirmation.

Off to one side, Stuart had been conversing softly with the Lhasa. Now he returned to whisper into Jen's ear.

"Jen, Angel is a real angel."

She replied absently. "That's a very sweet thing to say, Stuart." "So, Jen, what can I help you with today? A ring, maybe?"

Probably just a coincidence to offer her that, Jen decided. If it was intended as a joke it was decidedly off-kilter. "Well, I have this locket with me and…."

Stuart gave her a nudge. "I'm serious. Angel is an angel."

Impatient and anxious, she all but barked at him. "Stuart, alright already, stop."

Despite the fact that he had kept his voice deliberately low, Mrs. Walley had plainly heard what he had said. "He's just being truthful, dear." She gestured at the dog that was sitting on the counter munching on a beef-flavored cookie. "Angel actually is an angel. To be more precise, he's Harold, my husband." She gazed fondly at the Lhasa. "Harold did so love his treats."

Despite the locket, despite Stuart's transformation, Jen was not quite—not quite—ready to believe everything someone told her. "Okay. Your dog Angel is your deceased husband Harold. So, what does that make you? An angel's widow?"

"Don't be silly, dear." That maternal smile again. "Although I have learned a few things in my time, and in my time with Harold. Take that locket, for example. It's a conduit. That's the best way I can think of to describe it."

Jen raised both hands and turned her head to one side. "Okay, Okay, I get it. Enough of this dream. I am going to wake up now. I'll be back in my house, in my bed, and we'll start this day all over again. Not a problem. Wake up, Jen! Wake up!" She closed her eyes and covered them with her palms.

There followed a silent pause as she stood there. After a moment she patted her face, removed her hands from her eyes and opened them. Mrs. Walley stood there; waiting, patient, everyone's favorite cookie-baking biker aunt.

"Good morning, Jen! You awake now?" Leaning forward slightly she peered closely at the younger woman's face. "Yes, I can see that you are, even if you are a little bit numb. Perhaps that's just as well. Can I finish?" Jen might have nodded in response, albeit almost imperceptibly.

"When Harold was getting very ill and all his doctors told us it was only a matter of time, he was in a great deal of pain. We were told that his condition, and his pain, would only grow worse. Eventually he would have slipped into an induced coma ameliorated only by massive doses of painkillers until he passed on. Upon hearing that, a friend of mine—let's call her 'spiritual'— gave me this locket and told me to wish for some kind of better outcome. I could not wish Harold's condition away: the locket is not a healing tool it is a transformation conduit. I had to think of some kind of alternative." She took a deep breath.

"So I wished for Harold to become Angel, my companion." She gestured toward the Lhasa, who gazed back at her in a way that could only be described as devotedly. "He hasn't a worry in the world because now I can care for him and—he's happy.

Completely happy. And we are together. Not as we once were, but in a way that's really not that hard to understand. We watch TV together, we eat together, we take walks in the park together." She smiled. "It's way better than visiting a gravesite once a week." She pointed toward Jen's neck. "Pretty powerful locket, isn't it?"

Reaching up, Jen clutched at the locket resting against her upper chest. "So—this locket. Did that."

Mrs. Walley nodded sagely. "The one and only. Its power demands the respect it deserves."

She nodded. "So, I have the locket now. Why me? Why did Arthur give me something like this?"

"Well, I kept seeing you and Arthur around town together and I could tell something just wasn't right. That necessary *spark* seemed to be missing. And as someone who has experienced their own personal tragedy I felt I had to do something. But I couldn't think of anything to do—until Arthur came into the store."

"So *you* did this? You deliberately sold Arthur this devil locket? But why?"

"No devil is involved, dear, and I had to do it. He was going to buy you a ring!"

Jen gaped at the other woman. "What? That would've been perfect! And none of this—this 'other'—would have happened."

Mrs. Walley was shaking her head sadly. "It would have been worse. I've seen you and Arthur together numerous times, Jen. I can see things, sense things. To put it in contemporary terms, the vibe between the two of you was all wrong. All the empathy, all the real affection, was one-sided. No, that's not quite true. You were both in love. You with Arthur, and Arthur with Arthur. He's not the right one for you, Jen. Deep down, you've known that for years, but you still kept holding onto him. You were the bright candle, and he was the candle box, and he kept closing in on you. He would have snuffed you out, Jen. Your inner light was dying."

Looking on, a confused Stuart began to whine. It reminded Jen that she was not alone.

"She said 'inner', Stuart. Not 'dinner.'" Jen turned back to the older woman. "Suppose I throw logic and reason to the winds and accept everything you say at face value, especially your take on Arthur and I. What about Stuart? Are you responsible for his transformation, too?"

Mrs. Walley's tone turned stern. "No, dear. That was all you. Sometimes things do not go, um, as intended. I had no idea who you might prefer as a real alternative to Arthur. You wished for a guy like your dog. Then you went to swapping pictures, using not one of another person but of the same individual you had already wished for, causing even bigger problems. The locket is not sentient. It just responds." Her gaze turned to Stuart, who looked sad and lost. "Boy, did it ever respond!"

Holding out the locket so she could look down on it, Jen mumbled as much to herself as to Mrs. Walley. "Jewelry like this should come with a warning label. You know. 'Be careful what you wish for' or somethin'"

"Don't deviate, Jen. You miss the point. The purpose of the locket is to help its owner find their own spark, reach their own destiny. It's all about you; not those around you."

Jen reminded herself why she was there, why she and Stuart had come to this place. She still wasn't sure that finding out it was owned by someone she knew was a plus or a minus. Time, and perhaps another better considered wish, would tell.

"Mrs. Walley, we came here today hoping someone would know what the deal is with this locket and switch Stuart back. That's all. Everything else, about Arthur and I, has to take a back seat to that. For both my sake and for Stuart's. *Is it possible?*"

The older woman considered. "I don't know. The locket is still the locket. I suppose it can do it, but…."

Stuart cut in. "Jen, Harold says you already made a wish. So you can't wish me back to my real self."

She looked sharply at Mrs. Walley. "Is that true?"

The shop owner looked contrite. "This is true. I remember the woman who gave me the locket telling me that. One wish per person."

Jen refused to accept it. She could not accept it. Doing so would mean a lifetime of awkwardness both for her and for Stuart. She could not vouch for herself, but he certainly deserved better. He had coped with his transformation as well as one could expect, but had never made any secret of his unhappiness.

"Oh, c'mon. There's gotta be *something*. It's not fair." She pondered a moment. "What about the woman, the friend, who originally gave it to you? Wouldn't she maybe know something?"

"Perhaps," Mrs. Walley admitted. "Unfortunately, she passed on several years ago. And as far as I know she never used the locket on herself or anyone else. I don't know that for a fact, of course. She might have used it to wish herself into a younger body. A horse, maybe. "

Stuart winced. As if he weren't suffering enough as it was.

"Of course," the older woman continued, "there *might* be a solution. A way around the incontestable restriction. I'm bound not to tell you what that is. The friend who gave me the locket made me promise." Holding up a hand she wiggled her fingers at Jen as if to suggest the answer was close at hand and not all that difficult to discern. Jen's expression twisted.

"You're not gonna tell me, right? What is this? Sorceral charades?"

Using one index finger, the other woman wagged it from side to side like a windshield wiper. She was smiling, though whether encouragingly or at Jen's obtuseness her visitor could not say.

Revelation struck a moment later. "I've got it!" Whirling, Jen jabbed a finger at Stuart. "*You're* gonna make the wish!"

Mrs. Walley was delighted, though her tone a touch sardonic. "What a great idea! Who would have thought of it so quickly!" She looked toward the counter. "Harold, these kids today are so smart." Responding, the dog called Angel barked approvingly.

A great rush of relief passed through Jen. Or maybe it was just gas. Either way, it appeared that a means had been struck to return the world, or at least this tiny portion of it, to something resembling normality.

"Let's just do it now and end this nightmare."

Standing straight and still nearby, Stuart waited for Jen to proceed. Lifting the chain holding the locket over her head, she paused a moment to marvel once more at its seeming ordinariness. Then she popped it open and removed the picture of the human Stuart. Fumbling in her wallet she chose a favorite photo of his canine self and used her fingers to carefully tear and crop it down to a size that would fit in the locket. Pressing it into the open compartment in the locket, she snapped it shut. As she slipped the chain over his head Stuart followed her every move. The locket came to rest against his upper chest.

She stepped back, suddenly overwhelmed by an unexpected rush of emotion.

"Stuart, I'm really gonna miss this version of you. Yes, you brought more than a little craziness into this world, but you also brought with you all your unconditional love. I will miss the human form of that. But I do miss my handsome, furry, four-legged Stuart Louis. I know you've been miserable and confused like this. That's been the hardest part of it all: seeing you so unhappy. I think it's time you were happy again. So—are you ready? Let's make that wish."

Reaching up, he took hold of the locket in one hand, stared hard at it and—let it drop.

"No."

She gaped at him. "No? What do you mean, 'no'?"

"I mean not yet." The look he gave her was little different from those he had favored her with when in his natural form. "I miss my dog life more than you know and want nothing more than for it to be as it was before. But there's one wish that a few little dogs I know need to come true before I make this one, and I can't make that happen if I change back."

As if preordained, Jen's phone rang. Taking it out of her purse, she looked at it for a moment as if she had grabbed something alien. Then she recognized the number, and answered.

"Mom?" Lowering her voice, she whispered to Stuart and Mrs. Walley. "It's my mother."

"We guessed, dear." Scooping up Angel, the older woman said nothing more. But her smile was eloquent.

Looking at the phone, Jen watched as her mother panned the camera around the dog park. There were quick glimpses of blue sky and green grass. As her mother leveled the phone Jen was able to see construction workers, a couple of bulldozers, at least one large but still empty dump truck, two or possibly three mobile TV news teams and their support vans, and a highly vocal crowd of protesters apparently being led by Jim the guitarist.

"You better get your butt over here to the dog park right now," Sylvia was telling her daughter. "They're about to start digging and knocking down trees. It's all hands on deck."

"Okay, mom. Understood. We're on our way."

Stuart was already heading for the door, the locket resting innocently against his upper chest. "Let's go."

Jen started to follow, then turned back toward the shop owner. "Thanks, Mrs. Walley. I think we know what to do. See ya at the park?"

The older woman smiled. "We're already there."

🐾　🐾　🐾

Jen was not sure how many traffic laws she broke driving to the park. She knew it was likely in double figures but as long as she wasn't stopped she did not care. Finding a space was more of a problem and she ended up double-parking behind a Smart car.

Given the diminutive size of the tiny vehicle parked head-in in front of her, maybe no one would notice. At this point she didn't care. Let them tow her. Far more was at stake now than a simple fine and retrieval fee.

She saw Cindy almost immediately because she was on camera with Sanchez, the reporter from channel 2. Not wanting to interrupt the interview, she led Stuart on past. Focused on the reporter's questions, Cindy didn't see her friend, either. Both voices carried clearly in the afternoon air.

"I'm Maria Sanchez and we are live! As you can see, the people of Newport's oldest dog park are taking a stand. We are here with Cindy Shapiro, owner of a dog-infused café, The Barkery. Cindy, what's going on?"

Despite the microphone shoved toward her face, Cindy kept her poise. Thanks to the time it had taken for the news team to set up their equipment she'd had a few moments not only to compose herself but to prepare responses to some potential questions. So the first one did not catch her off guard.

"Thanks, Maria. The Barkery is a wonderful café and meeting place for dogs and their people. We've been here a number of years now and I can safely say that our reputation reaches far beyond Newport and its environs. We are open Monday through…."

Having conducted innumerable similar interviews in her career, Sanchez knew when to cut off a self-aggrandizing speaker. Shapiro had already been allowed more than enough time to promote herself and her business.

"I mean, what is happening here today at the dog park." With a sweeping gesture she took in the crowd. "You and your own dog Cupcake have been coming here yourselves for many years, am I correct?"

"Oh for sure," Cindy replied with enthusiasm. "Like so many other local dog owners it is our home away from home. It's especially important for those near here who live in condos and apartments and don't have access to a yard. Not everyone who lives in Newport is a millionaire, you know. But even millionaires bring their dogs into The Barkery, which is just a few blocks from here. It's open weekdays from…."

Passing by the interview, Jen couldn't help overhearing and rolled her eyes. *Oh god, Cindy always finds the camera….*

A familiar face stood out in the crowd and she waved. Espying her at nearly the same time, Sylvia waved back.

"Hi honey! Hi Stuart!"

While the noise of the crowd eliminated any truly quiet spaces, mother and daughter did manage to find a spot a little less frenetic than most.

"Jen, I called Arthur and told him you're mad and need to talk with him right now. He's on his way." She smiled.

Jen did not. She was privately aghast. "Why did you do that? Why *would* you do that?"

Sylvia was taken aback. "I'm trying to help here. His parents?" With a sweep of her arm she took in the dog park. "They're not involved in this transaction."

Jen's brow furrowed. "But—they're Daly Enterprises. I thought for sure that…."

"Not this time. Not on this development. It's solely his project."

"I knew it." Jen clenched her teeth. "They're testing him. To see if he can handle a project like this on his own, including the controversy. They knew what they were doing all along." Spotting another familiar figure, one surrounded by chanting, sign-wielding protesters, she broke away from her mother. "There's Jim—I gotta talk to him."

Hanging back, Stuart watched her race toward the leader of the protesters. Standing beside him, Sylvia flashed a flirtatious wink. "Well, professor Stuart, let's hope this works."

He returned the wink with a blink, then hurried to catch up

to Jen. It was plain as he headed in their direction that she and Jim had already seen one another.

"Jim, what's going,?" Jen's anxiety level rose another notch as a bulldozer started up nearby, the driver conversing with an on-site mechanic as they ran through a pre-dig checkout.

His expression was grim. "Looks like they're going to level the ground today. Take out the trees, the play tunnels—everything. When they get done there won't be anything left but a flat dirt field. The city can't do a thing. Only the developer can."

"The city, hmm?" She flashed him a sideways look. "Well, I guess you would know. You work for them."

He was more than a little bemused. "Huh? What are you talking about?"

Stuart was about to join them when he found himself cut off by a pack of dogs. Not that Sweetie Peters, Gizmo, Cupcake and Marley constituted much of a pack. Working together they would have been hard-pressed to bring down Freddy the squirrel, much less a caribou. But they had plenty to say.

"Stuart Louis," Sweetie Peters began, "this is your time. Only you can speak for us. We could lie down in front of one of those machines and our humans would just put on leashes and pull us away. You're not on a leash, physically or verbally. Talk human like you've never talked human before. Get up there now and be the hero I want to roll around in the grass with." She batted her eyes at him. "Mi amor."

At this, Stuart let out a howl of happiness that echoed throughout the park.

Leaning toward Gizmo, Marley gave the chihuahua a nudge. "How do you refuse that?"

"She's good," Gizmo admitted. "He cannot resist. Mi amor? No one resists."

Looking up at Stuart, Cupcake took a step forward. "I got a dozen beef and bacon cookies for you, Stuart. Set them aside all by myself."

He turned sharply to her as Sweetie let out a joyful bark and Marley's ears went up. Cupcake hastened to explain.

"But not now. They're for the after party. After you've saved the park."

He nodded somberly. "*If* I can help save the park. *Our* park. The one we let humans use." Turning, he started toward the makeshift stage that had been put up by the protesters. "Wish me luck," he called back to his friends.

The quartet unleashed a series of encouraging howls. Above it all he heard Sweetie Peters bark out, "I believe in you, Stuart Louis!"

Looking back toward her he smiled broadly. He would have blown her a kiss but was unsure of the exact process and he was too far away now for a snort of appreciation to be heard above the crowd noise. The smile would have to do.

As he approached the stage area, Sanchez spotted him and pointed excitedly. "Look, there he is! Newport's very own dog whisperer. I'm Maria Sanchez."

Standing nearby, it was a bit too much for Wanda, who muttered under her breath. "Girl we know you're Maria Sanchez. Why she always gotta introduce herself? " She started edging her way through the crowd toward the reporter.

Sanchez continued breathlessly, the latter a respiratory technique frequently employed by reporters to add tension to a situation where none actually existed.

"We've seen his work at The Barkery after a video of him talking to dogs went viral—which you can find on our webpage. Just enter "dog whisperer" to see previous reports, including follow-ups by me. But who is he, really? There doesn't seem to be much known about him beyond his extraordinary ability to work with dogs. Is he an animal trainer? An ex-circus performer? A revelation from the canine hinterland? Stay with me, Maria Sanchez, channel 2, as we try to find out."

Taking that as her cue, Wanda pushed past one of the station techs to confront a slightly startled Sanchez.

"You want to 'find out' about him? Well, I'll tell you who he is." Ignoring the reporter, she looked directly into the camera. "His name is Stuart. Stuart. Remember it. He's every dog's best friend. And yes, they talk. They tell him everything. That's who *he* is. There's an understanding there that passes understanding. I don't pretend to understand it myself, but they *talk* alright."

Sanchez finally managed to squeeze in a couple of words. "And you are?"

Wanda seemed surprised to have the interview directed toward her, but she responded with barely a moment's hesitation.

"Wanda James from Totally Clips. Newport's braid queen, number one in the sun, straight outta Compton, who can...."

Showing surprising strength, the reporter shoved her off camera. "That's Wanda, number one in the sun." A gesture at the cameraman directed him to turn back to the crowd, away from Sanchez—and Wanda.

"They're coming in from everywhere, ladies and gentlemen. Word travels fast these days and I'm told that pet lovers are gathering here from all across Orange County. I see at least one sign from the OC SPCA, another from WWF—I haven't seen this many acronyms since the last Democratic convention. It's getting wild out here, people." The cameraman pivoted to focus on her once again. "And now Stuart the dog whisperer is taking the stage."

As he slowly climbed the makeshift stairs, several hundred phones magically appeared, drawn from purses, pockets, and belt-mounted phone holsters. All eyes on him now, the crowd was abuzz.

"He talked to my Mitzi!" one woman declared loudly, as if her miniature schnauzer had received a benediction from a canine pope.

"I heard he almost caught Freddy," added the man next to her.

The voice of a small, red-haired boy rose above the din. "He's an ice cream thief!"

Someone started chanting, and it took only a moment for the entire crowd to pick it up.

"STUART!...STUART!...STUART…!"

Standing before them all, he tapped the microphone; a trick he had learned from watching television. Sweetie Peters and his other four-legged friends lined up beside him. In the crowd, several people sighed and commented, assuming that his unique skillset had allowed him to arrange the lineup. None of them knew that his friends had assembled near him of their own volition.

"Hello, everyone." His human voice still sounded strange to him, but it was the only one he had and he intended to put it to good use. "I'm Stuart, but I guess you know that by now. I was asked by the dogs who call this park their home away from home to speak to you today. I wish it were under more pleasant circumstances."

Sudden movement off to his left caught his eye. Sitting up on its haunches and balancing itself on its tail, a certain obstreperous rodent was staring back at him from off in the grass.

Freddy.

Stuart tensed immediately. Quickly sizing up the situation, Sweetie Peters took a step forward. The audience heard soft barking. What the would-be speaker heard was….

"Focus, Stuart Louis. Focus!"

She was preparing to bite him to get his attention, but it proved unnecessary. Gathering himself, remembering the crowd, he turned away from the tempting, teasing rodent and fought to remember what it was he had come to say.

"Do you know how much the little dogs of Newport Beach love this park?"

The crowd roared. "HOW MUCH?"

" Too much! It is for *this* park that they wait anxiously all day for their humans to come home and bring them here. It is *this* park that they dream of when napping at home. It is this park that provides them with the space and the time and the fresh air and friendship that many of them can't get anywhere else. *This park.*"

"And bigger dogs, too!" Marley added, in a couple of vocalizations that sounded to the crowd like a succession of sharp woofs.

Stuart acknowledged his friend's comment. "That's right, Marley. Big dogs love this park, too. Every dog has the right to go pee-pee here!

As the assembled animal-lovers cheered, the squirrel moved in so close that it was impossible to ignore him. This time all of Stuart's friends tensed, but the subject of the squirrel's attention kept control of himself.

"Excuse me one second, folks." When he crouched down, only a few people in the front could still see him. "Please, Freddy—not now. I'm trying."

Instead of flaunting his tail, which was the standard visual cue to spark a chase, the squirrel spun a tight circle while squeaking madly. In response to his acrobatics a second, slightly smaller squirrel emerged from below the stage. She was accompanied by three miniature versions of herself and Freddy.

"Ah, of course." Straightening, Stuart returned to the microphone. With one hand he indicated the assembled squirrel family. "Freddy here is asking me to remind you that the park is not just for dogs. Squirrels live here, too, along with what we would call other urban wildlife. Where else can you find that in Newport?"

The unexpected camaraderie was too much for his friends. To a dog they began barking at Stuart. He stood his ground.

"Be nice, guys! Freddy's been here longer than most of you . Besides, we're all on the same side here."

In response to this, his friends went quiet. Only Gizmo continued to try and stare down the squirrels, barking his head off. Stuart had to smile.

"Oh, c'mon, Gizmo. It's their home, too. If they're gone, who are we gonna chase? You? Cupcake can catch you blindfolded."

Not realizing that the on-stage interaction between dog whisperer, dogs, and apparently very brave or very stupid squirrels was reflective of an actual conversation, those in the front of the crowd close enough to observe the goings-on laughed again.

"If our park becomes a shopping center," Stuart continued, speaking forcefully into the microphone, "will any dog owners here patronize the place? Will you be customers?"

"NEVER!" The nearly unified response was followed by shouts of defiance and a few off-color exclamations that caused the producer of at least one mobile TV team to momentarily mute his channel's sound.

Standing off to one side, an especially well-dressed figure did not join in the roars of rebelliousness. Though he had been present since the very beginning of the demonstration he had not said a word. Not until his phone rang and he was compelled to answer.

"Yes, mother," Arthur Daly murmured into the phone. "Yes, I understand. He does? Okay, put him on."

CHAPTER FIFTEEN

Much could be said about the décor in the expansive living room. While it was located in a house in Newport Beach, a good deal of the furniture and artwork would have looked more at home in an apartment on the east side of Manhattan's Central Park. The couches and chairs were too big and too regal, the paintings on the walls not a bit abstract or even California impressionist, and the lighting entirely artificial. If nothing else, it fully reflected the tastes and personalities of those who dwelled within.

Sitting in a leather recliner only slightly smaller than a Volkswagen, Charles Daly (whom even his friends dared not call "Chuck") was holding a remote to flip channels on the sizable television mounted on one of the living room's few patches of wall not otherwise occupied by a pretentious painting or print while gripping a phone with his other hand. Meanwhile his wife was reposing on a curving neo-Victorian white couch only slightly less blindingly bright than the Persian cat she was brushing.

"Arthur," Daly senior growled into the phone, "your personal project is on the TV, son. On multiple channels, replete with unpleasant overtones and commentary by ignorant pundits." He paused a moment to squint at the big screen. "I see that a remote truck for The Animal Planet just drove up. Great. You're souring the company name."

Pausing in her interminable brushing, his wife called out from the couch as her husband activated his device's speakerphone setting. "The purpose of all this was to allow you the opportunity to run a project from the beginning and entirely by yourself. To prove yourself—with characteristic Daly discretion."

Arthur's voice echoed tinnily through the room. He sounded far more irritated than intimidated. "Mother, you're the one who dislikes dogs and strongly suggested I develop the dog park. I may be running the project by myself—but it didn't start with me. You're the one who pushed me too…."

His father interrupted. "I guess it's all my fault for letting you handle this yourself."

Irritation turned to exasperation. "Well, what do I do now? Not only is every dog lover in Newport here, there are people from all over the county. I see signs from Santa Barbara and La Jolla. This isn't some rabble I can just ignore. There are people here with influence."

His father grunted. "Why do you think I'm concerned?"

"Dogs, yuk." Shifting her bottom on the couch, his mother made a face. "Such dirty animals." She favored her Persian with a maternal smile that a human child would have found smothering. The cat, to its credit, ignored her. "Not like Miss Priss here, who is always fluffy clean." Looking toward her hand and his phone, she raised her voice to ensure that Arthur heard her clearly. "Do something, Arthur. It's still your project. Figure it out. After all, it's only money. *Your* money."

From his place of concealment, he hung up. Scanning the crowd, his eyes inevitably came back to the man on the podium. The dog whisperer. Jen's "college friend". Everything that had been going so well—the development, his long-term relationship with Jen—had so quickly gone to hell. Why? How? He stared at Stuart as he struggled with one particular conundrum.

Why do I not remember him?

In the vastness of the living room, Arthur's father stared at his silent phone a moment longer before turning to his spouse. His words were calm but his tone suggested something else.

"The park was your idea—dear?"

She did not meet his gaze as she began brushing Miss Priss a little harder, a little faster. The cat began to fidget. "That girl of his and her dog," she muttered. "Simple girl, plain dog. It's possible I may have suggested…."

🐾 🐾 🐾

Stuart was likely not familiar with the expression, "He had them in the palm of his hand", but he could see that people were listening to him. The longer he talked, the more people in the crowd ceased their own conversations and turned their attention to him. And more importantly, went silent to listen.

"…And remember," he continued, "there is no bond like the one between a dog and their person. No connection so close, no relationship as strong and pure. A dog never argues with their person, never complains, never insults. A dog only gives love. Jen Jensen knows that. Hector Ramos knows that. Cindy, Nina, and Wanda all know that. So does Jim, who has led the way in organizing this protest gathering. But probably not cat owners."

A few boos rose from the crowd. Standing with Jim, Jen began waving wildly in Stuart's direction, but there were too many people between them for him to see her. It's doubtful her cautioning would have made a difference anyway. Stuart was what he was.

Just then he was shaking his head. "Oh, c'mon. I mean, cats? Really? Nah…."

Near the back of the crowd, reporters were having a field day interviewing new arrivals. To a one, they were vociferous in their objections to leveling the park and putting a shopping mall in its place. As one newcomer declared flatly….

"Newport has a surplus of shopping, and you can't walk a mall."

"Well put, sir. We'll get your name in a minute but first…," and she flashed yet another radiant smile at her cameraman, "I'm Maria Sanchez at Newport Park, and you're watching live on CBS 2."

Stuart didn't know it, Jen didn't know it, but *everyone* was watching. If not the redoubtably self-promotional Maria Sanchez, then one of the other reporters working for one of the several other television stations who now had remote setups in place in the parking lot. The protest gathering had by now gone viral. Influencers were competing to see who could get live footage out first. One had arrived on a bicycle but was unable to penetrate past the outer ranks of dog lovers.

Jen breathed a sigh of relief when Stuart digressed from dissing felines and returned to the much more important matter at hand.

"The point is," he was saying to the now wholly attentive crowd, "there is only one person who can save this dog park."

"You, Stuart Louis, you!" Sweetie Peters declared, though the people in front heard only enthusiastic barking. He smiled down at her.

"Who?" someone in the crowd inquired. The question became a general refrain. "Who—yes, who? Tell us? Who is it?"

"It's the one guy who will spend the rest of his life in regret if he doesn't make the right choice. The one person whose yes or no will determine whether these machines assembled here start ripping up grass and trees or leave quietly." Raising his free hand, he pointed. The gesture held all the drama of Siegfried identifying the dragon.

Following Stuart's gesture, the crowd espied Arthur in his

alcove. Boos began to rise from those nearest him. He managed a feeble wave while trying to shrink back out of sight. Unexpectedly, it was Stuart who quieted the incipient mob.

"He's here now. Right over there. But hold on, everyone. Give him a chance. Keep in mind that he's never had a dog and his mother has (his expression turned to one of extreme distaste, as if he had just eaten something so disgusting even a hungry coyote would refuse it)—a cat. A big, fluffy, white one."

Behind him, Gizmo jumped forward. "Ese gato no es bueno!"

Marley put a paw on the chihuahua's tail. "Easy, amigo. The crowd is already riled up. We want them to listen, not riot." Reluctantly, Gizmo retreated, his visceral dislike of felines unabated.

Stuart gestured to Arthur. "Arthur, would you come up here? Give him a hand, everyone!"

Reluctantly abandoning the questionable safety of his hiding place and seeing no easy way out, Arthur moved grudgingly toward the stage. He was accompanied by a mix of claps and boos. Enough people wanted to hear what he had to say to assure him safe passage. As he approached, Stuart continued to soothe the crowd.

"Folks, be nice. We can bark all we want, but in the end everything is up to Arthur. He's the decision maker." He looked over at the man standing next to him, who thanks to Stuart's crowd-calming words was now looking a little less uneasy. On the far side of the throng, every camera was now turned toward the stage and every reporter was preparing for what might come.

"Land developer Arthur Daly of Daly Enterprises is going to speak," announced Sanchez. "We're live from Newport Beach and I'm Maria Sanchez. Follow me on Instagram, Twitter, Facebook, TikTok and Bumble." Each of the other reporters standing with their respective teams was prepping their listeners with a similar introduction.

Clearing his throat, Arthur steadied himself and spoke into the mic. "Hello everyone. I'm Arthur Daly."

From the crowd there issued a few boos, a few claps, and mostly, an expectant silence.

"I came here today," he continued, "to level the park, clear the property, and begin construction of a shopping center. The crowd boo. Please understand this to be nothing personal, just business."

Like a pot beginning to boil, the crowd started to murmur. No claps greeted his declaration. Watching Arthur intently, Jen found herself wondering where he was going with his appearance. After all, he did not have to speak, was not compelled to address the assembled. He didn't even have to show himself. As soon as Stuart pointed him out, he could have turned and left without saying a word. Yet here he was, up on the stage beside Stuart, preparing to tell the crowd—what?

"But after listening to the eloquence of my old college friend Stuart here and seeing how much this park means to all you good folks and nice people, I started thinking." He paused to let his words sinking in as the assembled seemed to lean toward him.

"'Thinking'?" someone said aloud.

"Yes, thinking. Thinking that since I'm not a dog person and grew up surrounded by many cats, I guess dogs were never really my thing. It was never me, you understand. Just the household where I was raised. It was always cats; never dogs, and...."

"'And'?" someone else in the crowd prompted him.

Arthur took a deep breath. "So for the sake of someone else I really care about...."

"Someone else?" half a dozen onlookers said aloud.

Standing beside Sylvia, Jen abruptly took on the look of a trapped animal. "Oh please, please, I hope he doesn't say me."

Her mother was shaking her head in disbelief. "I can't believe he's even up there. Something's gotten into him."

"Yes, for that person," Arthur continued, more loudly in hopes of not being challenged with prompts from the crowd, "I have had a change of heart. There wasn't much of that in my household, either, but things change and people change. I've changed."

Jen covered her face and considered joining the squirrels up in the trees.

"Who already?" someone in the crowd demanded to know, belying Arthur's futile attempt to shut down queries from the amassed.

For a moment a cringing Jen was sure he was pointing in her direction. But his hand moved to encompass everyone present. She relaxed, but not completely.

"You," Arthur declared forcefully. "Every one of you and everyone who enjoys the company of a dog. So I say to you now; enjoy this dog park for years to come. I promise you that from this day forth Daly Enterprises will not build a shopping center nor anything else at this location. Not a mall, not a drugstore, not so much as a kiosk. It was dedicated as a dog park and as a dog park it will remain."

The crowd erupted. Not just clapping this time, but full-throated cheers and hoorays interspersed with a few not-safe-for-work expletives, but all of them laudatory. People were hugging one another and not a few had tears of joy and relief in their eyes. A couple of hundred years earlier they would have hustled Arthur off the stage and borne him triumphantly through the streets (which today would likely gain a citation for blocking traffic and unlawful assembly). Hardly able to contain himself, Stuart looked down and put one hand to his eyes. Up in one tree, a cluster of squirrels were going nuts. Racing up onto the stage, Jen enveloped Stuart in a huge hug. At his feet, Sweetie Peters was jumping up and down with sheer delight.

"I love you Stuart Louis! You're my hero!"

Out in the parking lot, reporters were turning to face their cameras. "For the people. There you have it, folks. Proving that at least one developer has a heart. I'm Maria Sanchez reporting for Channel 2 news." She sniffed, a bit ostentatiously. "With a tear in my eye."

Looking drained and not a little relieved, Arthur saw that Jen was watching him.

"You did the right thing, Arthur. Against all expectations. "There is hope for you."

He exhaled heavily. The cheering from the crowd had abated only slightly. "I know. But I'm afraid I'm done, Jen. Doing the right thing doesn't always result in a win. My family entrusted this project entirely to me and now I've gone and abandoned it. Publicly. It will take a long time for them to trust me with anything like it again."

She offered him a warm smile. "As pretty bright guy I know once said, it's just business. You'll be okay." She gestured toward the still celebrating crowd. "Look at the response you got. Every one of those people is going to leave here thinking of Daly Enterprises as that rare creature; a benign developer. Your company just gained more in good will in this part of the world than it would ever have made developing yet another shopping center. Speaking as a realtor, I know how that will play out with planning and zoning commissions and other city and county offices. You actually won today."

The dour expression that had dominated his face began to fade as he digested her words. "You know what, Jen? You may be right."

With a final nod, she turned and left the stage. Stuart took her place.

"I think the dogs here really like you. It's not your fault you were raised with cats." He smiled. "Who knows? Maybe one day you'll meet a dog you can talk to just as easily as you and I are talking right now. You think one day you and I can get together here at the park and throw frisbee?"

He broke off as he noticed that Stuart was wearing a locket. He frowned. The world was full of lockets, but….

"Are you wearing the locket I gave Jen?

"Uh, yeah." Start began to back up. "'Cause right now, Arthur, you're closest to my heart, uh, I gotta go."

"But…?"

Departing with impressive speed, Stuart had already left the stage. Arthur tracked him as he moved through the crowd with people clapping him on the shoulder and fist pumping his hand. Even at a distance he looked a little frantic, as if something other than the day's events was driving him. At least, Arthur told himself, he hadn't run into Jen's embrace.

Actually, Jen was standing with Jim. Both were trying, and failing, to contain their mutual excitement.

"Jen, you guys did it! You and Stuart!"

Picking her up in his arms, he twirled her around twice as he hugged her to him. She was already staring into his eyes when he finally set her down. "We did it, Jim." For a moment everything else vanished: the crowd, the ongoing celebration, the park, the air itself. He smiled then, turned, and walked off to share in the congratulations of others who had helped to organize the demonstration. As he left, a waiting Arthur Daly took his place.

And promptly got down on one knee, gazing up at Jen. She stared at him.

"Arthur, what are you doing?" Grabbing his collar with both hands she urged him back onto his feet, looking around to see if anyone had noticed the gesture.

"I'm doing what I should've done a long time ago," he told her. It was a true statement, albeit delivered in a calm, assured manner. A professional manner. A business-like manner.

Non-plussed by the contractual offer, she let go of his shirt. For a moment she hesitated—but only for a moment. She knew it was time to do what was right: not what was easy.

"I'm not the one for you, Arthur. You know that. Somewhere out there, there's a beautiful, compliant, business-oriented cat lover just waiting for you, and I'm sure you'll find her. But right now, I need to go find Stuart. And *not* for the reason you might be thinking." Letting him go, both physically and emotionally, she turned and headed off toward the crowd, turning only once to call back to him.

"Forget about business for once and just enjoy—joy. You have a lot going for you, Arthur. I'm just not a part of it. Goodbye, Arthur."

Confused and unsettled, he started to go after her, only to be intercepted by….

"Hi!" Like a blunt stiletto, a microphone was thrust in face. He recoiled, but only for a moment. The wielder of the mic was—attractive. The Daly genes kicked in. "I'm Maria Sanchez with Channel 2 and you are Arthur Daly of Daly Enterprises. Do you mind if I ask you a few questions off-camera?" Without waiting for a reply she grabbed him by the arm and guided him away from the crowd. Though still confused, he allowed himself to be led.

"Where are we going?"

"Just a brief interview, Mr. Daly. About today's remarkable events. I won't keep you long, for the interview." Smiling broadly, she flicked off the microphone. "I hear you're single. Is that true?"

Criss-crossing her way through the area, Jen searched the crowd, the parking lot, but there was no sign of Stuart. Nor did he respond to her repeated calls. It was only when she began looking for him in the park itself did she come across his Bloomingdale's outfit. First the shoes, then the socks, then pants, underwear, and finally the once crisp now wrinkled shirt. All laying on the grass in a somewhat perfectly straight line. As if someone had taken particular care to get undressed and toss the garments behind.

Or someone had simply somehow run out of their clothes.

"Stuart!" She was frantic now.

A black and white shape exploded through the crowd dodging left and right between the legs of celebrating protestors. Jen's heart pounded as she recognized that familiar square head galloping toward her, leaping into her arms. Reflexes allowed her to catch him as he began wildly licking her face. The impact caused her to stumble backwards and she finally fell to the ground with him on top of her. In the course of her downward descent the licking never stopped.

"Stu!" Struggling to see around the hyperactive tongue she finally managed to get a good look at the terrier. Her eyes widened. "Potato Head! You're back!" She hugged him hard, forcing him to get creative with the tongue assault. "I missed you, buddy! I love you, Stuie Louie Lou Lou! You saved the dog park bud! And maybe me a little bit, too."

Climbing to her feet, she brushed grass from her clothes while Stuart bounced around her as if he was on a trampoline. Eying him, of one thing there was not the slightest doubt: he was overjoyed to be a dog again. As she petted him he ran back and forth; teasing, taunting, delighting in being on four legs once more. A slight shadow fell over them as she looked up.

"I see Stuart is back from the farm." There was only a hint of knowing sarcasm in Hector Ramos's voice. His expression told her everything she needed to know and she smiled in return.

"He is, Hector. He *is*."

Looking down, the cop watched as Stuart bolted and Ringo began to chase him, the two of them racing 'round and 'round a nearby tree, happily barking and play-growling.

"I'll figure out how to write this up. I guess as a standard Missing Persons. People will pose questions about the whereabouts of the 'other' Stuart, but eventually they'll get tired of asking. Especially when no one files any kind of follow-up. Especially when you're the only person who knows the, uh, 'missing' individual. It'll just go away, quietly. I've seen it happen before."

Her expression turned somber. "I owe you one, Hector."

"I think we're even." A whistle brought his patrol partner back to his side. Tongue lolling, the German shepherd looked up at Jen. "Ringo certainly thinks so, and that's good enough for me." He took hold of the dog's leash. "Let's go, Ringo. It's another day on patrol and we have work to do."

In their wake Jim arrived, with Sweetie Peters trotting along at his feet. Making an immediate beeline for the other terrier, she began licking his face. He did not draw away.

"Look who's back!" Jim exclaimed. "We missed you, Stu." Bending, he scratched the back of Stuart's head. The dog leaned back in pleasure. "He's one handsome fella, right Sweetie?" He straightened.

Head close to Stuart's, she whimpered gently. "I never doubted for a minute you would save the park, Stuart Louis."

"All in a day's work, mon chérie."

Pushing out her front paws, she gazed intently at him. "Now that's really French. I'm going to faint."

Instead, she moved forward to rub her head against his. He responded in kind.

"Look at them," Jen said affectionately. "They love each other."

"They do," Jim agreed. He turned away from the nuzzling dogs and toward her. "So, Jen. I've been thinking about buying a bigger house with room to expand my music studio and I think you'd know where I could find one."

She blinked, perplexed. "'Music studio'? You have a music studio?" He nodded. "I thought you worked for the city. For the dog park, to be specific."

He chuckled softly. "Funny how people think that. I guess it's because of the amount of time I spend here with Sweetie Peters or picking up bottles and other people's trash . "Both!" Jen added. "I'm a music producer and songwriter with a few hits out there. You might even recognize some of them." He gestured at their surroundings, preserved now.

"I come here to compose melody and lyrics. When I get home at night, I put them together. If it all works; hey presto—a song. Coming here is way more inspirational than staring at a computer or mixing console all day. Not to mention that it's better for Sweetie Peters."

She was still confused. "But your shirt." She pointed at his chest. "It says 'PARKS MGT'."

He looked down at himself and laughed again. "I know. The darn 'S' came off in the wash. It should say 'Sparks'. My last name." When she didn't react, he elaborated. "Sparks Management."

Her jaw dropped. "'Sparks'? So *you're* the spark'." She mumbled to herself. "Oh, Mrs. Walley."

He frowned. "What?"

"Nothing, nothing." She put on her best professional smile. Though there just might have been a tad more to it than professionalism. "By sheer coincidence I think I have the perfect home for you and your studio."

He smiled back. "I had a feeling you would."

As mothers are wont to do at times when daughters wish they wouldn't, Sylvia chose that moment to join them. She looked toward open grass where two Boston terriers were romping as if they had just encountered one another.

"Glad to see Stuart here, Jen. I was getting worried about him." She scanned the immediate vicinity. "Where's Professor Stuart?"

"Oh, he had to leave. He said to be sure and say goodbye to you and that he hoped the little talk he had with you would have some beneficial results. He had to get back to his girlfriend."

"Oh." Sylvia didn't try to hide her disappointment. "He has a girlfriend?"

"A devoted one, apparently. Mom, meet Jim Sparks. He's a noted songwriter."

"Now Jen," he began.

"That's great," Sylvia said, cutting him off without a second thought. "Nice to meet you, Jim." No magician could produce a card as swiftly as Sylvia Jensen, and it was the same card every time. "Here's my contact information if you ever want to buy a house."

Putting his hand on hers, he gently refused the colorful slip of cardboard. "Thanks, but I'm already working with a broker."

She eyed him for a moment, then looked at her daughter and then back to him. "Oh. *Oh*. Well, I can't say that I argue with your choice. Same company, anyway. I'll leave you two to discuss, um, real estate."

"Thanks, mom." Taking Jim's arm, Jen led him away deeper into the park. Leaving off from racing around a tree, the pair of terriers proceeded to follow, trotting along side by side in their humans' wake.

🐾　🐾　🐾

Ordinarily, a public park was rarely rented out for a private event, but an exception was made for Jen and Jim due to their spirited defense of that very same park. The public all but demanded it. Besides, it was an excellent way for the city to show off all the renovations and upgrades that had been made in the wake of Daly Enterprise's generous donation of the land.

One involved the gazebo where the wedding was taking place. Dressed in everything from tuxedos to shorts and beach sandals (Southern California, in case you've forgotten), friends and acquaintances surrounded it. The gazebo itself was a gorgeous Victorian reproduction whose components and labor had been donated by local contractors and companies; dog lovers all. It was almost a match for the custom squirrel house that clung to a nearby tree trunk and was currently occupied by a family of five.

The altar itself was temporary, so it could be removed in order for the gazebo to serve a multitude of purposes. Jen stood chatting with her friends. They were all there: Cindy and Amanda, Wanda and Nina. Her mother, of course, and many others. Stuart and his friends clustered behind the altar.

"Might as well get started before the humans do." Ringo cleared his throat with a bark. "Do you, Stuart Louis, take Sweetie Peters to be your dogfully wedded spouse?"

"I do, I do ahooo!" he howled.

"And you, Sweetie Peters? Do you take Stuart Louis to be the biscuit of your eye, your one and only furry guy?"

"He had me at woof!" she responded eagerly.

"Then by the power invested in me by the State of California, K9 Division Newport Beach, I pronounce you legally mated."

Gizmo turned circles while everyone else barked and whined their approval.

"Oh, go ahead, Stuart," Ringo urged him. "Kiss the bride!"

A mutual face lick sealed the deal. Looking behind the altar, Jim could only grin.

"Seems our two friends are at it again. Sometimes you have to wonder what dogs are really thinking." He chuckled. "I guess that makes us in-laws."

She sighed and moved closer, throwing tradition to the winds. Or at least the sea breeze. "Just kiss me."

"Sounds like a good line for a song. But it needs punctuation." Whereupon he brought her close and pressed his lips against hers.

The reception also took place in the park. Extending well into the evening, Stuart found himself on familiar ground, by a familiar tree, gazing up into a star-filled sky that the ocean breeze had, for a little while at least, cleared of clouds and fog.

🐾　🐾　🐾

"Now how's this for a happy ending? Jen fell in love with Jim. Arthur's dating Maria Sanchez, Avery got his orange ball back and Derek his slippers plus he sold his house to none other than Jim Sparks. I wonder if the crazy birds go with it? Me? How did I get so lucky? I wound up with Sweetie Peters, the girl of my dreams."

She snuggled against him. "It's because you got your four legs back, silly."

"Goodnight, Sweetie Peters."

"Goodnight, Stuart Louis."

Guests and other park visitors were leaving as it grew darker. Among the few still remaining were Wanda and Marley. In the darkness a hint of glow caught her attention. There had been clothes spread out below the glow but they were gone now. Whoever had taken them had overlooked a certain small piece of antique jewelry, perhaps because its radiance was lost in the daylight.

Picking up the locket, Wanda opened it. It was empty and there was no one around. Shrugging, she put it in a pocket. A sly grin spread over her face as she did so.

"I'm gonna put a picture of Denzel in here."

Marley let out a bark that to Wanda sounded like—well, just a bark—and ran off. She hurried after him, yelling for him to slow down, the locket gleaming deep inside her pants' pocket.

ABOUT THE AUTHOR

Born in New York and raised in Los Angeles, Alan Dean Foster is one of the most prominent writers of modern science fiction & fantasy with over 100 published books. Alan's novels have been translated into more than fifty languages winning many international awards. His works to date include hard science-fiction, fantasy and contemporary fiction.

He wrote the story for the first Star Trek feature film and has produced many novelizations of well-known franchises such as Star Wars, The Chronicles of Riddick, the first three Alien films, Star Trek, Terminator: Salvation, both Transformers films and now, a Fantasy Rom-Com about a Boston Terrier named Stuart. Foster enjoys both classical and heavy metal music, equally.

He's a composer and has recently written several short orchestral pieces and two symphonies. More on Alan Dean Foster's adventures, credits and awards can be found at www. alandeanfoster.com

facebook.com/AlanDeanFoster

amazon.com/stores/author/B000AQ39HU

Printed in Great Britain
by Amazon